HOME TH

Tim Parks's novels include *Tongues of Flame*, which won the Somerset Maugham and Betty Trask Awards, *Loving Roger*, which won the John Llewellyn Rhys Prize, *Cara Massimina* and *Mimi's Ghost*. His non-fiction work includes the bestselling *Italian Neighbours*, *An Italian Education* and *Adultery & Other Diversions*. His ninth novel *Europa* was shortlisted for the 1997 Booker Prize. His most recent novel is the acclaimed, *Destiny*. Tim Parks lives in Italy.

Tim Parks

HOME THOUGHTS

VINTAGE

Published by Vintage 2000

2 4 6 8 10 9 7 5 3 1

First published in Great Britain in 1987 by
William Collins Sons & Co. Ltd

First published in paperback in 1988 by
Fontana Paperbacks

Vintage
Random House, 20 Vauxhall Bridge Road,
London SW1V 2SA

Random House Australia (Pty) Limited
20 Alfred Street, Milsons Point, Sydney
New South Wales 2061, Australia

Random House New Zealand Limited
18 Poland Road, Glenfield, Auckland 10, New Zealand

Random House (Pty) Limited
Endulini, 5A Jubilee Road, Parktown 2193, South Africa

The Random House Group Limited Reg. No. 954009
www.randomhouse.co.uk

A CIP catalogue record for this book
is available from the British Library

ISBN 0 09 928993 8

Printed and bound in Great Britain by
Cox & Wyman Ltd, Reading, Berkshire

FOR ALL THE BRITISH VERONESE
AND, OF COURSE, FOR RITA

'Oh, to be in England
    Now that April's there,
And whoever wakes in England
    Sees . . .'

Home Thoughts from Abroad
Robert Browning (1845)

'Why didn't he go home then?'

'O' level student of English Lit. (1971)

What follows is entirely fictional: no reference to any living person is intended or should be inferred.

Part One

OLD ACQUAINTANCE AND NEW

If Sandro wasn't married, as he had let her know, casually (too casually perhaps? or rather, promisingly casually), then Julia might quite like to marry him. Amongst others. On a mellow October morning she wrote this letter to her ex-flatmate in London.

Dear Diana,

I'm in my room here. It's awful. The furniture looks like it's been carved out of used coffins. The bed is like sleeping in the bottom of a boat, crosswise. Would you believe the street is called Via Disciplina! It's narrow and the buildings are high, so that the sun only manages to slip through my window for a few minutes every day. It slides in like a bright knife and stabs a drab madonna on the wall.

(Julia felt self-conscious writing this first letter to her close friend Diana who worked in the East European Department of the World Service of the BBC and had translated a book of Czech poetry. The sun did not slide in like a blade. It was a great wedge of dust-swirled white light which never quite reached the grim madonna with baby Jesus raising one plump hand in precocious blessing.)

Still, I was determined to find a place in the centre. You go out to the suburbs here and you may as well be in Hemel Hempstead. Really.

So, what's cooking on the social side? Well, there's a rather sexy-looking Italo-Canadian I met at the assistants' get-together party. Name of Sandro. My age, more or less, big soft brown eyes and a really cool transatlantic voice. So he'll be candidate number one. Who knows, I may make motherhood yet before the great axe falls. Keep you posted.

I wonder if I'm going to miss London life. I suppose it's inevitable. So many things are. I do hope it's not all going to be a silly mistake, or that I'll just mope and be lonely. I didn't realize how adventurous I was being till I actually got here and sat down in my room.

Don't forget to make me pay my part of the last phone and electricity bills. My mum can draw a cheque for you on my account.

More soon. Big hug.

JULIA.

PS. See, I didn't mention you-know-who. . . .

Dear Lenny,   (she wrote then to you-know-who)

I miss you so much, I really do. If you knew. Can't you change your mind? I've been thinking of you all the time. It's terrifying how clearly I see you. Your carroty hair, your freckled nose. The way you close one eye in the sunshine. The smell of that ancient tweed jacket. How will I ever forget?

Lenny, it would be so easy if you came out here, a fait accompli. I know I promised not to hark on about it, but couldn't you? Couldn't you just this once take a big plunge, Lenny?

I love you always. You know I do.

Your own JULIA.

Dear Mum,   (she wrote in tiny print on a postcard)

I've found a nice little room here and am very cosily settled in. The teaching starts Monday, but for the moment I'm enjoying just soaking it all up. Diana'll probably be asking you for a cheque for some bills. Don't worry I'll pay you back. Give my love to Mike when you see him. Love. JULIA. PS. Am wearing the sweater. Thanks a mil. J.

———◆◆◆———

Alan explained that he had invited one of the new lettori to dinner. Or rather a lettrice. 'She seemed very lonely.'

Elaine rolled blue eyes. Was it possible that with both the kids, not to mention HER, Alan was still inviting people to dinner?

'I'll cook,' Alan said, and apparently it was.

Alan had a big, square, patriarchal face with magnificently thick eyebrows and hair that bristled up in a stiff virile brush. His wife was small and slim.

Julia came and talked too loudly and too long all evening. She heard herself talking too long and too loudly. She made mental notes and criticized herself, but she didn't stop. She had come to Italy, she was saying, because she had been with a man who liked being with her, yes, but was too obsessed with his adolescent fantasies of nymphets and vamps to guarantee her any happiness or security, though he was of course now begging her to come back; because men always wanted to have their cake and gobble up every last crumb of it too.

'Good for you,' said Flossy, who was likewise well-built. She spoke through a thick cold and had tissues tucked under her sleeve.

Elaine, whose body, despite two pregnancies, conformed exactly to the unhappy Lenny's supposed fantasies, smiled slyly at Alan over the bald head of a baby she was holding.

Alan said: 'Couldn't you just leave him and stay on in London?'

To which Julia came back sharply that Alan obviously didn't understand women in love.

Elaine's smile, framed in hennaed curls, took on a told-you-so schoolgirl's dimpling. Julia didn't know that in his time Alan had written three plays for the radio, two of which had been broadcast, and all of them about women in love and based on his ex-girlfriend who had tried to kill him when he left her.

'That may be' – Alan had the competitor's weakness of picking up any glove of challenge that landed at his feet (even if perhaps it had been dropped there by accident) – 'but London is a big place, I mean. . . .'

'Right, but you try finding a place to live. Leave your flat in London and you may as well go to Timbuktu. You know they've started advertising houses in Scotland in the *Standard* right next to the local flats-to-let section. The desperation factor. Bungalow in Renfrewshire, same price as a year's rent in Kensington.

'Not to mention finding a reasonable job,' Julia went on (had she taken a breath? It seemed not). Alan and Elaine, who owned a one-bedroom flat in Hampstead which they rented out through an agency on company let, couldn't have got a word in edgeways had they wanted to. And all three listeners now had the impression that Julia had been living and perhaps even working with her man of the adolescent fantasies, and had thus had to give up everything to get away and punish him. But this was not the case: because Lenny lived with his wife and two children in a three-bedroom so-called luxury flat the Fortis Green side of East Finchley High Road.

'A woman' – who but Julia? – 'okay university degree' – two-one from Bristol – 'two languages, dynamic as any man, eager, efficient, etc; what happens? You go to the interview, if they're interviewing women at all, and the first thing they ask is when you plan to have children. You say you're not planning them, the last thing you want is kids, you're not even married, and they don't believe you, they. . . .'

Rightly so, thought Alan.

Rightly so, part of Julia was admitting as she got up steam.

Elaine was complacently tracing out the line of tiny Margaret's sticky-out ears.

Only Flossy was in wholehearted agreement and would have told her own lifestory here had Julia allowed herself to be interrupted, had she herself not been stifling another sneeze.

'They even make snide remarks about not having to be married to be pregnant, Christ, there should be some drug to bring on menopause early and a certificate to go with it: "We hereby guarantee that Julia Helen Delaforce, although capable of giving men pleasure in all the normal and many abnormal ways, is henceforth to be considered one hundred percent infertile, in that. . . ."'

They sat round a painted wooden table in the kitchen chaos the Bexleys always lived in. Alan accepted the now broader told-you-so smile on his wife's face, though it was rather annoying how she radiated this silly, happy girl's complacency, as if everything that happened and got said was a trick she'd won at his expense. His own opinions on feminism, which had to do with its being a false consciousness and a wilful determination to feel aggrieved (though he wouldn't deny that life could be pretty unfair to the fairer sex) were too complicated to bear dinner-time explanation to two such fiery souls as Julia and his younger sister Flossy. He mixed wine and Ferrarelle.

Towards eleven-thirty Julia said, as if at last throwing the conversation open to all:

'So what becomes of the long-term ex-pat?'

One hand balancing Margaret to burp on his shoulder, Alan was at that moment twiddling urgently through the short-wave dial of an ancient Grundig on the window sill; until, amidst science-fiction whistles and bursts of static, a voice broke into this untidy Italian kitchen and with a curious sing-song formality announced: 'Oldham nil, Crystal Palace (pause) nil.'

'Oh shit,' said Flossy, sneezing into her handkerchief, 'we've missed the first division.'

Elaine asked Julia if she could cook, because next weekend they were going to have an apple-crumble competition. Another friend had brought some all-spice back from England. Alan was an ace apple-crumble man. Elaine rather liked Julia, though she couldn't have said why, perhaps because she was the only other person she had met in Italy who smoked roll-ups.

Julia said truthfully she couldn't cook to save her life. Walking home along the narrow Via Disciplina it occurred to her that she hadn't remembered to ask about Sandro. Because she was fed up to the back teeth with married men, and somehow precisely the way he'd told her like that had had her suspecting the contrary.

Every time Julia left company she always experienced a vague sense of shame, which was stronger or weaker in relation to the amount of alcohol she had drunk. And this was another thing she was fed up with. Unless, it came to her, finding herself mirrored a moment in the bright black panes of her bedroom, unless what she was really fed up with deep down, beneath all the other failures and disappointments, was simply herself. It was not, to be precise, her body that distressed her, though God knows she'd been short-changed there. No, she was quite simply sick to death with the feeling, the consciousness, the every waking day moment of Julia Helen Delaforce.

So of course it was herself she had wanted to leave in leaving England.

In which case she'd got off to a bad start spending the whole evening griping. (Lenny was a Palace man. Diana cooked apple crumbles when she invited her BBC friends.)

Elaine and Alan had two beautiful young children.

At 3 a.m., having calmed down Robert after one of his nightly squalls, Alan stopped a moment in the sitting-room to scribble:

'If Bishop Tutu is a prisoner of hope, then I am a prisoner of happiness.

Life lacks intensity. Groans under the routine.

Yet this is domestic bliss, is it not? The happy home.

I have suffered the misfortune of being given everything on a plate.

Love, family, job. A padded cell.

What on earth to do?

I feel like someone in a Tchekov story, dreaming impossible Moscows.'

Not feeling especially sleepy, he picked up *Corriere della Sera* and re-read the Juventus–Verona day-before coverage. Was nobody going to catch Juventus? If only Verona had kept Fanna. Reading, chewing a knuckle, he felt vaguely guilty and returned to his notebook. He stood over it. He put pencil against paper and waited. But the truth was that Alan Bexley felt oddly incapable of writing these days. Perhaps because it was seven years since his ex-girlfriend had tried to kill him.

Sandro was ten minutes late for a lesson he would leave five minutes early. Fifty students faced him. He climbed onto the dais and grinned.

'Right then,' he said, 'gerund uses with prepositions,' and he gave out a page number in Thomson and Martinet. (There was no other word but gorgeous for the girl in the third row. Let's hope she's one of the eager, questions-after-lessons kind.)

Before lunch he knocked discreetly at the notorious Professoressa Bertelli's door. The professoressa was an ill-kept paranoid woman in her late fifties.

Sandro, whose face was usually grins and radiant self-satisfaction, found a worried, diligent tone to ask if she had any ideas how he might improve his techniques and rapport with the students. He felt he wasn't getting the best out of them, nor they from him.

A few minutes later Professoressa Bertelli invited Sandro to lunch and over tortellini followed by veal chops (because they stayed, as residents will, with the tourist menu) she told him in a hushed voice about the conspiracy there was against her in the department and this disturbing business of them putting powder in her eyes. If he knew of a faith-healer. . . . But the mafia always got there first. The church that is.

Sandro, who had been forewarned, was understanding, his conversation banal and soothing. He said that having to work with others at this kind of intellectual level could prove very trying. There were pressures and responsibilities and questions of personal integrity which naturally created areas of conflict.

'The Vatican,' Professoressa Bertelli said belligerently, and then she said that Professor Errico was a mean, corrupt bastard, if he would excuse her language, and a slacker into the bargain.

Accepting a splash of grappa and feeling his way more carefully than ever, Sandro remarked that the only shame was that the job wasn't offered on a permanent contract, because then one could give just that little bit more. There would be that feeling of total commitment.

And he said he was happy though that they had got to know each other. The thing was to nip misunderstandings in the bud.

Professoressa Bertelli was a big old woman with a heavily lined grim face where watery eyes swam suspiciously at the bottom of deep sockets. When she smiled, though – and this was rare – she would have a perfectly wholesome, even maternal expression, despite the decades of spinsterhood and deepening paranoia. She smiled now.

'Of course, we do very occasionally give someone a permanent research post,' she said, telling Sandro what he already knew, 'if all three professors are convinced that we have an exceptional candidate on our hands.'

With the meal finished, her mouth chewed slackly on nothing. She picked up a toothpick.

'Someone who can make a real contribution to the department.'

While she spoke, Sandro gave her the flattery of his soft brown eyes. Which obliged him to watch her. She powdered heavily and wore expensive frames. Her nose was a trifle shapeless, puffy, the mouth wide, even a little gross now as she stretched the lips to stab at a molar. But her shoulders were broad and well made and the breasts surprisingly high on her chest. What would it be like to go to bed with someone so old? Perverse, but interesting. The few times he'd seen older women naked in films, he had always been intrigued by the startling youthfulness of their bodies against the wrinkling age of faces and hands. Unless it was just the actresses they used of course, or they were playing around with the photography.

'I'll pay,' he said.

'No, no, God forbid,' she smiled.

'Really, I've been taking up so much of your time, Professoressa Bertelli.'

'Call me Roberta.'

'I think I really ought to. . . .'

'No, I insist.'
'But I insist.'

Later and no poorer he stood on the Roman Bridge in dazzling autumn sunshine. The air was clear glass. The surrounding scene would have been a 3D postcard but for the traffic: cream and ochre palazzi climbing above the Roman Theatre to Castel San Pietro on his left, the bell-towers and fancy battlements of the city to his right, with the river taking a great sweep over white shingle between. One problem, Sandro thought, assessing his new job, would be how to spend one's free time. Seeing as there was so much of it. And he decided to attend an evening course he had seen advertised at the university which introduced you to the world's greatest philosophers.

———◆◆◆———

Nov 10   *Beeb, Shepherd's Bush*

Dear Julia,

Thank heaven there's the BBC address so at least we can write. I miss you too. I was over at Diana's with the production crew on Sunday and everybody was asking after you. Needless to say we all think you've been a bit crazy going off so suddenly, leaving a good job, not to mention the nice situation with Diana – and in Kensington too. I know I must seem rather a blind alley in emotional terms, but maybe the problem is the way you think relationships should have so much direction and finality about them. You're so dramatic. You never want to swim with the tide. It always has to be Shangri-la rather than Shepherd's Bush. I mean, I don't want to sound mercenary, but you do realize that coming over to Italy for me would mean turning down £20,000 a year (another well-deserved raise last week) not to mention abandoning a wife, two children and five years of mortgage payments. Whereas if you came back we could see each other as often as you like, within the limits of the decent and reasonable (which you must admit aren't too awfully limiting). In fact, at Diana's we all agreed to write you letters asking you to come back, so you'll be getting a lot of post soon. Everybody loves you, even if you always insisted on thinking otherwise, and the school'd be bound to find a way to take you on again, with your experience. So think it over.

What else? Diana's got yet another new boyfriend. Stuart. Doubtless she told you. She does seem to have something of a fixation for these banking/insurance types (the dreaded Ronnie!), which is odd considering her background and that avantgarde guff she translates. Awfully argumentative bloke. He took us all on (me, Sally, Rob, Barry and Kat), saying the media should be run on market principles and from what he'd heard from Diana the Beeb could reduce its labour costs by 30% without the public ever noticing. Can you imagine translating Czech poetry on market principles? But everybody was too kind to say it. Anyway, he's the first bloke I ever met who not only admitted to voting Thatcher last time, but said he would next too. What hope the nation!

Diana lapped it up with that big, ever-hopeful ever-happy beam she always has; sometimes I think she finds these guys just to annoy us. But then the food is always so scrumptious and she must be the only person in London on less than fifty grand who has a rooftop terrace. (It was warm enough to have at least our aperitivos (!) outside and Barry said if he had a terrace like that he'd never dream of going to Italy – yes, Barry and Kat <u>are</u> together again – take note.)

Well, it's 11 and I guess I'd better be getting a move-on. We've got a tough schedule today. The old pre-Christmas interview-the-tramps crap. We're supposed to follow a couple of old winos around for a month and see how mean everybody is to them. Probably turn into a pub crawl. Look, give me your phone number as soon as you've got one and I'll give you a bell. Licensing fees are up so a couple of calls isn't going to break the bank. And do come back Julia. You're such a London person, I can't really imagine you surviving anywhere else. I know you think I'm a casual bastard, and I am. But life'll show you I'm right in the end. Plunge-taking is not what it's about. Getting by more like.

I love you too, Julia. I really do. Green eyes.
LENNY.

PS. I forgot to mention the best bit: Sally and this Stuart had a really (but really) wild argument at the Grenadier when he said he couldn't give a damn if Sadler's Wells closed (you must have heard about that). She started shouting at him and walked out and Barry and Kat had to run and get her back. You see what you're missing! Love again. L.

—◆◇◆—

November 30th *Via Disciplina*

Dear Diana,

Everybody's written telling me to come back but you! (Even Barry! I didn't know he could write!). Yet funnily enough you're the only person I can feel bothered to write to myself. Anyway, as far as coming back's concerned – no way! The truth is, I think I've finally found the good life here. The job is outrageously easy. 8 hours straightforward language teaching and 4 hours 'ricevimento' when you're supposed to deal with your students' problems, only they hardly ever turn up, so you just end up chatting to whoever's around. For which I get the magnificent sum of one million, two hundred thousand lire a month (I'm a millionaire as of yesterday!). If your maths aren't up to it, it all works out about a hundred quid plus a week, which is really okay here, so long as you don't have expensive tastes – and when did I have time to develop those at Christ Church?

The university situation is so classically 'Italian' you wouldn't believe it. There are three professors in the faculty: one's just plain mad – a woman around sixtyish who's convinced everybody's stealing her books and putting powder in her eyes and beaming ultrasonic whatevers at her desk (honestly!). She should be certified, not teaching. Then there's Scudellotti, an effeminate ditherer, fiftyish, who just goes on and on and on in a sing-song appalling English that creases you up if you make the mistake of thinking about it; his line is that it's impossible to get anything done because the other professor, Errico, will never agree with him and is only in the job for the money and doesn't love literature like he does, etc. etc. Errico's a gnome of a man who commutes from Milan and is always asking you to do translations for some agency he has; a bit of a shark, very Latin, and with a roving eye too, but not unpleasant. So the upshot is, Errico and Scudellotti are always trying to enlist Bertelli's, that's the woman's, help so as to get a majority decision over the other, only she's so out of her mind she thinks they're really conspiring against her. I could go on but it would take forever to tell everything. Makes Christ Church politics seem pretty tame anyway. Only somehow it meant more there. This feels more like a soap opera, as if you could never really be a part of it. As if it wasn't really happening even. Perhaps because it's not my country. (I do hope there are advantages to not being able to take things seriously. Everybody was always saying I took things too much to heart.)

Apart from which I've found a couple of friends. There's a girl called Flossy, younger than me, who teaches a few hours at the Oxford School and is quite a character. She used to be a member of Militant Tendency and spent almost a year with the Greenham women before coming out here. She's living with her brother and his wife and kids at the moment, only it seems the brother doesn't appreciate her that much (he's a really pompous arsehole, the 'you-just-need-a-man-(like me)' type, thinks he's a writer apparently – yawn – a normal ex-pat delusion). Anyway, we agreed we'd live together as soon as we can find a place big enough. My only worry is that she may be a bit too anti-men and turn them off coming to visit and so on, which is rather throwing out the baby with the bathwater, if you see what I mean (though who would deny that the bathwater is usually tepid and scummy and generally fit to be thrown out?).

So what do I do with all this time on my hands? Well, I spend a lot of mornings just mooching around the streets here. There are thousands of tiny cobbled back-alleys and always something new to look at, some shop tucked away somewhere, some curious piece of architecture. Would you believe there's a hunch-back goes round sharpening knives on a moped with a kind of rickety counter attached and a revolving whetstone geared up to the motor? Good for a horror film. Then I got myself a canary for company, everybody has them, and hung him in a cage by the window. I called him Napoleon because of the way he puffs out his chest. Maybe it was a mistake though because his whistling's driving me bananas, and of course I'll have to find somebody to look after him if I go away. I suppose, to be honest, I do feel a bit spare sometimes, but it's bound to take a while to settle in. At least it's a clean start, which was the intention. And no tube!!!

Oh, my tennis racket. Will you check if it's still behind the sideboard, and if it is, can you see if there's some safe way of posting it. I'll need exercise in spring to prepare for the beaches! And one thing, Diana, for when you do write. Even if he does come over, please don't mention L. I really want to make it a clean break. I don't want to hear of him or from him ever again. (I'm working on this Sandro.)

Love – J.

PS. There seems no point in making you envy my weather every time I write. Take it as given.

December 4th   *Kilburn*

Dear Sissy,

Could you please write and tell Mumsicle to GET OFF MY BACK! She's getting like the IMF. 'I'll only give you money if you do what I say, cut your hair, wear a tie (A TIE! – I had to go to my dictionary), keep the right company, don't drink so much, etc. etc.' (MUM = Money Under Menace.) She keeps coming round to the old pad here which is pretty hem-hem-barrassing and even offered to wash mine and Brünhilde's clothes!!!! IF THERE'S ONE THING I HATE IT'S MAR-TYRS – not to mention the underlying insinuation (or does she want to examine for stains?). Mum seems to go backwards in time and is now cruising her way through an especially prudish patch of the 1880s.

Otherwise all wellsy wellsy well, howbeit college exams and exhibition looming and dooming and glooming and sooning!

I hope and trust you're getting on well enough with the dagoes on the further shore. I'm thinking of going to HAMER-ICA myself when I've finished here – the land of hop-on-ortunity – if only I can get the old meany-greeny-weeny-backs together (don't tell Mumsicle – she'll be trying to give me even more money to keep me – or perhaps that's not such a bad idea . . .).

Lance and Trev think I should try modelling! Brünhilde is against. What do you think?! Can you imagine Mum seeing me towering in Y-FRONTS by the bus-stop at Tally Ho? S for sensational, n'est-ce-pas?

Love and stuff and nonsense.

MIKE.

———◦◦———

Alan sat in front of a screen that glowed neon green. Despite ear-plugs he was aware that the babysitter was playing 'Bash the Nasty Rabbit' with Rob and that Flossy was teaching her Marble Polishing Machines Representative in the sitting-room. He distinctly heard, though the ear-plugs filtered off the background and made the voice seem immeasurably distant, a confident 'No, I daaasn't' (at least they weren't at the stage to be stumbling through her old copies of the *Morning Star*). Elaine would be out doing the shop in a thin windless rain. He imagined a slim figure struggling with an umbrella and two heavy plastic bags.

So what possible justification could he have for wasting time trying to write this trash that even his agent didn't want to see any more? A half-hour and he had only a few lines. He read them, moving down a line at a time with the winking (mocking?) cursor.

'Can boredom be a revelation? It may seem a contradiction in terms, but it certainly felt that way for me. Perhaps I mean revelation in the way illness is a revelation. There you are suddenly with a high temperature, a vicious pain beneath the ribcage. You vomit. And in the space of a few hours your whole life changes. You. . . .'

If it changed though, you wouldn't be bored any more, would you? Dying perhaps, but not bored. Was it really worth printing off this mulch? Maybe he should try thrillers, at least there was a pot of gold at the end of that rainbow.

Alan picked up an airmail edition of Monday's *Guardian*. What he needed was some more artistic company. Stimulation. Experimentally, just to see what it felt like, he opened a new file on the screen and started typing: 'Dear Mr Waterman, I write with reference to your ad in the *Guardian* (Dec 9th) for the position of copywriter. . . .'

What was he doing in Italy in a dead-end job? And what was worse with a time limit attached that would cut him off at precisely the age he became more or less unemployable in the UK? He'd come out here to write (it was the ease of the job that had fooled him) and all they'd done instead was have children.

He had allowed his energies to be dissipated. He had lost his way in life. Friends back home were leaping up the career ladder and he was teaching lousy students where not to put adverbs, getting no useful experience and merely filling wastebins with this trash that no word processor could make saleable.

'I am thirty-four, studied English at. . . .'

The phone rang. Alan felt an unmistakable sense of relief at being dragged away from himself.

'Pronto.'

In Flossy's manically neat hand, the blackboard over the phone showed his duties for the day. WASH DISHES. BATHE

ROB. PAY GAS BILL. They wanted the man to work of course, but they would never let you write the rota.

'Pronto?'

'Al,' Colin said, 'the fuckers're sacking again.'

———◦◦◦———

When she found it was Sandro she had buzzed in, Julia couldn't help feeling the kind of self-satisfaction that comes from seeing how just a half-dozen pleasant smiles have had their desired effect. She was particularly gratified to think that only a few moments before she had put on the new grey wool dress that showed how, away from London parties and with all this bike-riding Flossy had got her into, her body was trimming down into some kind of decent shape. Diana-shape, she thought.

'Sandro. How nice.'

But Sandro's usual grin was soured to a beaten-dog grimace this evening. The two clean rabbity teeth and the Harrison-Ford set of self-satisfaction were not in evidence. In running-shoes, black cords, black sweater and swept-back black glossy hair he preferred a rickety chair at the table to the armchair she offered and, sitting forward with his hands tapping an urgent beat on his knees, might have been a young priest trying to make the impossible compromise between his duties and a modern image. He looked worried and awkward.

'It's cold up here I'm afraid. I bought one of those electric radiator things but they haven't delivered yet. Can I get you something hot, or would you like wine?'

She poured wine and he thought the way she held her body so self-consciously, dressed so formally, might be in direct proportion to the way that same body left so much to be desired. (Perhaps the philosophy course was sharpening his mind. Nietzsche was his favourite so far: 'Beyond Good and Evil'. A great shame he hadn't had time for the stuff before.)

Julia sat herself cross-legged on the bed, only to find she had to push the new dress down harder than she expected in her lap. As usual she was aware of her mistake and as usual that painful awareness put her in a defensive throwaway mood. Rather abruptly she said: 'How come you came to Italy anyway? I thought Canada was supposed to be so wonderful.'

Sandro's grin returned, though ruefully: 'Seems I'll probably be on my way back there before very long. That's why I came over.' And he explained what had happened. He had a very earnest way of leaning forward when he spoke and giving the impression he was being perfectly frank about something people couldn't usually be trusted to be frank about. The listener felt privileged. Julia was reminded of student days when she had always seemed to be sitting cross-legged on beds or cushions in makeshift rooms talking to the kind of men who preferred earnest talk to discos.

'So the principle they're bound to apply,' he finished, 'is the principle of last in, first out. Easy decision. No problem about serious criteria. And that means us. At the end of December.'

'They can't do that!'

'I know, we've both travelled a long way to be here; we've left good jobs; we've spent a lot of time and money finding places and getting set up. They can't do it; but they will' – Sandro finished even more earnestly and dramatically – 'because this is Italy. They can do anything they want to you here. It's chaos.' He drummed a beat on his knees with a comb and the knee twitched up and down too. 'We'll be out on our asses without even the money for the flight home.'

Julia stared. Sandro's announcement had done her the favour of allowing her to forget her self-consciousness. She lifted a forefinger to her mouth and tugged at the nail. The brightness of her green eyes in the alarmed pale face was quite suddenly and surprisingly rather attractive.

'So what we've got to do is this: we've got to get to the professors and persuade them that the last-come-first-go deal is unfair and what's more impractical for them. The job has a five-year limit, so if they have to cut, the people who should get the push are the ones nearest to the end, get me? Otherwise

27

they'll be having to recruit new people again in just a year or so. Whoever's in their fourth or fifth year, out.'

'And who's that?'

'I don't know, but it's not us, is it? So that's got to be our line.'

Sandro pushed an urgent hand through glossy hair and his dark, almost black eyes took on a magnetic depth. More nervously, Julia curled her left hand over and behind her head to gather and then toss her hair so that it swung round and fell freshly washed on the front of her left shoulder. This brought out a stubborn sweep of jaw and neck to the right, as well as somehow drawing his attention to her breasts.

'But we've got to do it without getting up the other lettori's noses. Because we'll need them if it comes to a strike. If you see what I mean. Nobody's going to strike for no cuts if they think we're just trying to shift the great axe onto their necks. We've got to play a careful political line with the professors and then maximum solidarity alongside the others.'

Julia said she wouldn't know what to do if they fired her. For a moment she savoured her bewilderment as Sandro would be seeing it. Hard done by. Defenceless. But then she realized she was excited too. Destiny, perhaps, was telling her to go straight back to London, where she belonged. And to Lenny.

'Well, until they actually tell us anything, we've got to go on teaching, not give any sign of being resigned, or even expecting it'll be us to go.'

'No. Have you spoken to any of the others?'

'Only Scudellotti. There's to be a big meeting tomorrow at twelve in the faculty. I thought I'd better catch you first.'

And then with a sudden change of plan, that might or might not have had to do with the moment she tossed her hair like that, so that it caught the light against powdery whitewash behind and let her neck show suddenly long and marbly down to a respectable cleavage, he asked if she wouldn't like to go out and have a drink. 'Before the battle starts.'

'You didn't go to Oxford or Cambridge,' he enquired, as they walked down flight after flight of stone steps.

'God forbid.'

'Because I'm getting pretty pissed off with the Oxbridge brigade.'

'I know what you mean.'

'It's like a conspiracy. I mean, this constant crap about raising standards, as if they were the only ones capable of teaching at a high enough level. You can bet your life they'll make sure none of them gets the push – Manwearing, Habershom, Bexley and that crowd. Scudellotti licks shit for the Cambridge crew.'

'The whole of England,' Julia said with a sudden conviction that surprised even herself, 'is an Oxbridge conspiracy.' Lenny for a start, she thought, with his May Balls and Downing Association dinners. 'That's one of the reasons I left actually.'

'Stinks,' Sandro remarked, grinning confidence again.

December 14th   *Via Disciplina*

Dear Lenny,

No sooner do you – do I – get on a gravy train than it derails and I get thrown off. They've gone and cut two places here and seeing as I'm the most recent arrival it looks like I'll be one of the two to go. Which'll leave me high and dry. No point in going into the details because it's all so complicated. The fact is they never give you proper contracts here precisely so they can fire you at short notice. None of the foreign teaching assistants have contracts.

Anyway, it's all forced me into thinking what I'm really doing here and what I'm going to do for money in the New Year. Should I come back? Like you said, everyone wrote (even the illiterate Barry) saying I'd made a big mistake and they missed me playing charades – Barry said he missed the cocktails I mixed and the way I'm always hitching up my bra-strap (how does Kat-Kat put up with him? Probably only because he threatens

29

suicide every time she walks out, one ploy you must admit I've never tried). So, yes, I thought about just chickening out and getting the next plane home, because I do miss you all and it was very nice of everybody to write. I miss my room in Kensington, my spider plants and ferns, and I miss the big flowery comfy couch in the living-room and the stereo and the drinks cabinet everybody has to put a bottle in when they come. I even miss Diana hogging the phone with her bankers and insurance agents and bothering us all with readings from that dreadful Dolovov man – remember? Barry used to call him 'Do-leave-off' and he never seemed to notice.

But the point is, London would mean you again Lenny. It would mean loving you and wanting to be with you and having to share you with all the things you consider at least as important as me: Liz, squash, your teeny-bop typists and stupid current affairs programmes (I <u>don't</u> miss BBC TV). And I can't take it any more. You said life is not about plunge-taking. Probably you're right. But it's not about 'getting by' either. Getting <u>somewhere</u>, more like, building up something, making home. I mean, we've known each other 11 years now (can you believe it just took me five whole minutes to work that out?) Eleven years Lenny! We had a history behind us before you even met Liz. And after 11 years we still have this awful on-off relationship with me loving you achingly in a stupid little-girl way that makes me sick sometimes (because you're no great shakes, for Christ's sake) – and you still keeping me at arm's length, fitting me in carefully with your schedule, as if there was some pretence to be kept up, when Liz has known everything for aeons and screws around herself anyway and even the kids know in their own kids' way. You said so yourself. The truth is you only ever stuck with me because you were flattered by my loving you, because I was the only one that ever did. But you were scared as well as flattered. You were scared of anything intense (like when you pissed off on that stupid Nigerian project when your mother was dying, I couldn't believe it, simply because the whole thing terrified you and you didn't know how to behave);

so you left me and went and married fun-and-games dumb Liz who cared for you even less than you did for her. Serves you right.

Anyway, I've been thinking about all this and I decided, even if they do fire me, I can't come back. It's been so sweet, Lenny, our love these past years, but really so torturous too – and so exhausting. If I just think of all those times outside Khan's waiting for you to turn up in that 1100 you should have got rid of ages ago (you're such a miser with your £20,000 a year), or the Friday nights doing ditto in the lounge of the B&B on Hendon Way, I feel like screaming, I really do. Somehow it was always me doing the waiting, and I feel it always would be. So, I want to sort things out a bit more sensibly. Not that I believe in finding yourself or any of that rubbish (God knows what there is to find), I just want a situation with a job and a group of friends that isn't full of agonies and contradictions.

If you had the guts to come out here it would be different (you know Liz's going to inherit enough money from Daddy's roof tiles to put both boys through Eton ten times over, so don't come any of that financial shit). If you came out here, or invited me back to live with you, it would be all my dreams come true – and why not? (It could be Shangri-la <u>in</u> Shepherd's Bush.) But I know you won't.

Sorry if it's not a happy letter, but that's how I feel this morning. Anyway, I can't see as you deserve any better.

I love you still though. God knows why.

JULIA.

PS. I can't believe you went and wrote that <u>crap</u> about the school taking me back. I thought I'd told you a million times I'd die if I had to do another term with gruesome George. What the hell do you think I went to all those interviews for? For the pleasure of telling farty businessmen I was never going to have kids? The fact is, Lenny, you just want everything to go on the same way forever and ever with you hedging three million bets at once and everyone else eating shit out of your hand.

31

I'll close this before I start sticking pins in photographs.

PPS. Don't bother defending yourself.

PPPS. If I had a phone, I wouldn't give you the number, shithead.

With only ten minutes to go before the big meeting, Julia sealed one of the five envelopes already prepared with Lenny's BBC address and marked 'Confidential', then took a postcard from the assortment she kept in the drawer under the table and dashed off: 'Dear Diana – scored Sandro – great rejoicing – love J.'

Only as she was slipping the two messages into the battered red box on Via Venti Settembre did she notice that the card showed what looked like a great stone horsetrough with the legend in four languages:

> La tomba di Giulietta
> Le tombeau de Juliette
> Das Grab der Julia
> Juliet's Tomb

How the English did like to be different, she thought.

— •◦• —

Alan and Elaine had been sitting on the sofa of their gloomily furnished front room for some twenty minutes. They watched the two great windows opposite where the evening's twilight seemed to be bleeding away earlier and faster than usual, drawing dusty colours from pre-war furniture, darkening the face of a bruised and bleeding Santo Stefano on the wall above. They sat on; neither reached out to snap the light at the switch behind the sofa; they were enjoying the sense of sad peace that comes from watching natural light fade and familiar lines dissolve into shadow. Now only the panes themselves were clearly visible, looming larger and silver grey, as if they held the sky itself and what was left of light.

'Julia was hellishly belligerent,' Alan took up the conversation of some moments before.

'You can see why.'

'Nobody had actually *said* anything about firing her. Officially we were meeting to discuss two places cut by Rome; cuts the department can implement as it chooses. Or fight.'

'But she's not stupid. The latest arrival's always the first to go. She's got every reason to be angry if you ask me.'

'Yes. Angry, yes. Of course. We're all angry. Fine. But anger isn't belligerence, is it? What I mean is, it was as if she'd just been waiting for an opportunity to go hammer and tongs at everybody. And being new, she's got no idea how things work here. She doesn't realize the cuts will probably never happen. The Italian government's famous for giving in to everybody. She must have talked non-stop for 15 minutes.'

After a moment, Elaine laughed: 'You're such a bumbler, you know, Al, with your fine distinctions. I can't see any particular difference between anger and belligerence. I quite liked Julia. It seems she has every right to make a fuss. She gave up a job to come out here, for heaven's sake. It's a pretty shitty situation.'

Alan left a short space to let this criticism roll off his back.

'Anyway,' he resumed, 'her line was, instead of firing the two new arrivals, which nobody had said we were going to, mind, they should fire the two people nearest the end of their five years.'

'Who are?'

'Me and Colin.'

After another short silence, Elaine said: 'Fair enough in the end. We could go home.'

'Right, it's fair, and even logical, *if*, which I doubt, the worst does come to the worst, but it's not the sort of thing you say at a lettori's meeting, is it? and anyway it'll never get a majority because it would mean accepting the legitimacy of the time-limit on everybody's jobs, which is exactly what everybody's determined to fight. In fact, not even Sandro supported her.'

'But it's not the lettori making the decision, is it? It's the professors.'

'Of course, theoretically, it's the professors. But seeing as they'll never agree and seeing as they hate making unpleasant decisions, they'll sell us a line of shit about democracy and ask us to decide.'

'Makes for a bit of drama.' And laughing again, she added: 'Why not have a balloon debate?'

'Julia would love that. She's the sort who'd be asking to be thrown out just to prove her theory that everybody was against her in the first place.'

'Perhaps they are.'

'Well they certainly are after what she said today.'

'So what's this Sandro like? Tell me about him.'

'Thirtyish. Maybe more. Bit smarmy, but he seems quite straightforward. Italo-Canadian, so he has the advantage of speaking good Italian already. He agreed with Colin that we should go on strike against any cuts.'

'Colin playing big Scottish chief.'

'Right. In his Glaswegian Italian the Frogs and Spics are always saying they can't understand. They didn't want to strike of course because nobody's been cut from their departments. Pascal started talking about a responsible attitude to the students, which was funny coming from him; Krauts all in favour though, so that's how the vote'll go.'

Elaine said then she often wondered if Colin and Marina really got it on, him being such a beery old fart.

'He was saying in the bar afterwards she still insists on keeping Janet in their bed. He seemed pretty pissed off with it all. Said he wouldn't mind if they did throw him out. Give him the push he needs to make a move.'

'At forty-whatever with four kids.'

'Well, his angle is, you shouldn't ever let yourself get into feeling trapped anywhere, whatever the situation.'

'Yes, yes,' she laughed. 'Bullshit.'

Alan said then that actually he wouldn't mind going himself

if they fired him. He was wasting his time at the university. Nobody wanted to learn anything and nobody cared. The whole thing was a farce. It was easy money of course, but there was a terrible danger of becoming polluted morally, if she saw what he meant, just taking money for doing next to nothing. Sometimes, maybe, you had to chuck in something you didn't want before you could find something you did.

'You've only said that about a million times.'

There was a twinkle in her eyes as she told him this, which was annoying, and likewise her prim little nose and little puckered lips were annoying him this evening, this bright, practical airy happy look she had, when their future was at stake.

'I know.'

'So just decide. Don't fuss over it. I'm dying to go back. Why wait to see if you're fired? That amounts to letting your future be decided by an administrative muddle.'

'We can't afford to be impulsive, though, can we?'

'But what's impulsive about deciding to go back?'

'It's just I'll never have any time for myself, like I have here.'

'You're always saying you don't have any.'

'But imagine how little I'd have commuting to a job and crawling home half-dead in the evening. And then having to face the TV on top of everything else and see the idiots who've made it on Channel 4.'

'Then stay here and write. See if you can get a permanent contract.'

The brisk logic of this turnabout was exasperating.

After a moment Alan tried: 'But you don't even like my plays.'

'Not particularly, but I know they're what you want to do. So okay.'

'But you just said you were dying to go back. I can't stay here thinking I'm making you stay when you don't want to.'

'If you want to, I want to.'

'It can't be as simple as that.'

'Look,' Elaine said, 'if I want to go back, then I'll go, you don't have to worry about me when you make your decisions.'

'But we're married, for Christ's sake, with two kids; of course I have to worry about you. I mean, how can you say one moment. . . .'

'All I want is for you to do what makes you happy – as long as it's more or less viable financially.' And she leaned across and planted a kiss on the corner of his mouth.

'Ellie,' Alan said, taking her hand and realizing he was a prisoner of his ambitions. Ambitions he might well have grown out of. What was more, she refused to make his decisions for him. 'Ellie,' he repeated, drawing her to rest against his shoulder.

They were in the complete black dark now, except that the darkness had a gloss to it where the windows were. They sat on another five minutes and he threw an arm around her. Suddenly he said: 'Do you ever think of the stars?' She said not particularly, why? He'd heard something on the World Service about anti-matter. Whatever that was. One of the silly science programmes. The possibility of a whole universe made of anti-matter. But the point was, whenever he tried to think of the stars, he couldn't, they were unimaginable. Not so much the stars, but the spaces between them. 'The interstellar spaces.' He felt dizzy trying to imagine them. The only way he could get anywhere near was by feeling he was falling, falling through those spaces for ever. Those impossible distances. And what he couldn't decide was, whether he felt elated that the world was so magnificent and fine and he was part of it, or appalled that it was so large, infinite, and infinitely beyond his grasp or ken. That he might as well be dead in a way.

'Here we are in our tiny domestic box of bliss,' Alan said, 'our home, looking out on that darkness, I mean, do we feel attracted, drawn out there to those pinpoints of light, or repelled, forced to take refuge and cling here? Or even more disturbingly, both, torn?'

Did one go on from Italy, he might have added, an ex-pat all your life, or flee home to cosy pubs, mortgages and the kind of contacts who'd be bound to find you something some day?

Along Via Quattro Novembre, all the lights went on together and a beam of sodium yellow cut a new angle through the room across a clutter of toys on the carpet. From being part of the vast evening, the space around them shrank to all the tidying up they ought to do.

'Oh shit,' Elaine said. 'We'll have to wake the menace up. It's five already.' And she said: 'When are we ever going to make love if we go and throw up opportunities like this? At least if we were in London we could dump the kids on Mum.'

Standing up, she said: 'Anyway, I thought you were going to do the shop, this evening. Moonface says she can't manage it when she's out with Robert.'

Coming back into the room a moment later with Margaret over her shoulder, Elaine laughed: 'Speaking of stars though, I tell you what I do feel like, a lager and lime in the Plough on Sandringham Ave.'

In his notebook, Alan remarked: 'My wife: sometimes it's as though I'd only met her yesterday and were trying to decide whether I really wanted to see her again.'

———— •◦• ————

Having discovered they were both Oxbridge haters, Colin invited Sandro to after-dinner drinks at his flat on Viale del Commercio. Instead of having him write down the address, Colin gave him a business card four inches by three, a postcard almost; this said:

Professor Colin M. Tinsley
Traduttore Scientifico
Viale del Commercio 371
Telefono: 55 98 64

Beneath the address was a series of curious signs in red that Sandro was unable to identify; a mixture of geometry and Arabic perhaps, or runes.

It was the first time he had been to the modern, industrial

side of the city; the air was spongy with thickening fog and the pale yellow squares of lighted windows floated here and there, floors above, as if detached. Why bother being in Italy if you lived here?

Tinsley had a three-bedroom flat, four children, a very attractive young wife and a heavy Scottish accent that seemed to have something to do with the thick, uncut marmalade beard he was constantly fingering with whichever hand wasn't busy holding glass and cigarette. Incongruously, he wore a canary yellow shirt and blue neckscarf, and his nose was noticeably long and curved. His wife, who Sandro had to make a conscious effort not to follow with his eyes, was shifting away dirty dishes that had doubled up as ashtrays; a little girl clutched at her legs while the older children trooped remarkably obediently off to their bedrooms, whence a strain of television. The air was thick with tobacco smoke, food smells and a doggy odour, for the Tinsleys had a dog too, a big mongrel that had to be cleared off an armchair to make room for Sandro. On the walls, posters depicted zodiac signs and astrological charts.

'Y'see, I'd go myself, I really would' – they were immediately settled with beers, Colin speaking rather loudly to drown the whines of his youngest daughter – 'I'm fed up with the place. Especially with silly farts like Manwearing and Habershom, wanting to teach the kids Gerard Manley Hopkins before they know how to say, I do, I don't. No, I'm ready for out, and I've got the contacts here, I mean, I could do it, it's only a third of what I make anyway, when you've got four kids, what do you want? and then I have been here seventeen years, bugger it. But the point is, of course, if I bow out, and I still might for God's sake, because you never know how you might feel tomorrow morning; Christ, I got married, I got divorced, I got married again, freedom means believing everything's possible – no, if I bow out, the government has won, hasn't it? That's the problem. They wanted to cut and they'll have managed it. They don't care where the cuts come. They'll have got their cuts. When these kids need teaching! Fact it seems that at their meeting after our meeting, Bertelli and Scudellotti were in agreement with that cow Juliet or whatever she's called, to keep you and her and ditch me and Bexley, who is, yes, a dithery Harrow-Bridge boy whose parents have got more money than sense, so he doesn't need the salary, but not a bad lad in the end, I mean, not at the Manwearing-Habershom level, at least he's conscientious, nice wife (haven't you met her? very attractive); they were ready to ditch us because Scudellotti hates my guts over me organizing the union and everything, only of course Errico blocked that because I do about half the work of his whole fucking translation agency, another thing I want out of, but there you are, I've got mouths to feed. No, what we've got to do is hang together. The kids need teaching. Things are already bad, but cut two lettori and the whole department more or less goes to pieces. That's the angle we have to insist on. Not a strike to save jobs, but to defend the kids' rights. And we've got to get the students on our side and the local press and TV – tell them what a scandal the situation is – and no more of this pathetic crap about which of us is going to go first. Because nobody's going to go. If we don't approach it that way then we may as well not fight it at all. We may as well just lie down and die right from the fucking start, sell the kids down the river and put our heads on the block.'

'I'm behind you all the way,' Sandro said into the first available space, 'that's exactly how. . . .'

But now, still wiping her hands on an apron she'd slipped off, Marina came back into the room, which immediately smelt of sex, Sandro thought. In tight trousers, she perched on the arm of the sofa beside her husband, slithered a hand inside his shirt and kissed him. Which only emphasized, with the one skin against the other, how much damage the years had done to that part of Colin's cheeks not hidden by his beard. As if he'd never left the Scottish wind or whisky behind. Smiling very attractively at Sandro, drawing the little girl who'd followed her onto her knee, she said in Italian: 'I bet you're Sagittarius,' and, surprisingly, was right. He grinned Harrison Ford's grin.

'Colin's Aquarius,' she went on in a tone that indicated this was a motive for pride. Her eyes were very big and hazel brown. 'That's why he left England. And Janet is Scorpio, aren't you, love. We timed it on purpose.'

Around ten-thirty a young brawny man named Beppe arrived bringing a box of tangerines, and apparently he was a green-grocer. There was a game of chess he'd left unfinished with Colin. The board was brought down from off the top of the kitchen cupboard and Sandro thought in Beppe's position he'd have resigned twenty moves ago.

Over chess and tangerine peel, the evening's conversations included discussions on: freemasonry, Nietzsche, the three secrets of Fatima, a long overdue revolution in the spelling of English vowel sounds (choir, fire, liar, lyre, higher), and the way the health service were dealing with a cyst in Marina's ovaries, all subjects on which Colin had the last word in a defiantly Scottish Italian.

———— •◦• ————

Jan 5   *Piazza dei Caduti, Quinzano*

Dear Mum,

Thanks for the birthday and Christmas cards.

I was so sorry to hear you've been ill. For heaven's sake, though, don't be so stubborn, go to the doctor, or better still, to the hospital so they can give you a proper check-up with all the tests and everything. It's ridiculous saying that doctors and hospitals just make you think of what happened to Dad. You both paid for the service all your life, so use it. It makes me quite mad sometimes to think of you ill and refusing to get help. Especially with all the charities you're always giving to.

I know I said I'd be back for Christmas, but then when it came round it seemed I'd only just arrived here and my finances were so low after paying rent and so on I thought it best to leave be, at least until Easter, especially seeing as everybody's on strike at the university at the moment, so we're not getting paid. Too complicated to explain in detail.

Mum, I know you were disappointed about my moving so far away and not being able to help out with the shopping and come to lunch Saturdays and so on, and I miss it all too. I know you also think I was silly to chuck in the security of the job at Christ Church. It was just that I was going crazy doing the same things all the time, always, and at the same time not knowing why I was bothering. Anyway, there must be more to life than job security. At least it's been an adventure coming out here, and a rest frankly – my London rut was so infernally busy. You said yourself I was always looking tense and worried.

Oh, make sure to write down my new address. I've taken a flat with that girl Flossy I told you about. We get on fine. We've gone on a really tough diet together because she has the same weight problem I have. The trouble at Diana's was she could tuck away chocolates day in day out till Doomsday without ever putting on an ounce or getting a spot. Some people have all the luck. Flossy's got me into cycling too, which must help.

Lots of love and write soon,

JULIA.

Julia felt guilty about this letter: she felt it was lacking in real affection. Perhaps because she had written it from the first in a spirit of duty. She re-read, pouting sternly as she did when she concentrated.

P.S. Please don't say you feel so depressed and lonely, Mum. At least you did have a terrific husband. I mean, everybody around is divorcing, cheating on each other, turning homosexual and everything, but you were both happy right through. I was thinking only yesterday of all our holidays together when we were small. I don't know why I should have been thinking that. Perhaps it was seeing an ad for family reductions on the trains. I remembered you knitting on the beach and the spluttering way Dad used to swim in those baggy red trunks he had and when he called Mike a young scallywag all the time. (I do hope Mike is putting in an appearance now and then, by the way – I shall write and tell him to.) It's always been the Black Rock holiday I remember best of all. When we lived in the converted bus and Dad killed all the hornets. We do have a lot of great memories, Mum, and what are they there for if not to cheer us up?

Love again. J.

By the way, as far as Mike is concerned, I can't see anyone German marrying someone as confused as him. So stop worrying. Let him sort out his own life. He's a bit of an idiot, but he's always had a wonderful way of falling on his feet. I just hope I shall too.

------◆◆------

Jan 5th   *Piazza dei Caduti, Quinzano*

Dear Mikey,

I've written to Mum, telling her not to worry about you, but she's bound to be a bit lonely still and I'd put up with her as much as you can, if I were you. Let her knit you sweaters and come round occasionally. What does it cost? I know you feel bitter about the way they pushed you into doing economics and then went berserk when you changed. And of course you're right. Dad acted in his usual dumb, traditional, ignorant, high-handed way. I know you also feel bitter about me not helping you in the fight. And probably you're right again, though I had my own personal problems at the time, and anyway they always ignored me and spoilt you silly, you male-child you! so I didn't feel particularly eager to help (plus you were old enough to fight your own battles, for heaven's sake). But what I'm trying to say is, even if you were right, why make Mum pay for it now, never visiting her and so on? She's a fine person, even if she does live in the last century, and although I don't believe in God, or in anything really, I do think we have an obligation to be generous towards our parents. I couldn't say why. I just think that.

And I also think you'd make a great model! You're always posing, aren't you, and there's no point in pretending you're not handsome. What I can't understand is how none of the family looks came my way. I'd give a lot for your eyelashes. So have a go. If it stops you being reliant on Mother, maybe you'll find you can get on with her again.

Everything's fine here. I'd ask you to visit if you ever had any money!

Love to you and Brünhilde.

Your sis, JULIA.

Jan 6th   *Fortis Green*

Dear Julia,

I met Diana and somebody called Stuart in Hampstead last week and they told me you'd gone to Italy. Lenny hadn't told me anything of course. Very silly of him. He tries to keep up this veneer of propriety when I've told him I'm perfectly resigned about the open marriage situation until the kids have grown up, and then it's each for his or HER own. Oh yes.

They've taken me on at the Adelphi again. Just a small part. Costs a fortune in babysitters and I had to give up the badminton league, but it's good to be under lights again and there are lots of parties.

Well, I just thought I'd write to wish you luck. I think you did the right thing going. Verona does sound romantic. Romeo and Juliet, no? One part I'll never play again!

Best of luck and no hard feelings.

LIZ.

In conversation with Sandro as they stood at the Faculty door handing out leaflets, Alan was explaining the novel he was writing; or maybe it would be a play. The point of the thing was, what does a person do when he suddenly discovers his life has no meaning, offers no excitement, has no direction. When, for example, after years of ambition and love and setting up home and having babies and all the things people do in their twenties and thirties, he suddenly discovers it is all hopeless and boring and senseless.

Sandro watched passing legs: 'Gets himself laid.'

'Right, of course, sex. But imagine we have an intelligent or maybe shy person, or just someone who appreciates that fucking around is only a temporary solution, that in a way it's only evading the problem. And then that it will hurt his marriage, his wife, his children, and he doesn't want that. He doesn't want to do anything cheap.'

Sandro was dressed in dark trousers with a crease, a turtle-necked white pullover and a short belted coat with fur inside. He said: 'At least he'll have some complications to deal with.'

Alan had an ancient college scarf thrown carelessly round his neck. His complexion was pink to Sandro's sallow.

'Yes, but negative, painful ones. No, I don't really see complications as an answer to boredom. Because the hero's problem is, he's too smart. He sees through the conventional protective strategies, the existential ploys.'

'He could emigrate, change job, start a new life. Ambitions. Hobbies.'

'Yes, that's what happens in fact. In the novel, if I don't make it a play. I thought of a terrific quote to put at the beginning: "Life is short, and yet one gets bored." Anouilh. Anyway, no, he emigrates, goes to India and things, new religions, meditation, you know the scene, filling up time, loads of Brits do it. We're doing it in a way, I suppose, coming over here. I'll make it a bit picaresque probably. Life is after all. But the question I'm asking is, what if, after a few years, the new place becomes old, if you see what I mean, becomes familiar, boring, and he's back at square one? Only worse. Because he can't just repeat the escape experience, can he? The next new place, new ambition, new woman, wouldn't be as new as the first. In the sense that he knows now that its newness is temporary. He knows that any superficial move would be just that, superficial. The problem is in himself. I suppose I'm just trying to explore the possibilities, turn that exploration into a plot. What does he do? That would be the book's tension. What does the hero do? Is there a way out of this dead end?'

'Psychoanalysis,' Sandro suggested; and after a moment, even more resourcefully, 'Suicide.'

But Alan said, on the contrary, this was precisely where the twist, the resolution would come. 'Exactly when the reader is sure the thing is heading for total disaster, marriage break-up, heavy drinking, drugs maybe, possible suicide, the hero finally discovers the real meaning of life in his love for his wife, his children.'

'Who he was so bored out of his mind with previously.'

'Right, yes. Only now he perceives them in a different light. He senses their value and he feels fulfilled. Complete. Finds a new intensity. Appreciates the depth of his love for his wife. Like the king,' he added, though this was pushing it a bit, 'in *The Winter's Tale*.'

'Perhaps because she's dying of cancer.'

This mightn't actually be a bad idea, Alan thought, with the way cancer was selling these days, but said: 'The real problem is to make the end convincing, to avoid a feeling of wishful thinking, of wilful optimism on the writer's part. Convey a sense of real discovery, belief, relief. I mean, I believe in the really earned happy ending.'

Sandro said: 'Uh huh.' And he said: 'I was reading Wittgenstein over Christmas.'

There was the tiniest pause before Alan said, 'Oh yes?'

'"On Certainty".'

'Don't know it. Can't say I'm big on philosophy. Time's the bastard. God, if I had time I'd read everything.' He pushed a hand up into bristling hair.

'Good book,' Sandro said. 'Gives you a new angle. What you

mean when you say you know something.' He waited and then went on. 'The idea is, there are some things that if they turned out not to be true, it would change your whole life, bring the whole house of cards down. And those are the things we say "I know" about, because otherwise we couldn't go on, if you see what I mean.'

Alan couldn't precisely get the relevance of this to his hero's predicament. Unless boredom was to be taken as one of those pillars of certainty? He asked politely: 'What did you do at Christmas? Have you got family here?'

Sandro lived with a great-aunt, he said. Sister of his grandfather who'd gone to Toronto in the twenties. They'd been invited to some old friends of hers. The great-aunt had a florist's shop, so she was always busy festive times.

'Nice,' Alan said rather at random, sifting titles now. The point was to keep up a constant mental pressure. Sooner or later the barriers must give way. The form would declare itself.

They handed out leaflets to a group of incoming students. The xeroxed sheets invited everybody to a meeting at which a vote would be taken on a sit-in. They told the students it was their rights and education at stake.

'If we don't get any joy out of this soon, I'm going to be hurting,' said Sandro.

'So is everybody,' Alan agreed with the same relished grimness. 'Hurting' might be terrific as a title. And he invited Sandro to dinner.

Some half an hour later Alan was in Scudellotti's office where he told the professor he was ready to leave the job himself if that would make things easier for everybody. Scudellotti was an effeminate man in his late forties with an over-eager, boyish face and manner. He wore English tweeds, rimless glasses, and a grass-green tie. Under no circumstances he said, under no circumstances could they afford to lose someone of Alan's academic background and artistic commitment, when there were others like – but he wasn't going to name names – who had no qualifications whatsoever, no ambitions or commitments apart from their salaries; and he was furious, he said, with Errico and Bertelli, quite livid, because there had been two very obvious candidates to get rid of right at the start and if they'd made a decision, a simple clear-cut decision, it would have nipped the strike in the bud, so to speak, if one could apply such a delicate metaphor to something so clumsy and unpleasant and fundamentally selfish, and that would have been very much that. Speaking of which though, seeing as there were no lessons, there were one or two things that might usefully be done in the library, ordering new books and so on; they were particularly thin on eighteenth century background. Alan slipped a large block of catalogue cards into his bag.

'Will do,' he said, and when he was at the door Scudellotti said it would be absolute folly for him to go now, a golden opportunity thrown away, because he really was the only, the only candidate for the permanent research post they had.

———◆◆◆———

'Alan,' Flossy said through a thick cold, 'doesn't like the strike because he has the hots for all the sexy little things who go to his Romantics class. And he only does the Romantics class because it makes him feel more important. More literary. The lettori aren't supposed to teach literature, only language. It must cost him two hours a week in extra preparation.'

She said: 'Sandro always has to be waited on when he comes round. Have you noticed. He gets brought his dinner, you even mix his whisky for him.'

'Alan does his big moral thing,' she said, 'about wife and kids and believing in marriage because it's the only sensible way to run your sex life, he says, without hurting people and so on, but the truth is he only married Elaine on the rebound after this Mary, the one he wrote the plays about who tried to kill him with the paperweight. He's so proud of that. Anyway, if you watch him closely, he's always staring at women. If she lost her figure, he'd be out before . . . before. . . .'

'Decency is always a veneer with men,' she said. 'Or always something they have the wrong reason for.'

They pushed their bikes up the last steep curves to Roverè. The day was splendidly still with the vast Alpine panorama falling around them in bright cold sunshine on fields of glistening snow. Julia puffed and panted and her breath froze. Her lungs felt as if she were swallowing acid. Flossy had dark stains of sweat under tracksuit armpits.

'What I can't stand though is the way they both accept that he is the genius of the family, that he's the one time has to be made for, these blessed three creative hours a day he has to have, when she's just as smart as he is. Men always seem to think they have a monopoly on ambition and artistic pretensions. And the thing that infuriates me about Elaine is the way she's content to play smug second fiddle and coo over the kids as if that were all life was about, as if any idiot couldn't have kids. Not to mention the way she repeats what he says all the time. Really. Soon as anyone gets angry and tries to wake her up of course she just says they're frustrated.'

And Flossy said: 'He complains about Thatcher and what she's done to the arts, as if that were anything compared with what she's doing to the working class, and then he goes and gets Robert booked in at Harrow. I can't believe it.'

The small town of Roverè appeared as they rounded a curve; holiday houses and old farm buildings were scattered scruffily in melting snow along the uneven ground where various slopes and valleys ran together. The stillness suddenly had a sound of running water.

'You know, the way Sandro washes up after every meal reminds me exactly of my father, before we got a dishwasher that is. Punching his ticket and nothing more. Such a dumb grin of self-satisfaction for having rinsed a few plates. You can bet it's the dear old aunt washes all his underwear.'

'Rabbity teeth he's got,' she said.

'Speaking of which, I thought maybe we could do a wash

when we get back and see if we can't fix up a line in the bathroom.'

And wiping her nose on her sleeve, Flossy said: 'Seems a bit less steep here; think you can make it if we stay in low gear?'

At which Julia finally found the breath to gasp: 'I just hope to God there's a bloody bar open when we get there.'

———◆◇◆———

January 25th   *Piazza dei Caduti, Quinzano*

Dear Diana,

Suddenly everything seems to be going wrong: the job, the flat situation, Sandro, even the weather for heaven's sake. It's been foggy and wet and utterly miserable for days. Of course, I knew Italy wasn't permanently paradise, but I didn't expect this. People would be complaining on the Edgware Road. It has a way of going absolutely still and dull and damp that makes you think the sun will never shine again. As if the season had pulled an ugly face and got paralysed. At least a windy morning on Kensington Church Street was invigorating, even if it did blow your umbrella inside out.

So, the job. We've been on strike a month over these cuts. Since Christmas. It's a ridiculous situation. The cuts were made by the government but left to the faculty here to implement, and I think if the professors had just said, 'Okay, you and you, out', that would have been the end of it, because all the ones left would have been so pleased it wasn't them. But like I told you before, the professors can't agree about anything, so they told the lettori to decide amongst themselves. Can you imagine? If there'd been a couple of volunteers everybody would have been happy, but of course there weren't. They all pretend to be very socialist (doesn't everybody?) and it's actually terribly funny because we have these meetings together with the assistants from the French and German departments, so everybody has to speak Italian, though nobody is, and somehow the way we all stutter along with our awful accents just makes the hypocrisy even more obvious, especially one horrendous fifty-year-old, ginger-bearded, hawk-nosed Scottish bloke who seems to think he's Mick McGahey. He must have left England in the sixties I imagine and it's all still workers rule, ok.

I rather stupidly tried to get some sense into the affair by suggesting that since we do so few hours, maybe the salary for eight could be divided by ten and everybody could stay, but I think they thought I was crazy, or desperate, or a government infiltrator or something.

So we ended up going on strike for our gravytrain. I must say, it is nice having a gravytrain, but it's pretty embarrassing going on strike for it and having to pretend to be angry. I mean, I could really have got into a good juicy strike at Christ Church, but this is silly. Anyway, somebody rang the newspapers and TV and they interviewed a few of the lettori speaking in Glaswegian, Oxbridge, Parisian and Ruhr Valley accents – God knows what the local wops made of it – and the newspaper did a whole two-page spread called, Our Fight for International Culture, and none of this had any effect at all. Most of the students don't come to lessons anyway, never mind read the papers. We arranged a sit-in and only twenty-odd turned up, all from the Young Communists' Association. The TV people came and we all tried to sing the Red Flag, except that the Italians were singing it in Italian and the English in English and nobody had their hearts in it anyway, so when it was time for the building to close, we gave up and everybody went to the bar where the Scottish bloke got drunk and swore and slapped everybody on the back and talked about psychological stamina and low points and high points and pacing our protest (with foam in his beard and veins showing in his nose!) What a bore! God knows how it will all end.

The result for the moment is that I'm spending a lot of time at home with Flossy in our flat, which is a bit out of town in the main square of a village called Quinzano where some masochist of a priest rings the churchbells at 6.30 every morning and incredibly nobody seems to mind. It must have been quite a nice square once, only they ruined it with a big war memorial with awful futurist heroism mosaics that just block the view and get pissed and scribbled on by the local yobbos (everywhere you go there are local yobbos, like Coca-cola and Tampax). Our flat is on the first floor of an old place overlooking the monument and has three big rooms plus bathroom, kitchen and balcony, so it's a great improvement on Via Disciplina, if not quite up to Peel Street standards. At least I can get away from Napoleon's whistling by sticking him out on the balcony.

The only trouble is Flossy. I know you used to say I was a misery, but you should see her. She goes round with this quite terminally glum and bitter look all the time. When I met her I thought it was just the thick cold she had, but now I've discovered she has the same terrible cold all the time (she has allergies) and the same doggedly baleful rather suffering expression. You remember when I was with you I used to get furious about the way you didn't share my views and would put up with those awful conservative men. I used to think it would be nice to live with another feminist. Only now I'm with Flossy she's just so insistently negative and bitchy I find myself saying the kind of things you used to say, and so we both end up rubbing each other up the wrong way.

Maybe part of the trouble is we're on a pretty drastic diet and watching like hawks to see the other doesn't sneak to the fridge, etc. (we have a weigh-in Saturday mornings and stick the figures on a chart. Childish, but it works). What's really maddening though, is that even when we're arguing she insists we do everything together, shopping, cycling, cinema, cupboard-cleaning, the lot. She never leaves be. (And after arguing we have to 'analyse our attitudes'!) She can't let go of the idea that we ought to be the best of friends, as if we weren't just flatmates but lifetime bosom buddies as well. The only time I get any peace at all is when she meditates, on what I don't know, or when she goes off to town to teach. Anyway, when Sandro comes over she's always starting political arguments (she has this indignant, short-sighted look when she argues and bites her tongue, which makes you feel quite sorry for her until you get used to it); but the bottom line is that she never takes a hint and gets out, the way we used to (remember Raunchy Ronnie?). I was afraid it would scare him off at first, but he seems to quite enjoy it, which is actually rather worse. He eats peanuts, watches the TV here (which somehow manages to be worse than the Beeb, but don't tell the boys) and gives the odd smug reply, until Flossy finally stomps off to the bedroom in disgust. I get furious with her for grinding on and on so much, and furious with him for being so sarcastic and not caring whether we're ever alone or not and watching so much dumb stupid television. In fact I'm beginning to think he's a bit of a lump.

You remember when I first came I said how attractive he was? Well, it's worse. He really is super-handsome: these dark brown, almost black, liquidy eyes, a lovely soft, just ever so slightly twangy voice, good strong shape to his face, good cheekbones, always smiling a bright pleased-with-himself smile, clear complexion, slim strong physique (he's started going to a gym), and then he just oozes charm – the kind of man you (I) can't believe is spending any time with you at all, as if you'd suddenly found Harrison Ford in your bed (there's a resemblance).

So what on earth's wrong? you may ask. Well, it's odd, but the thing is we just don't seem to be getting anywhere. Nothing is happening. What I mean is, we've been to bed together quite a few times now and he's very nice and good and everything, but I don't seem to be really falling in love with him and he doesn't act as if I was his girlfriend or anything particularly special. He just comes round maybe twice a week without having to be invited, but then without inviting me anywhere else either, and he eats while we starve ourselves and then he sits in the armchair and watches TV or talks politics, or about the strike, grinning and being sincere and smug at the same time and drumming on his knees with a steel comb (which makes me nervous); and he seems perfectly happy, as if our friendship had nowhere else to go and everything were just the way he wants it. There's no intensity or urgency at all: and it's sad, because it makes you feel, however awful it all was, maybe you can never replace the intensity you left behind and the friends you knew for years and had a real feeling for. I suppose really it was a mistake rushing into things, getting myself a new lover and flatmate so fast. You meet people here, Flossy, Sandro, and you imagine they'll be to you what other people have been to you in the past. You're in a hurry to change, to set up home. Only then you find they're not what you expected at all and that you can't simply choose to be intimate with them. Or sometimes it's as if none of us were quite all here, as if part of Sandro was in Toronto with someone he's not telling me about, part of Flossy on Greenham Common, part of me in Khan's (what an awful thought, curried!), and all of us vaguely angry with each other for carrying each other even further from the moments that mattered.

Or maybe I'm just depressed. Everything seemed to start so well, then just went to pieces. I was even missing the way we used to argue over who should clean what yesterday. Flossy writes up a terribly meticulous rota, and tapes it on the fridge door, the idea being that if everything is programmed down to the last dot and comma there'll be no reason for arguing. But it's not much fun and we seem to end up cleaning the place about ten times more than it needs and then arguing all the same anyway.

It started me thinking how we two became such good friends sharing that flat together and rowing about who to invite to dinner and whether it was worth translating poetry; the strange thing is I never really noticed till I left. I suppose I was always hankering after the impossible with you-know-who. I never sat back and enjoyed. So that now I spend half my time trying to decide why I don't just get the bus to the airport and fly home before I've collected too much baggage to be able to carry it on my own.

Best love, Di-pie. J.

PS. Can you do me an enormous favour? I'll understand perfectly if you can't, but I'd be so grateful if you could. Can you go and visit my mother? She wrote to say she'd been ill, but I'd like to know how seriously, and the only way is for someone to go and see her. When she's well she plays hypochondriac to get attention, and then when she's really ill she pretends she isn't because she's so scared of dying. I'd ask my brother, but he's so anti-family one can hardly rely on him. If you could just drop in for ten minutes and see if she's alright that would stop me worrying.

PPS. I heard your bit on Roumania on the Beeb. You sounded just like you (what a clear-bell voice you have!). It was as if you were right here in the room! Flossy says the BBC is the voice of the establishment. I thought of L and told her no, it wasn't. It's the voice of inertia. The funny thing is she always has to listen to the football results to see how Brighton are getting on. It seems so out of character. Apparently her grandad used to take her and brother Alan when they were very young. Thank God nobody took me. The time she wastes. And they always lose. Still, it's the only chance I get to tease her about her false consciousness.

PPPS. I'm 10 stone 3. 8 pounds more for the target. I'll send you a photograph if I'm still alive.

———◆◇◆———

Feb 10th   *Vicolo Storto*
                                                37100 Verona

Dear Martha,

Lots of thanks for the kind letter. Yes, they are many years that we are not seeing each other now. I hope that you and Vittorio are fine.

You say that Sandro is not replying to your letters. But he is living still here with me. He is not gone away. He is out very much and works very much and I think he is happy. He is smiling always. The young people today is not easy to understand, but

54

Sandro is polite and he gives me always the money for staying.

You say that you do not know why Sandro is leaving the Canada. He is not saying nothing to me about this matter. If he will say me something, I will write to you once more again.

Un caro abbraccio   ZIA LIVIA.

———◆◇◆———

Julia met Elaine on a day that was suddenly beautiful after early fog. Elaine was steering a little boy on a pushchair over Ponte della Vittoria when Julia spilled out of the crush of the 14 bus directly into her path. Immediately they invited each other for cappuccinos and pastries. Elaine was looking little-girlish, despite a difficult night. She wore old jeans and an untidy parka jacket, her curls were flat and tousled, but her walk had a lively flounce about it that made her seem at once fresh and feminine, and her eyes were bright. Julia was made up and carefully dressed, because she had decided to replace the ritual of eating breakfast with the rituals of rubbing in creams and choosing clothes, in the hope that the renunciation of cereals and toast would somehow prove less torturous. However, and strangely, it was not until she had taken the first bite from an attractive apple turnover, bouncing Robert on her knee, that she remembered her diet and burst out laughing.

'If Flossy could see me now!'

Elaine said she had never got on with Flossy. Partly because she had tried to monopolize the children and boss everybody around, and then because with the colds she always had it was hardly good for them. Added to which, to be honest, she was jealous. Even if it was costing a fortune in babysitters now she was gone.

Julia said she actually liked Flossy very much and had a lot of fun on their bike rides: it was just a bit hard to live with her, and then she had that kind of battlecry, do-or-die feminism that seemed to have no place for men, which was rather throwing out the baby with the bathwater, as it were. She felt quite sorry for her.

'Oh that's just a show. You should see her when she gets a crush on someone. It's appalling. She positively simpers.' And Elaine said Flossy's problem was that when she fell in love with a man he was always married, or anyway in some way unattainable, and Alan's theory was that unconsciously she did this on purpose so as to have an excuse for the inevitable rebuff, which really depended on her being cussed and not very attractive and having that cold all the time.

Julia remarked that she was always falling in love with married men too, though she hoped not for the same reason.

Elaine said cheerfully: 'Well, I shouldn't bother falling in love with Alan. He's so busy with his writing he doesn't have time for his wife and kids, let alone a mistress. Sometimes I wonder if he's actually noticed we're in Italy, he spends so much time pecking on his computer.' She laughed: 'It's funny how he's convinced he's such a good husband. But men are like that.'

They rolled cigarettes, regretting Old Holborn and Golden Virginia – Drum was nice, but pretty boring in the end – and Elaine said that sex was anyway fairly relative once you'd had two kids. In fact if it wasn't a contradiction in terms she'd suggest kids as the best contraceptive known to man. Her tits were ruined. The bra companies probably promoted childbirth because you could never do without them afterwards. It had been the greatest mistake of her life, she added breezily, having the kids, because they cut your freedom down to a minimum for ever.

'Don't you?' she asked Robert.

And he said, 'Mummy,' and broke Julia's heart.

Julia asked what did Elaine think about the strike and Elaine said Alan said it was just a farce with all the lettori going in more or less every day to ingratiate themselves with the professors so they wouldn't be the ones eventually fired. Alan of course was too proud and wrapped up in this play he was writing to go and do the same thing, more fool him. Sandro it seems was the expert; he'd started doing translations at an incredibly low rate for Errico's agency and offered to help Bertelli with this course book she always told people she was preparing and never finished.

Julia didn't know about that.

Elaine said actually she would be rather thankful if Alan were fired, since then they would have to go home. She had been talking to a student at the Cambridge school, only the other day, who had just come back from London, and as he listed the places he'd visited, Covent Garden and Portobello Road and Soho, she had suddenly felt tears pricking her eyes. She really very nearly did burst into tears. 'I thought, but those are *my* places, that's *my* city. That's where *I* should be living. Honestly, for a moment I thought, if I don't go back soon I'll go mad.'

She added: 'I have so many friends in London.'

Julia said she did too.

They paid and left. Elaine, walking away scruffy and un-combed with her two-year-old boy, was more attractive than herself, Julia thought, despite make-up and careful dressing. No need for childbirth to force her into bras.

But she didn't mind, the way she might have done ten years ago. And she was happy about Italy today. She liked being here. She liked the different streets and smells, the change in air; and she liked a creeping romantic feeling which had to do with its all being over; where the 'it' was something more than just Lenny, Christ Church and Kensington. She had subtracted herself from all their scrutiny was the thing perhaps. She didn't have to try any more, the business of getting through in a way you could bear thinking of others thinking about. Walking down Via Cappello past Roman remains and gipsies begging, she felt at once free and strong and utterly beyond help.

———— •◆• ————

Dear July-poo,

Something awful has happened, though I suppose rather funny and exciting too. I'm pregnant.

I hope that's sufficiently earth-shattering?

By Stuart, who I don't even think I've told you about so far.

Find a phone somewhere and call me reverse charges. I want to talk.

Love DIANA.

———— •◦• ————

The gym walls were all mirrors so that the chrome of weights and work-out machines seemed to stretch away in all directions. Likewise the bodies of the women doing their exercises. For although the exercise class was open to all, there was a tendency for the men to stay on the weights and leave the aerobic jumping about to the women. Thus, heaving in front of his mirror (*mens sana in corpore sano*), Sandro could watch not only the attractive flexing of his own muscles, but also the scissoring open and closed of fifteen pairs of legs, one of which, and by no means the least inviting, belonged, as he had discovered two weeks before at Alan's dinner party, to Elaine.

In the bar, though officially it was time to hurry back and take over the kids from Alan, she asked why he had left Canada.

He said everybody here was always asking him that.

She said this seemed fair enough. Her curls were still damp from the shower and framed a pretty upturned nose with a suspicion of freckles summer would no doubt betray and a small quick mouth; plus there were the blue eyes she had handed down to both the children. She looked more a girl than a woman and she had a girl's light flirtiness, made more attractive still just now by the pink afterblush of forty minutes' aerobics and a hot shower.

He grinned brilliant rabbity teeth and drummed a beat on the bar with his steel comb.

'I won't tell you.'

She pouted. In her smaller, apple-cheeked face a pout had something pleasantly provocative about it; above Julia's broader jaw the same gesture merely gave the impression of a scowl. Marina had also pouted, he remembered when Colin started complaining about her keeping the daughter in their bed. It was a very female kind of expression. Made you think of blow-jobs. Even Professoressa Bertelli pouted when she puzzled over her incredible book.

'That's mean.'

'I am mean. Anyway, you'd never know if I was telling the truth.'

(Question: do homosexual men pout more than heterosexuals?)

'Why shouldn't you?'

'Well, for example, Julia told me she left England because it was all an Oxbridge conspiracy and she couldn't get a job.'

'So?'

'But then Flossy told me she'd left because of a man.'

'Ah.'

'And Colin's wife told me he'd left Scotland because he was an Aquarius and too creative for restrictive British society. But then Professor Errico told me he'd left to get away from his first wife and the kids, only then she followed and dumped the kids on his doorstep.'

'Oh, is that the story?' Elaine laughed.

'And of course your Flossy says she left because of the Thatcher government, but I don't believe her.'

'No, don't. She was broke and Alan offered her room and board in return for babysitting so he could get some work done.'

'So it seems everybody has a reason for not telling the truth.'

'And what's your reason?'

'That would be telling, wouldn't it.'

'Well?'

In her teasingly bright smile he saw a row of small, just slightly uneven white teeth.

'Tell me why you left England first?'

'Alan heard about the job. He wanted to have a salary as well as plenty of time to write.'

'And you just came along.'

'Yes, I thought it would be nice.'

'Nothing more murky or interesting than that?'

She giggled: 'No, why ever should there be?' Then she said: 'Alan says though that for a lot of people, when they change countries, they don't do it for any particular reason, but just because deep down they want to do something drastic.'

'And why should they want to do that?'

'He says it's for the same reason people get into terrorism and things. Just an impulse to do something drastic. It comes into his book apparently.' She laughed, 'Or like when I feel like throwing the baby out of the window.'

'Sounds like potted Kierkegaard to me,' said Sandro, who knew no other kind, and he asked, 'Why do you always tell me what Alan says anyway?'

'Do I? I suppose it's living with him.'

'I suppose it must be.'

They were both silent a moment, draining glasses of mineral water and lemon.

'So now,' Elaine said, 'you were going to tell me why you left Canada.'

'The opposite reason from Alan's theory. To avoid doing something drastic.'

'Which was?'

'Oh I'm not telling you that,' he laughed, and he walked her back as far as Via Quattro Novembre.

February 12th   *Friern Ave.*

My dear Julia,

Thanks for your letter. I'm so glad you've moved into a nicer flat and found someone you like living with, as living on one's own is never much fun. I'm always trying to think who on earth I might live with. I thought maybe Joan, but of course she'd never leave her house with all the memories it has for her, nor me Friern Avenue. So here we sits.

Now, dear, you mustn't worry about my health; I'm sure I never do. I just had a touch of high pressure and my leg was playing me up with perching on the step-ladder painting the ceiling in the lounge. I had some men in to give me an estimate, but it was outrageous, even if they weren't going to pay the tax. The windows will be the next thing. The condensation's got worse and I notice that if you push the pane it rattles. I must keep the place decent though if I'm to go on having the Thursday Night Prayer people over. Apparently Giles, you remember the verger at St Luke's, knows somebody who can come and do it. I hope he isn't unreasonable about the price. One of the things I do find most trying now Dad's not here is dealing with men about money. At the car service place they are so cussed and I sometimes think if only I was used to swearing and could come out with some foul language from time to time then they wouldn't play me up so much.

I'm sorry if I sounded depressed, love. I didn't realize I did. You know how it is. And you mustn't feel guilty about not coming to visit. I know that part of the reason you went away was because you thought if you weren't going to marry and have children you didn't want to get stuck looking after me in my old age. You never said anything about going away before Dad died. If I do get infirm, as God willing I never shall, I shall go in a home, I promise, and not be a burden to anyone.

Mike came round at the weekend with a pair of trousers that needed the zip mending and we agreed on a new pattern for a cardigan. He had that dreadful girl Brünhilde with him again. One doesn't want to be unkind to the dear child but she does have such a nose. And she dresses so scruffily. She was wearing something that looked like an underskirt, in tatters at the bottom, and then a long yellow sweater that she must hang weights on every night to make it longer and more shapeless than it already is. Her hair is always so tousled it's difficult to see if there was ever any plan or purpose behind its cutting in the first place, a real Strewell-Peter look, which, no doubt, unbeknown to the likes of me, is 'in'. Still, there's no point in wondering what the world's coming to, I don't suppose, when it seems to have been there for such a long time already. Actually, in reply to what you said, I'm not so much worried about his marrying her, because I can't imagine him staying with such a plain girl for any length of time; no, what terrifies me is the idea that she'll go and get herself pregnant or something and he'll desert the poor lass. Oh well, I suppose, as Mike says, it's none of my business and I should keep me-self to me-self.

I think a lot about our holidays too. They were jolly times, though when I'm looking at the photographs I suddenly find all I can remember is the awful fag it all was before we had a car, getting you packed and in the train and then down to the beach every day and washing the salt and sand out of your clothes. Never mind. You'll say I'm just getting to be an old miz so I'd better stop.

All my love as always.

Write soon.

MUM.

Oh, I forgot to say. Diana came round with that boy you once used to have something with. Leonard. Apparently they'd been to interview a foreign writer who lives on Grove Avenue and thought they'd drop in. Fortunately I had some fruitcake left over from Christmas so we had tea. Leonard kept complimenting me on the pattern I was doing on the machine (for Mike), so we agreed I'd make one for him if he pays for the wool. He is a delightful fellow and it was nice to see him again after all these years. I could never understand why you were so crazy about him before, but now I think I see. There is something rather fresh and manly about him.

Love again. MUM.

I just re-read this and realized what awful scrawl my hand-writing's becoming. Age. I'll have to get someone to fetch Dad's old typewriter down from the attic. I didn't expect to have to become such a letter-writer in me old age.

———◆○◆———

Julia learnt she had been fired from Colin who came round to talk about it. He drove over in his Cinquecento and had one of his boys with him, a handsome, silent sixteen-year-old. The boy stood by the window watching the square and when Julia spoke to him it turned out despite his name of Alistair he spoke no English. It was raining and people cycled by under umbrellas.

Colin sprawled in an armchair with his head back on ironed underwear. His hair was tangled and obviously unwashed, his beard bushed out wider than his cheeks and made them seem unhealthily fat; the nose was hooked into a caricature. With a flamboyance his body couldn't match he was wearing a bright green blazer complete with badge, black cord trousers and damp tennis shoes. Across the passageway, Flossy emerged from her new idea of combined bath and meditation in a pale blue dressing gown, her plump flushed feet slapping on the tiles. She stood in the doorway, swaying slightly, arms folded.

'Fucking shit,' Colin was saying.

From the kitchen, the BBC was talking, as it so often would, Julia had discovered, about irrigation in Africa; in much the same way as at home it might be telling of a burst water-main on the Hornsey Road.

'Who's the other then?' Julia asked, not entirely unhappy with life opening up like this. Unless it was the ground beneath her feet. 'Sandro, I suppose.'

'Well, that's the whole point, isn't it. What the cunts have done is said they'll reduce the cuts from two to one, on condition that the strike ends. Which was what they always meant to do most probably. Double your cuts, offer to compromise, seem reasonable. Typical ploy. The professors got together and agreed on you, which is the first time they've agreed on anything frankly since I've been here.'

'Thanks,' Julia said. 'What about the strike?'

'That's the other thing, isn't it. They've all voted to go back to work.'

'What! When?'

'This morning. We called an emergency meeting. I tried to get in touch with you but you're not on the phone.'

Colin began to hunt through his pockets for a cigarette. At the window his son watched out at where rain pattered down on the faded heroisms of the ugly monument.

'Bloody typical,' Flossy said, examining a tissue she'd found in her sleeve. 'They take a vote without even hearing the interested party.'

But Julia was simply thinking how inscrutable people were, even when they wore their hearts on their sleeves.

'The thing was, because there's no point in not being frank about this, nobody thought you were really seriously determined to fight for the job. I mean, you haven't given a big impression of commitment to the strike, you haven't been at all the meetings, you haven't picketed; and people felt if they stayed out it'd better be for someone who was going to throw them-selves into it heart and fucking soul. I mean, hassle with the professors, the newspapers and so on. Get in there. Make their case felt. We thought the whole cause would be lost before it started.'

He puffed smoke out through the fringe of his moustache.

'You mean only those willing to make a fuss about it get their free ticket back?'

'Look, love, it's a compromise. Everybody's been out for a month and a half, they haven't been paid, it seemed the right offer to accept. Then Manwearing and Habershom were very much in favour and took the rest with them. But we all agreed to do our best to hand over some private lessons to you. Oh, and it seems Errico mentioned to Bexley about giving you some hours in a private school he's opening.'

Flossy said, 'At half the fucking money.'

Colin said nothing.

'I'll get in touch with him then,' Julia said and smiled. 'If I don't just take the first plane back.'

'No need to go to extremes,' Colin said quickly and seemed quite genuinely concerned now. 'Listen, come over tomorrow evening if you want and we'll talk about it. See what we can do. Us ex-pats have to look after ourselves. It's not as though we're just going to let you go like that.' And he gave her his card.

'Freemasonry ciphers,' Flossy said while Colin punished the starter motor below the balcony. 'He told Alan he makes a mint interpreting for Italian and American masons when they discuss their deals.'

'Really? Lucky him.'

'No, it's probably a load of old bull. Typical male identity assertion crap. Alan tells him he's a writer so he has to be an international freemason, as well as union leader. He lives in a pigsty so the masons obviously aren't doing any deals for him. Listen to his car.'

They listened.

'Is one allowed,' Julia asked when it finally started, 'to treat oneself to a cake when losing one's job?'

———◆◦◆———

Feb 14   *BBC Broadcasting House*
                                              Portland Place

Dear Julia,

You're wrong. It's twelve years. December '73, not '74. And why do you have to call me a shithead? As if I'd always meant it to turn out like this. As if I was having a great time. I've never liked this part of your character, the way you are justified and nobody else is. Remember that after the first of those twelve years I did offer to marry you. I was always against the abortion. It was you insisted you didn't want to feel you'd trapped me,

65

that I wasn't ready for a baby, I was still a boy, that you wanted us to get our careers started before having children, that you didn't even know if you believed in marriage because it always ended up with the woman taking the subordinate role, etc. etc. (and there were a lot of etcs). You said we should marry in a year or two's time and what was the National Health for if not for saving idiots like us from making monumental mistakes. And then you were so depressed and miserable afterwards, not to mention downright bad bloody tempered (as if it was my fault) that naturally I ran off. I'm not saying I did the right thing. It was just that at twentyish, having a woman two years older than me weeping her eyes out and threatening suicide and scratching her cheeks to shreds (it's not much of an exaggeration) was too much for me. I think probably it would be too much for me now too. So I took a year off and met Liz. The fact is, we might have lived perfectly happily ever after, if you hadn't had that abortion. Or alternatively if Liz <u>had</u> had one. Because after you, when she got pregnant, I just gave up right away. I felt marked out by destiny. As if lightning had struck twice (the old N.H. can't save you from the stars). Except that she did it on purpose, of course; she was wild about having a baby, to show she'd grown up, which she never has. Then as soon as it arrived it was a different story. Doubtless you'll be gratified to know, if you didn't already, that it was Lenny here changed ninety percent of the nappies while Liz was at the gym trying to get back in shape for some part they never gave her.

I think even a few months ago I would never have brought up any of this. Partly for your sake, but mostly, I suppose, because I like to avoid the tragic side of things. Why harp? Everybody is always so triumphant about breaking down taboos, but there must have been some wisdom behind them. Some things are better buried. So we never talked about it when we met again, did we? Why should we have? What was there to be gained? But your going away now has taken a lot of the normal fun and company out of my life, honestly. (It annoyed me, you know, the way you kept implying your going away would somehow solve problems for me. It's not as if I had a great marriage to fall back on, or as if I was really screwing all the little girls at the Beeb all the time as you so obsessively imagined.) No, your going has put me in a retrospective mood. Maybe the truth is that when one breaks off seeing somebody in the present, you suddenly start thinking of their lives chronologically, not just them as they are now, but all their lives before, and it becomes a story. And when it becomes a story, with a beginning and an end and all the changes and disappointments between, then you just feel smothered in sympathy for them, as if the whole thing were a crime, a trap, and they the victims. (It's something I think when I get on the tube to come home sometimes: you see the people all crowding in, pushing and shoving and breathing fumes and they seem two a penny, superfluous, and most of all, in your bloody way: you think, a few hundred more, a few hundred less, who cares, life is cheap; and yet if you could just see any one of these people's lives singly, chronologically, grasp its story, where they come from, how they got here, in these clothes and shoes, wearing this ring, this face, then they would become heroic, desperate, moving. Or at least some of them would – might.) Anyway, I can still see you, Julia, so tremendously clearly, in your yellow bathrobe face down on the bed in that miserable bedsit in Orchard Street, beating the pillow with your fists; I can still see your green eyes when you turned and said those terrible words, that you were damned forever for having killed the baby, that never, never, never would there be a baby like the one you'd killed. I remember the bed had one of those red candlewick coverlets and there was your Mexican hanging on the wall opposite the window that Diana's got in her bathroom now, the thing with the green and orange sombreros. And you tore off your St Christopher and chucked it at me and it went out of the window and down onto the outhouse roof.

Perhaps I shouldn't write all these things now it's so long over and we haven't talked about it for centuries. But I thought you might like to hear that I'm not such a casual bastard as to have forgotten. I shall never forget. The truth is, Julia, at night sometimes, in bed, I write you a thousand letters in my head that never get sent. And I think maybe everybody does this: that around midnight, or one o'clock, Fortis Green Road, East Finchley, Cricklewood, all of London, may be whispering with insomniac messages that would smother every G.P.O. sorting office if only they ever got sent.

Still, enough of that. Back to your usual Lenny. I'm in B.H. today for a change (we had a game the other day to see who could think of the best alternative meaning for B.H. Barry came up with 'Bloody Hell' predictably enough. 'Big Hotel' was one that had a kind of innocent ring of truth to it. 'Blind Hope' was the winner though, suggested by yours truly). Anyway, I had to come and talk to somebody here about a doc we're planning on the history of botanical classification (!) (about which I know nothing) – the kind of lightweight crap people watch with interest and then promptly forget. Ask them anything the next day and all they remember is the idiot presenter's face popping up in cornfields and museums and African jungles – of course these programmes only get proposed for the travel budget. So much for the myth of educational television. You have to laugh really when you think how seriously we saw our 'careers' in the old days (all of ten years ago!). Me, the film director. You were going to start the world's first intelligent women's magazine (and Barry used to get you mad by saying such a thing was a contradiction in terms). Now it boils down to not much more than so many tube tickets and how big a mortgage the salary will fetch. Perhaps I should suggest a doc on the psychology of job satisfaction. Get the team a trip to Japan at the very least.

I'm going over to Diana's tonight. They took Liz back on at the Adelphi (talk about the casting couch!), so she's out every night and the kids are more or less living with my parents (what can one do but feel the obligatory guilt and get on with it?). It would be ideal if you were still around, a completely free field, but there we are.

Diana's affair with Stuart is flourishing. He may be a belligerent, suave, fascist, overdressed little sod, but he really does seem to love her. A certain doggy look comes over his scrubbed, well-organized, sensible yuppie face when he arrives in his double-breasted Italian raincoat with the overblown shoulders (he drives the horrible Renault Fuego of all things, has a phone in it and calls her from all over the place to revise his ETA – 'estimated time of arrival,' I finally discovered). In fact, I get the impression he's moved in permanently now and I noticed Diana's got a new ring which has a very definite diamond sparkle to it. Not bad going in three months. Makes your heart melt. How long it lasts of course will depend on Diana's famous whims (remember the demise of Raunchy Ron, right in the middle of your party!) The amusing thing is the way he, Stuart, always comes in a dark suit and tie while everybody else is in jeans and Diana in those awful Indian smock things, not to mention the now green highlights in her hair – so that he looks like he's barged into the wrong studio. The asinine Barry keeps calling him 'Boss' and luring him into discussions on probable futures markets for such unlikely commodities as pale ale and vaginal deodorants, but he doesn't seem to mind or even notice really. Actually I can't help admiring the guy for his comformism, or v.v., depending on how you look at it. (Hopeless at charades though, couldn't even get Mill on the Floss the other night.)

So, on with my life. There was just a sniff of spring in the air this morning. Something fresh rather than merely cold about the platform at East F. Spring used to be such an excitement. Now it's just a relief. However did we get this way at only 31?

Thinking of you I bought a bottle of Valpolicella for this evening, plus Amaretto for the famous drinks cabinet.

Best love as always.

Your LENNY.

PS. Happy Valentine's. I almost forgot.

—◆◇◆—

Dear Julia,

Diana told me last night about you having a boyfriend, this Canadian bloke. I felt pretty hurt I suppose – which is stupid in the circumstances. I've been thinking about it all night – Liz not home till four as usual. I imagine it means you won't be coming back; something I hadn't bargained for really. I never thought you'd stay away more than a few months, because it seems your whole life is here. Christ Church, Diana's, Khan's. I feel ridiculously sad, as if I hadn't fully realized you'd gone till now. Still, I do hope it all works out for you.

Love,

LENNY.

Do write and tell me more about your life there. I love to hear from you.

———◦•◦———

Alan considered his driving a sort of secret sin. In his dealings with others he prided himself on his reasonableness, the even-handedness with which he could cope with arguments, his generosity (towards Julia, for example, passing on his best private student, towards the Third World in periods of televised famine, towards all the people he so frequently invited to dinner). He likewise prided himself on his ability to keep a conversation bouncing about, even with difficult combinations of people (in terms of group dynamics he was the low-profile orchestrator, a polite question here, a warm response there, a convincing interest in the lives of others, rarely reciprocated), and of course on his determinedly moral attitude to his private life, his marriage in particular, despite the way other young women could be so heartbreakingly enticing (the quite wonderful Antonia, for example, who seemed to dress on purpose to make mental undressing easy – a feat in winter time – and Sara too, who in the course of their private lessons did nothing but lament her husband's prudishness); then there was his conscientiousness (no truck with the so-called 'ora accademica' of 45 minutes – he gave the kids their full whack), his sense of responsibility toward his children (two hours' play every day, despite the fact they had ruined his career when you thought about it – or even when you didn't), his determination not to be guilty of forcing his wife (though she was willing enough) into a merely subordinate, domestic role (it had been connections made at the university had got her her two hours a day at the Cambridge School, with him standing in as babysitter more often than not); and finally, and perhaps most meritworthy of all, there was his underlying resignation, his determination to fail gracefully, if fail he must, not to become (or at least be seen to be) bitter, not to become one of those ridiculous middle-aged men who gave themselves airs without any track-record, who complained about establishment mafias, nepotism and down-right, bat-blind foolishness on the part of producers and script departments (though all were true); to accept, in short, what life brought, resisting the boredom-prompted temptation to self-destruct, the dark desire to throw the whole pack of cards up in the air, go a-whoring, empty the bank account, take a plane at random from whatever airport; no, somehow he would stay on even keel, with Elaine, not questioning exactly how much he might or might not love her, whatever that might mean; somehow, heroically, he would hold the whole thing together, come what may, trusting that life would find a way to reward so much common sense and altruism. And this without even a suspicion of religion, nor any easy metaphysical or otherworldly props, apart from that implied precisely by this vague trust that he was doing the 'right' thing, that any other course of action would be 'worse'. It was a self-image he was cultivating of course, there was repression involved (quite a lot actually), and play-acting; but it really was the best self-image he could think of.

In his car, though, this angelic Alan became a demon. Mr Hyde found a breathing space. It must have been – for Alan was a remorseless and fascinated self-analyst, invented and reinvented himself daily – that in the car, in the heavy traffic London and then surprisingly Verona too had always confronted him with, he was overcome by a sense of the obstacles life had put before him, of the obstacles we all are to each other, of the appalling clamouring one on top of the other, one behind, beside, in front of the other, life inevitably is (like the notice-board at the university where everybody simply pinned their announcements over the ones already there, regardless, or the shortwave bands on his radio where voices shouted each other down across the fraction between one megahertz and the next). So that a car double-parking in the heavy traffic flow along Lungadige Matteotti was all the distractions, rejection slips, dirty nappies, incompetence and sheer cussedness that had for-ever blocked the trunk roads of his ambition. Quite definitely life was too short for this, for 'U'-turning coaches and broken traffic lights, and yet . . . and yet when he was at his desk, at his screen, working, when genius should have shone, he did get bored, caught himself thinking of football for some reason, day-dreaming Juventus-Liverpool, producing nothing. And curiously this awareness of his own shortcomings only increased his rage when he got into traffic, increased his determination to lay at least some of the blame elsewhere. Did it have to take so long to turn a corner? Was it really possible that that illegally parked arsehole was going to block the citybound lane while he went into the tobacconist's and bought himself a pack of cigarettes? Alan hit the horn. Hard.

This tension was exacerbated by his starting late for every journey. Deliberately perhaps, however much he cursed himself. Before going to the university he would hang on as long as possible in front of the sphinx-like glow of the screen, which seemed, rather than cooperating, to be hiding his novel (if it was a novel) in some recess of its memory – how passive and voluptuous white paper and a sharp pencil had been! (But there were so many corrections to be made.) And coming back he started late because, buttonholed by the eager few after lessons, he couldn't help but feel a sense of responsibility, and self-esteem, and so launched into liberal explanations, advice, suggestions, reassurance about exams, etc. He ran out of the building, chased down the street in heavy rain, dodging carelessly through umbrellas, leaving the pavement and squeezing between parked cars to get round groups of students, covering, as if it were a race (but life was), the three hundred metres to where he had wedged their filthy Citroën Visa into the first available space. The babysitter had been told only till six-thirty. She had somewhere to go afterwards. There was Robert to feed. Had Elaine asked for any shopping? 'About Britain' was at quarter to seven if reception was good. Or was it 'Sports Report' Thursdays? Better still. Elaine would be at the gym till almost 8. A half-hour grappling with the screen maybe if the kids stayed quiet.

He fastened his safety belt, perhaps the only driver to do so in all Verona, as if this last responsible gesture might somehow ward off the evil spirit about to take over. It was not that Alan ran red lights or pulled out of side-streets without looking – as so many people would in Italy – more that every moment in the car was galvanized by a constant sense of competition, an acceptance of every challenge, refusal to be squeezed out of this lane, pushed out of that, refusal to let the idiot overtaking on the inside get away with it. 'Dick!' he shouted. 'You fucking cunt. You absolute arsehole.' Somebody lost – Ancona plates – was inching along, slowing everybody down; indicating left a Seicento turned right. The door of a Mercedes swung open sending a cyclist careering into his path. 'Can you believe it! Christ and shit!'

But a particularly risky piece of driving on his own part, maybe only just squeezing back in after overtaking, or an abrupt switch of lanes to creep through a light at the last of last moments (*rosso fresco*), would immediately leave him ashamed of himself, he would grow suddenly tame, respectful, letting in a truck stuck in some side-road, accepting the grinding stop-start all the way home as a kind of punishment.

Yet the next time he climbed in the car it was the same again: the hurry, the anger, the tension in neck and shoulders, the

73

curious feeling of possession, of something to exorcize, being exorcized perhaps. Perhaps the whole of his orderly life depended on these moments of wild aggression and yelled abuse as he fought his way to the university and back. Perhaps all his dedication to home and tran-tran was a rationalization of fear, and the person he punished when he drove, not all the other idiots, but himself, punished himself for his lack of courage, his mediocrity, punished himself for being lost in this stupid, tin-pot, picture-postcard, provincial heap of medieval detritus. Shit! And Fuck! And Cunt!

— ◆◇◆ —

March 1st   *Kil-burn-and-plunder*

note phone number at last — *328 1234*

DEAR SISSY,

I met your old LOVERBOY yesterday, Lenny the Lion. Under what curiousest of circybumstances you might very welly hask. Fact is, your little BRUV has won a PRIZE! Yes, yes, the College Prize, no less — and the winning painting is going to the R.A.'s young ha-hartists' hexibition. So I goes to d'BEEB, dun I, for my hinterview, and this geezer sez, 'Are you not Julia Helen Delaforce's brahrther?' I didn't recognize him, frankly, but it turned out it was that freckly pop-eyed bloke you were knocking off at Homerton when I came up to stay after one of the arguments with Dad. 'Member? (no, I'm only here for the beer). Invited me to a party next week at your old flat, which was nice of him (you never did), though I don't suppose I'll go.

Haven't seen Mumsicle recently, though I had to phone the other week to ask for (guess what?) money. She seemed hokey-dokey. Brünhilde got fired at the Princess Alexandra for arguing with a customer (she poured a pint of McEwan's over him), so we're a bit short. (Prize money, one hundred and fifty measly squid, already squandered on clothes and paints.)

No time for any more, I only wrote to brag. Telegrams gratefully accepted. All flowers to. . . .

Your silly-billy-fillystein bruv – WHO PUT THE FORCE IN DELAFORCE

MIKE.   PS. If you're so damn worried about Mum, why did you leave? We all have our own lives to live.

———◆◇◆———

Dear Martha,

Is very kind of yourself and Vittorio write me the very long letter; is also very generous that you offer me the ticket with Sandro for Toronto in the summer. But I am very old for make trips. I must stay in the shop. Is complicated the ordering flowers. I cannot give to no-one else.

I said Sandro about your offer. He says he is not wanting to return in Canada very soon. I ask him why he is left and he says he is bored, he needs change. He says that is an existential question. I am laughing. The young people today are wanting to be very intellectual, but the problems are always the same things. He is laughing too. He has a nice smile. I do not think he is saying me all the truth.

I must say you that I am asking Sandro to leave my house. Is embarrassing, but I must explain, or you do not understand. He has a girlfriend that he brings her to the house. She is very nice, beautiful girl – I think an English girl – but she is married, she has the ring. Sandro is a very good boy in the house, he causes me no problems, he is very simpatico, but I say him I do not like these things in my house. You understand? Is complicated explain in English. I am not religious person. Are many many years I do not go to church now. But I do not like these things. Is not dignified. I say Sandro he must go and he is agreed. He will go when he will find the place. Is a pity because I like him, also for the company.

Excuse me that my English is not good. Next time maybe I write Italian if Vittorio remembers.

Un caro abbraccio,

ZIA LIVIA.

Dear Diana,

It's midnight. I'm in the Bexleys' flat, that's Flossy's brother's place. I thought I'd write to pass the time. It's all rather complicated, but something appalling has happened. This Alan has killed a child in a car accident and the police are keeping him. They couldn't get in touch with the wife for some reason, she wasn't where she was supposed to be, so a neighbour drove up to get Flossy to look after the kids, and I came with her.

I do feel so enormously sorry for him. What could be more awful? And it was his fault too, so it seems they might even put him in prison. Flossy and Elaine, the wife (she turned up after an hour or so), are out still, talking to a lawyer who's one of Colin's, that's the Scottish bloke's, students.

Like so many appalling things there's nothing you can say about it. You're left staring at the walls, thanking God it wasn't you. Though it quite easily might have been. Remember the nights driving back drunk from Ronnie's, the time we ended up in Stoke Newington? Anyway, I don't know why, but I've been sitting here in tears for more than an hour thinking about that abortion I had so long ago, thinking that I'm equally guilty in a way, maybe even more so, because I actually chose to do it. 14 weeks, 14 years, what's the difference? I remember for months afterwards all I could do was sit paralysed in my room, staring holes everywhere. Of course, I only started imagining the child when it was too late and every pram and pushchair on the street was an accusation. Just like Alan never knew about this child till he'd killed him.

I'm sorry, pretty grim stuff to bother you with over your granola. I suppose all I meant to say was, I think you're doing absolutely the right thing going through with it. Change the subject.

It was wonderful to hear your voice on the phone and I am so glad you're happy about it all. By the sounds of it Stuart is going to be great. Actually, after talking to you, I felt quite jealous, I thought maybe I should just chuck the pill and the hell with it. Maybe this time at least I could get the culprit to marry me and pull some financial weight. But I don't suppose I'll do it. What do you think?

Lenny, by the way, wrote a whiney letter saying you'd told him about me and Sandro. I'd rather actually you didn't tell him anything. I'd rather he was left entirely in the dark. He came a lot of stuff about memories and things and how it was me he really loved, but without offering to damn-well <u>do</u> anything about it. Which is vintage Lenny. At the end he just wished me the best of luck with my new lover, would you believe it, when from the rest of the letter you'd have expected him to be on the next plane. So that all it amounted to was making me nostalgic and then slamming the door in my face again. Which is not precisely what I need.

Best love – I envy you.

J.

PS. Can you believe what's worrying me now? When we left Quinzano we were in such a hurry I went and forgot to pull the canary in. I've just realized. So he's out on the balcony and it must be nearly freezing. I hope he's not going to be another casualty.

Julia paced the Bexleys' front room from midnight till two. She was struck by the fact that although they had been here upwards of three years, the place still had very much its original furnished look with only a veneer of Bexley over it: a photograph of the two of them in wedding dress outside an English country church; another, just a snap this, of a tubbier Elaine holding a baby in front of a modern-looking building, presumably a hospital; then the clutter of toys on the floor, a dirty bib over the arm of the couch, baby clothes. The furniture had not, as had theirs in Quinzano, been bought in a hurry to fob off the prospective tenant with the lowest possible capital outlay. It seemed more like the relics of a lifetime's poor taste some lonely aunt had spent her last years among and which the inheriting nephews and nieces had then had no idea what to do with. There was a massively heavy old table, dark, almost black and slightly warped, with ponderous scrolling on the legs; and then a cabinet in the same style that took up the whole of one of the longer walls with ill-fitting glass doors and shelves crammed with another decade's idea of china. The lower cupboards had had their handles removed, presumably to defend their contents from Robert's inquisitive hands. On the wall opposite, in a heavy gilt frame near black with dust, Santo Stefano lay haloed in a heap of rubble, leaking blood from every limb, while beside and above, disconcertingly near the ceiling in fact, a young last-century girl was praying by a marble tomb, tears glistening in candlelight.

They could at least have taken those down, for heaven's sake! They could at least have switched the ugly, smoked-glass chandelier over the table for a regular lamp-shade. Obviously they were doing no more than camping here. With the pedal-car on the floor, the rattles stretched between chair-legs, a pack of Elaine's tobacco, a line of Penguin paperbacks displacing green china on one shelf and an ugly computer screen on the table, there was a strong sense of collision, a collision of two cultures, two clutters. But there was no doubt about which was permanent, which temporary.

Or perhaps they liked living among other people's things, Julia thought, not having to project their own domestic image (they had abandoned their own flat back in Hampstead). Perhaps they liked the feeling of not having arrived in the place they were going to be. Wasn't that rather what she and Flossy were doing in Quinzano in their even less attractive muddle of modern sticks of schlock (not replacing the awful cover on the sofa because they didn't know how long they were going to stay – as if a sofa-cover was the most expensive thing in the world – and who knew if they wouldn't be there the rest of their lives)? And then Sandro too, lodging at his great-aunt's where she was never allowed to go because the old lady didn't like him bringing girlfriends. A method of self-defence of course. A bolt hole. Perhaps all the ex-pats, she thought then, had their reasons for not wanting life to begin just for the moment, their exile a kind of limbo.

Except that Alan was in it up to his eyeballs now.

As she had been once.

And it occurred to Julia that she had had the abortion for that exact same reason, because she hadn't wanted life to begin quite so soon. Only to discover that in doing so it had rather abruptly ended.

'Fucking nightmare,' said Colin later, as they squeezed into his Cinquecento: 'Overtaking on a solid white line. Lawyer says they could put him away for a year if they want.'

Julia remarked that Elaine seemed to be taking it very well, though it was kind of Flossy to stay with her, and privately thought Colin wasn't driving all that carefully either. The tiny car accelerated into the slalom of curves up the hill to Quinzano.

'Sorted out some work for yourself?'

'The odd private lesson here and there.'

'Make the bastards pay.'

Julia said nothing.

'You didn't go back though, eh?'

'Not just yet.'

'Everybody's always talking about going home, me included, but they never do. Place is a quicksand. You come for the fun, like to the beach, and then find you've been sucked in. We're stuck. Same anywhere you go, I suppose. Place where you are always turns out a bigger trap than you imagined.'

They pulled up in the square in Quinzano. The ramshackle buildings looked more ramshackle still in the blend of moon and sodium light. The stone-slab balconies with their rusty metal railings, the leafless vines twisting up the walls, the broken stucco and barred ground-floor windows, gave the place a gothic look of dark possibility. Which was also romantic.

'Still, not much to go back to in Thatcher's Britain, is there?'

'I can't imagine it'll suddenly be so enchanting the day it become's Kinnock's Britain,' said Julia, who had always voted Labour, but resented reductive arguments when she wasn't making them. 'Anyway, you've got all your family here, I can't imagine why you should want to go back. You've got it all settled. Home is here now, isn't it?'

At which, double-parked in the square at 3 a.m., with Alan in a police cell and Napoleon freezing on the balcony, Colin launched into his lifestory. The greasy windows of the old Fiat misted over: the space filled up with smoke. And the point was, Colin insisted, the ridiculous, appalling thing was that the whole deal with Marina had been just a matter of convenience. 'I needed someone to help look after the kids, she was desperate to leave home. Then as soon as Janet arrived she forgot about me and the others right away. Still keeps her in our bed at three years old, spoils her silly. I never get a look in. Sex-life, kaput.'

Julia wondered if all this mightn't be the preamble to a pass. How life went on. She said: 'Who was that bloke arrived just before I left that night I came over?'

'Oh, Beppe.'

'Nice man.'

'The local greengrocer. He's into karate.'

'No, really? I thought he was very nice.'

'Terrible record with women. Nobody seems able to stick him for more than a couple of weeks.'

'Don't tempt me. I'm one of the world's great masochists.'

'You know,' Colin said, as Julia opened the door – he was scratching vigorously in his beard – 'if they go and put Alan away, the university'll probably ask you to substitute. I'll put in a word, if you like.'

Julia climbed stone stairs. On the door, a note said: 'And my dinner? SANDRO.'

Napoleon wasn't dead. Not a Russian winter. Over bread and cheese, Julia turned on the radio and found the World Service, faithful as ever, braining Britain amongst insolent hoots of interference.

If, she thought, as Sandro said, you only 'knew' those things which, if they weren't so, your whole perception of the world would change, then the BBC must be one of those things, a great old rusty cultural anchor.

——◆◆◆——

March 25   *Peel St.*
                                              Kensington

Dear Julia,

Diana always lets me read all your letters. I feel like an old friend. I know she never writes back, so I thought I should. Especially because we have some news. We are getting married on July 5th. You are invited of course. The ceremony is going to be in St Marks, Lewes, at 3 o'clock on Saturday afternoon. Diana didn't want a church wedding but all the parents insisted. Anyway, I think you have better memories. Then a month's honeymoon. We're thinking of going to Hawaii. I suppose Cornhill can do without me for a month.

What else? I'm not very good at writing letters frankly. Usually I begin: 're. your enquiry of . . .' and the sec fixes up any mistakes I make on the dictaphone. Well, I hope she does. Anyway, I'm staying at the flat here now, which is a big saving. Diana entertains a lot with her friends from the BBC and I've started playing squash with them at a club off Oxford Street. Barry is best. I think he could go professional frankly, except there's no real money in it if you're not in the top twenty worldwide.

I can't think of anything else. I hope all is well with you and that you're a long way from all this terrorism stuff we keep hearing about. Oh, Diana says to ask what happened about your job and the strike and everything. She always says you should come back and that she misses you. I am very much looking forward to meeting you of course.

Yours STUART.

enc. wedding invitation

Hello, July-poo my love. I don't suppose it's worth offering excuses for not writing since I'm hardly likely to change my ways. Just adding a note to say your brother came round. Why did you never tell us about him! He's excruciatingly handsome and really proved quite the heart and soul of the party until his odd girlfriend threw up and he had to take her home. Poor Stuart had a dreadful argument about the arts with the BBC boys, I thought they would come to blows, and your Michael supported Stuart, which, as an artist, was rather sweet of him I thought. Said he didn't want to be supported by the Arts Council, only by people willing to pay good money for his pictures. Good luck to him! See you soon.
DIANA.

When you come back I'm going to persuade you to stay back!

March 22nd   *Piazza dei Caduti, Quinzano*

Dear Mike,

Congrats of course!! You can finally tell the world, told you so. Please do stop writing in that silly style, though. It makes you seem about 15. I often wonder why we have such different characters, having grown up together, and why, in particular, I feel about a hundred, but can never think of you as being more than 20. It occurred to me the other day that pensions should be handed out on a 'you're as old as you feel basis' – I'd never have to work again.

I'll be back in England in July for Diana's (my old flatmate's) wedding (I believe you've met her now). I'll take you and Brünhilde out to dinner to celebrate the prize.

Love
BIG SIS

PS. Don't for Christ's sake try and make me feel guilty about Mother. I left London for all kinds of personal reasons it would take forever to explain. We do all have our own lives to live, it's true. But I don't see how this releases us from certain – I don't want to call them obligations, but in the end I feel they really are. (I shopped with her every Saturday morning for the last five years! One does these things.)

———◆◆———

While Flossy meditated each morning, Julia watched the postman do the rounds of the square. He sat on a Vespa in blue uniform and peaked cap, pointed beard on his chin. Infuriatingly, just before their block, he stopped at the Bar Centrale, and if he had to ring the bell for one of Mother's packages, woollies usually with progressively more complicated patterns, his breath smelt of grappa and his smile was readier than it might have been two or three blocks before.

Marry the postman. Lead a local proletariat life washed down with strong wine and Grappa Giulia (her namesake). Why not?

Dear Mum,
    I did not leave because I don't want to look after you in your old age. Whatever are you thinking of?

But even before he came into the square she could hear him buzzing along the street behind the block parallel to it, and immediately felt a kind of exquisite tension, anticipation and impatience. What was she waiting for? Some improbable capitulation from Lenny? The news (what news?) that would bring her home? Which world was she living in anyway? Each day the postal service called her bluff with messages that were never quite *the* message.

Dear Julia,
    I finished Leonard's pully and he came over to pick it up in the middle of the Thursday Night Prayer Group, so he went off to the pub until it was over and then came back. He got Dad's old

typewriter down from the attic for me, which was nice, and we ended up chatting together over one coffee after another until midnight and gone if you please. I did him a polo neck with a. . . .

If she put the espresso pot on and the milkpan just at the moment he switched off his Vespa to go into the bar, then she would be able drink her coffee over whatever fortune brought her a few minutes later: the first gas-bill, for example, incomprehensible and extortionate; a postcard from Barry in Bombay, presumably holding a microphone up to misery ('You wouldn't believe how hot it is, best, BARRY'); a copy of 'La Provvidenza', addressed to the late last tenant: 'How the Saints Intercede for Us – Sant' Antonio and San Zeno.'

The stroke-victim lady on the ground floor put her balding head round a door bristling with security devices. 'Is there anything for me?' 'I'm afraid not.' 'Pazienza.' 'Buon giorno.' 'Buon giorno.'

And what could she be waiting for?

Climbing the stairs, Julia regretted her Christ Church job, how busy she'd been and the sense of direction and responsibility that timetables, exams, parents' evenings and Burnham gradings gave; but she regretted it as one regrets an illusion. Was it possible that she had given so much time to that, to GCEs and the battle with George over teaching methods? And if she had managed to find a career job in an office, rather than coming here, to fill her life full of phonecalls and cigarette smoke, business lunches and address labels, what would it have meant?

The distance here, her being so far away from Kensington and the ILEA, seemed to make all her past life so numbingly small and insignificant. Excepting, always always excepting – (why had Lenny reminded her?) – the abortion.

Julia stopped on the landing. How old would the child be now? Ten? Eleven? A boy or a girl? And remembering Alan and the trial he was facing, it suddenly seemed quite incredible they had let her off so lightly. Quite incredible, after killing a child like that. For nothing.

Tears brimmed. She turned to Flossy's rota for salvation. Divided into morning and afternoon, as once it had been at Alan's, she read: 'FLOSSY: BATHROOM FLOOR, THE WASH. JULIA: DO SHOPPING (VEGGIES, FRUIT, CHEESE, KLEENEX), PAY ELECTRICITY BILL, WASH KITCHEN FLOOR.' She would pick up some ice-cream too, in case Sandro came, plus the wherewithal for a fruit salad for herself and Flossy.

Dear Diana,

Just a short note to say congratulations. I'm all in a rush here. About the job – didn't I tell you? – they fired me (just when the strike plot was thickening, it ended), but I decided to stay all the same. I've got some private lessons and translations and I suppose I'll find some more. Too complicated to go into in detail (I seem to be writing that every letter, but the truth is, how can you fit your life onto a scrap of Basildon Bond?). Anyway, I'm happy here.

I'll see if I can make it to the wedding. If I do, I want to be bridesmaid. Okay? And once again, congrats. Who would have thought when I left in September you'd be marrying within the year!

JULIA.

PS. The angelic Mike may not want money from the Arts Council, but he certainly scrounges enough of it off his mother! Don't be taken in. He's just another charmer.

In deceptive sunshine, cold one moment, scorching the next, she cycled with Flossy to Lazise on Lake Garda. Twenty miles. The constant pressure of her feet on the pedals was a satisfactorily heroic way of killing time and the companionship of another masochist doing likewise was reassuring, even though, in single file and with the mad traffic there was, they couldn't communicate. Unless, Julia thought, it was precisely the non-communication that made it companionship, rather than bickering and argument. Because it seemed sometimes one only needed to find a subject of conversation to have fallen out with Flossy. Although, peculiarly, and in a way she wasn't sure she liked, the more they fell out, the closer, somehow, they seemed to become.

It was cherry-blossom weather with a light breeze blowing the first bees about, and throughout the journey the hills to their right were electrically bright in spring sunshine. Life could be so tantalizingly beautiful; you felt quite furious not to be a part of it.

When they were sitting stiff and sweating by the lake-side, Julia announced that Sandro had asked if he could come and live with them. On a temporary basis. He couldn't put up with his great-aunt any more. She was always going on about what the neighbours would think if he didn't have his shutters open by eight o'clock and, if ever he tried to have a lie-in, she came in and woke him up. Added to which she went in for a lot of emotional blackmail, wanting him to spend time with her, etc. etc., eat all her stodgy cakes.

Flossy's muscular legs in tracksuit trousers dangled from the parapet. Breathing through her mouth, eyes streaming hay-fever, she had her head thrown back to catch the sun, sweaty hair plastered to her skull. She wasn't sure, she said after a moment, that she really wanted to share the place with a man. When she turned, her eyes were balefully big and slightly hurt.

'Neither am I really.'

They watched the lake which sparkled sharply close by, then melted away in a haze where Salò must be.

'He'll never marry you, you know.'

'Who wants him to?'

Flossy took off her shoes and wriggled her toes.

'You don't even like him. All you want is a baby.'

Julia stared at where fishing boats gave an idea of the horizon.

'Because you don't know what to do with your life.'

'Snap.'

'Well, at least I know what I don't want. I'm not going to get involved with some crappy man who reduces me to a domestic role and considers his own personal prestige the most important thing in the world, leaving me with the kids and the cleaning.'

'But you're a maniac for housework, Flossy! You love it.' Suddenly, surprisingly, Julia found herself brimming with warmth for her friend, and she took her hand. 'And you love children too. Look at you with Alan's. You're all over them.'

'But not men,' Flossy said sharply, and Julia said: 'Oh come on, God, let's have a beer. A big one. The hell with Sandro and the hell with the diet. Some fun for heaven's sake. Some life.' And she stood up, tugging Flossy after her.

In the second bar, towards evening, she wrote on a postcard: 'Dear Lenny, Having a wonderful day getting drunk by the lake here. It looks just like the picture. We're trying to chat up some German motorcyclists with very sexy leather pants. If you knew what you were missing. . . .'

And she sent it to his home address.

------◆◆◆------

Alan rose at three to give Margaret her feed. When she was through he burped her for almost fifteen minutes, put her back in the cot and waited until her breathing was even; then went to the front room. In his diary he wrote:

'Oh to recover yesterday's boredom!'

Terrific irony for his book of course.

Only it seemed so appallingly cheap to write about it, to use it.

A child had died! It was as beyond imagining as the stars. It was a nightmare.

Why hadn't something *given* for Christ's sake?

He wrote: 'The hero, call him that, kills a child, is mortified, tormented, destroyed, rediscovers the value of life pure and simple, rediscovers his wife, his own children, who he had previously seen as a trap, decides to dedicate the rest of his life to loving them and helping handicapped people. Just when he reaches this resolution, this clarity and liberation of mind, we discover the wife has cancer. Darkly, he realizes this is retribution for his sin, his presumption.'

He stood up, acutely dissatisfied. Of course, it always looked cheap in note form. It was a question of putting heart and soul into it. If one had such things. The truly terrible part of it all, though, was how such an appalling thing could have happened and he was still here fussing and jotting in his notebook. You expected at least a tragedy to solve things for you.

Nothing was special out of the window along the lamplit city street. The trees were in their places, the occasional car rushed. The gates and fences were in their places. Why stare after details? Nothing had changed.

He wanted to be haunted by guilt. He really did. He wanted to pay. But it was hard to feel it.

Perhaps with the court case.

Rather deliberately he crossed the room and pulled down the flap of a thirties cabinet with primitive veneer. A light came on automatically and spangled in tiny mirrored squares lining the inside. There were even a few bottles left behind by the late-lamented whoever he'd been (or she) that nobody ever wanted to drink but that it seemed impossible somehow to throw out: Sciroppo di Tamarinda, Erba, Lichior al Cafea. Alan took out a bottle of Johnnie Walker and because there were no glasses, drank a moment from the neck.

A child had died, was gone, was no longer available, was not to be found in sea nor earth nor sky, not by all the Shackletons, search parties, satellite photographs, nor sonars the world could muster. His clothes would remain, his shoes, toys, headphones, bike (albeit twisted), but that young boy was not to be found. Nowhere. Ever. It was going to take some time, and perhaps a lot of whisky, to absorb that fact in all its momentousness and banality.

'Alan,' Elaine said.

He felt his way, slightly dizzy, through the cluttered dark of the bedroom.

'Mmm?'

'I've got a confession to make.'

He mistook the tone of this altogether and giggled: 'You haven't gone and farted again, have you?'

———•◦•———

April Fools'   *Piazza dei Caduti, Quinzano*

Dear Lenny,

(Julia wrote to his BBC address)

What do you expect me to do? Remain chaste in memory of you all my life? I was thinking the other day when I heard about Diana getting married; it's as if we were all playing a game of musical chairs and eyeing ourselves a safe homey place for when the music stops. (By the way, Stuart wrote me a nice but thoroughly dumb letter announcing their wedding; she's obviously far too intelligent for him, so why on earth does she have to marry him? Women can have babies on their own, can't they? I even told her on the phone I'd be willing to go back and help if she was worried about managing. And I would, gladly. In fact if you see her, why don't you tell her it's not too late to change her mind, though don't say I said so. Oh, here's one that'll amuse you: Stuart said he thought Barry should become a squash professional of all things; my own feeling is he should be certified).

Anyway, where was I, yes, musical chairs: so, I suspect that for me the music will be stopping all too soon, it already has a rather flat-battery, mid-30s sound to tell the truth, and hence I'm trying out bits of upholstery here and there. Sandro is one of them. And don't imagine for one moment that you can sink into a cosy, self-pitying nostalgia thinking, she wasn't faithful, oh, if only she'd never left, how happy we would be; because the truth is I still love primarily you. The ball is still very firmly in your court, sweetheart. I'm going to prolong your agony of having a decision to make as long as I can.

So, Sandro is living here in the flat now (you did ask me to write about my life). He's handsome and rather lazy. A bit like a cat. Sometimes I wonder if I'm not keeping a pet. He has the same kind of natural self-satisfaction, natural charm, natural sneakiness. He makes me furious sometimes frankly, and he doesn't have any of your wit at all. Diana said once I would have sold my soul for the kind of puns you were always making, and she was right, Lenny, if only somebody had let me. Or maybe in a way I did. Because I often wonder where exactly my soul might be. Orchard Street?

So, he's handsome. He has thick glossy hair swept back California style and he wears sunglasses up on his forehead. Now it's getting warm here he dresses in the kind of light outfits you imagine tennis players wearing on their way to the courts, stylish, casual and pretty damn seductive to tell the truth. Partly because of the way he walks so straight. His conversation is likewise casual and stylish and his voice rich and seductive again (not high like yours), and he has a permanent smile which is half sardonic, half sensuous, but mostly just charming. Think of Harrison Ford in the first Star Wars and you've got it (how many times did we go to see 'The Empire Strikes Back', just to hear Darth hissing, 'Luke, this is your destiny!', and for weeks afterward you used to phone hissing, 'Jooleeeaah, thisss isss your dessstiny!' – and instead you see how wrong you were.) Where was I again? His film-star smile. He definitely lifts one side of his mouth rather than the other. It's the kind of smile that has you wondering what exactly there might be behind it, whether maybe he isn't a bit shifty, because it's always there. He's always smiling. Always always. And always friendly. Or maybe it's just I find it hard to believe he's living here with me: you always used to make it sound like you were doing me such a big favour being with me, telling me I ought to slim, telling me I should do exercises to stop my breasts sagging, buying me a bottle of pore minimizer once, of all things, as if I didn't have my own already. I can't believe I put up with it. Sandro, to his eternal credit, never makes any such comments. He seems to know how to treat a woman. (Can you believe I'm 33 and never until now have I found a man willing to share my postal address?)

Like I said though, he's lazy. Chronically. I think that's maybe why he's never been married or anything. Completely laid back. He gets up late, hangs around in his dressing gown, shaves every other day, spends hours in the bathroom, watches TV all evening drumming his comb on the coffee table, and if you ever ask him about his past he tells you he hasn't got 'a past', he's just been doing the same things all his life. In Canada it seems he worked as a translator at the Italian Consulate, but most of the time he was playing cards. Here he has the same job I had at the university and concentrates all his efforts on politicking in the hope of getting his contract made permanent.

Anyway, he's a well-trained domestic animal and we're happy together for the moment, in a modest, well-organized, limited sort of way. Cohabiting must be the word. Which is more than I ever managed with you.

So, does that tell you all you wanted to know about my life away from London? I hope you feel an April fool.

What else? Lenny, you did write some nice as well as some horrible things in that long letter. It's strange to think we've only managed to start communicating at a distance of 1000 miles and 7 months. Perhaps those are the only kinds of distances you feel safe at. Or is it that there's nothing left for us now but to analyse the past, nothing left to lose? And what makes me furious is I can see you actually enjoying it, enjoying that sweet sad feeling as you write for an hour before getting down to your silly anaesthetizing overpaid job. Where would we be without our ex-mistresses to tickle our hearts, the excuse of our wives to prevent anything ever getting serious, and the promise of all the sexy little office girls you'll ultimately be able to replace us both with so as to start the whole story over again and have a half-way decent pair of tits in your bed when you're fifty?

I know you Lenny. You'd like to be a nice guy, but you're not.

You say you write a thousand unsent letters to me on the

more insomniac nights. I suppose I do the same. In fact this is one of them. Funnily enough I read an article recently about some survey somebody had done on lovers. I was in the hair-dresser's. It said that lovers tended to be more critical of each other than friends were. 'The desire to improve one's partner is an indication of love.' Something like that.

I'm desperate to improve you, Lenny.

But I'll take Sandro pretty much as he is.

It's strange how you begin a letter one way, see it one way in your head while you're doing the dishes or making coffee or cycling home, thinking what you'll say; and then just writing it, it turns out totally different and a lot less inspired than you'd intended. What I meant to tell you about was this lunch I went to in the country last Saturday where we met this extraordinary bloke by the name of Beppe who teaches karate, breeds dogs, plays chess and runs a greengrocer's shop (an optimistic idiot who believes in life); it was a funny day and you would have died laughing (one thing I will confess to missing is laughing together with you, Lenny); but it'll have to wait, it would take pages. I also wanted to say how beautiful the spring is here with miles and miles of peach and cherry blossom and the swallows arriving right on Easter day, circling and diving over the river. Instead, as you see, I just ended up griping.

Thanks for visiting Mother. She'd make a pully for the devil himself if he gave her the measurements and bought the wool – but I don't suppose he needs one. Pop in if you've got the time, since it's not far from where you live. I like to think of you two having tea together in that awful front room with the embossed crown wallpaper and the 'all I can offer you . . .' Churchill jug. It's at once so incongruous and so natural. Why on earth shouldn't you have tea with my mother? Perhaps she'll convert you. Do be careful.

And Mike too! Diana told me you'd invited him to her party. Seems you've been seeing more of the Delaforce family than you ever did when you were with me (see what nice in-laws you're missing out on – even if we don't have the old roof tiles).

Actually, the truth about Mum and Mike is that she has spent the last twenty-seven years spoiling him and worrying about him – worrying about his girlfriends, that they were going to get themselves pregnant and corner him into marriage, worrying that he was going to ruin his hearing with playing the guitar so loud (he had a room-full of amplifiers), worrying that he was on drugs, worrying when he gave up economics to do art, worrying that the skinheads would beat him up because of his long hair, etc. etc. Mum has filled up her whole life worrying. By the time Mike was 24-ish she was beginning to worry that none of the girls would trap him into marrying and he'd be left all alone, and now he's 27 she's terrified that that German girl (the one who came with him to the party) will. Presumably you saw why. The only thing Mum never had the imagination to worry about was whether he was queer or not, which, as it happens, I suspect he is. He lives with two other oddballs in the worst part of Kilburn and they always refer to Brünhilde as 'the man of the house'. (An interesting and risqué documentary subject, Lenny: why do some women prefer gays? No freebie travel though; you could do all the research in Wood Lane.)

Anyway, having dedicated her whole life to worrying about Mike, when he left home and then Dad died, she realized she was going to be stuck on her own for her old age and so started angling for me to come back.

Which was fair enough, I suppose, and I do love her. Only I cringe at the thought of having my life end that way, before it even seems to have begun. At least here the pressure's off. I feel freer. (Though quite for what remains to be seen.)

Lots of love, Lenny. I think of you swinging back and forth on your BBC stool reading this, folding Basildon Bond (my last sheets) in your veiny hands. I can see the nicotine stains. (Aren't we romantic?)

Big kiss, Lenny.

JULIA.

PS. Am I mean? I re-read this, and I thought, what a mean

person I am, to you, to Mother, to Mike, to poor Sandro. It's only a thick skin. On se défend. I love you all.

———◆◦◆———

Sandro and Colin agreed, Bexley was on the rocks. They agreed that in any other country he would have been fired for not turning up to lessons, or worse still turning up drunk. They agreed that however badly things had gone wrong for him, his over-reaction was mere self-indulgence, and that whatever he did to make up for it he had certainly lost the chance of a permanent post after calling Scudellotti a 'testa di merda' to his face. They agreed that the underlying problem with people like him, because Manwearing and Habershom (what incredible names they had) were two more, was that their super-privileged backgrounds, and particularly educations, had led them to expect such glittering lives, and now that they found they were nobodies like all the rest they didn't know what to do with themselves. Pleased with this analysis, Colin and Sandro also agreed that the assistants' union should be strengthened and the kids *taught*, that they themselves should sit and vote together at all assemblies, that Laphroaig was better than any Kentucky bourbon, that Canada and Scotland were similar in that, having always been under the heel of larger nations to the south, their peoples had been spared the presumption that made the English and Americans insufferable – and then so many Canadians *were* Scottish, a cousin of Colin's, for example, who was into curtain-walling. They agreed that the business of the 5-year time-limit was a strike issue, that Julia was fundamentally a nice enough girl, though rather more cynical and sour than was good for her and just a bit aloof, and that Flossy was nothing more than a baleful dried-up old hag who might do worse than to see a psychiatrist or get a sex change. They agreed that beauty was supremely important in a woman, though not so much so in men, and that Elaine had absolutely one of the best bums that ever flounced in jeans; they agreed that Alan didn't deserve her, that it would be an injustice in the end if they didn't put him away for a while, killing a boy like that just to get home a moment earlier; they agreed that Reagan was mad; they agreed that anyway women, beautiful or otherwise, were all totally irrational, as witness Colin's first wife who had doted on the children and then abandoned them with him, and now Marina who had sworn blind she didn't want children and then had gone and had one while supposedly on the pill. They agreed that children were wonderful and ultimately the only true answer to man's existential crisis, but a tremendous sacrifice, especially if your wife insisted on keeping them in bed; they agreed they never wanted to leave Italy, its sun, its bars, its aura of classy eroticism, its food, its people, its wine. They agreed that Kierkegaard was more difficult and more intelligent than Sartre, that modern philosophy was off the rails entirely, that Nietzsche had a lot more going for him than he was credited for, and that pretty soon they'd drive back to Colin's and see if they couldn't get Marina to rustle them up a decent meal; they agreed that first though, while the kids were having theirs, they could do worse than to grab another drink while the going was good, and so Sandro called to a waiter through slanting sunshine across green table-cloths to bring them two more of the same.

Colin, for some reason the wine didn't allow him to remember, found he was wearing a red silk scarf and an old borsalino.

———◦◦◦———

April 2nd   *Piazza dei Caduti, Quinzano*

Dear Diana,

   The enclosed pack of paper was hand-made in Siena and the floral designs were copied from original medieval scrolls. It cost me a bomb and contrary to what you're no doubt already thinking, it is not a wedding present. It's a loan. I expect to see every sheet returned over a period of 12 months as of this day, with the modest interest of a thin coating of ink (I hope you'll use a fountain pen). And please don't write in concentric circles the way you used to when Ronnie was in America, my head might come unscrewed.

So, what's new? Not much. I suppose I'm writing just for the feeling of talking to you more than anything. I do miss you, flatmate mine, which is why you should bloodywell write back! Though I appreciate you'll be busy just at the moment.

Anyway, yes, last Sunday we went out to the country for a big lunch at this friend of Colin's, that's the Mick McGahey bloke with four kids. He came with his wife (second), who's a rather syrupy leggy thing, about twenty years too young for him, and their little girl, a thoroughly spoilt but hopelessly pretty brown-eyed brat who apparently still sleeps in the matrimonial (mark 2) bed – this was the object of interminable snide remarks on his part which were obviously not meant to be funny. So, there was me, the wife, Colin, Flossy, Sandro and the baby, all in Colin's Cinquecento, which if it isn't a record, it ought to be. Sandro managed to get himself jammed next to Marina, the wife, of course, in a position where the only place he could look was down her dress. Men's little pleasures are becoming so transparent as to be almost endearing. (Can you believe he's reading Kierkegaard's *Diary of a Seducer*?)

But the real discovery of the day was Beppe, our host. The guy is a greengrocer, only 30 apparently, but he looks nearer forty from all the work and weather. 'Vigorous' is the only word I can think of that really sums him up. He has so much energy, so much go and fun about him. I mean, all the English people here are a rather lost bunch, dithering about whether to go home or not, comparing London and Milan's weather in the paper (I do every day!), reading through the jobs in the *Guardian*, or at best considering their being here as a kind of status symbol (the art brigade, that is – can you believe there's a bloke called Adair Habershom who does abstract paintings on canvases ten feet high and swears by ginseng!). There's a great lack of vitality about. Even the BBC boys we know/knew are hardly vigorous, are they? I was thinking about this: the dominant attitude with Barry and Co. (myself included come to think of it) has always been a sort of savoir faire sarcasm which is supposed to have something to do with being modern. No, the only dynamic people I've met these last years are you, because you're erratic and full of a silly bubbly energy that drives everybody up the wall and makes them fall in love with you at the same time (remember when you did Coriolanus at charades?), and Flossy, because she's so bitter and so determined not to be what she imagines everyone wants her to be, that she's either pedalling like a maniac or depressed as hell or trying to show everybody else up as lazy by scrubbing the floor when it's not her turn on the rota and then expecting them to like her for it.

Anyway, Beppe is big, without being tall, full of muscles and energy, with a dumb, explosive laugh and he has green eyes not unlike mine, and a very busy, shiny, face, always changing expression and showing up rather bad teeth; he was trying to speak English (he's been taking lessons from Colin), and it was funny hearing him plough away so confidently through a million mistakes with a strong Italo-Scottish accent, contorting his mouth round the vowel sounds and obviously loving every minute of it, as if he were a dog performing a trick (Colin clearly considers him a proletarian protégé in the best old socialist tradition, though actually he must be quite rich).

Anyway, he fed us lasagna in this old farmhouse he's bought and is doing up. He'd made it himself and it was too greasy, but nice, and he just kept giving everybody more and more and being ridiculously insistent (bye bye diet) and pouring wine, etc. It reminded me of our best parties of old times. In the middle of everything – we were talking about that Alan being in prison (he's out on bail now) – an argument broke out about how and if a man could avoid being 'inculato' (homosexually raped), because there was a case in the papers about a bloke who got put in prison by mistake and by the time they found out he was innocent, he was in hospital having his bum stitched up (men!). Beppe said he thought if you really didn't want it, you could resist, because the anus muscles are so strong, so if you didn't resist, it was because deep down you really wanted it. Marina said she often thought the same thing about women who got raped, that deep down they wanted it (*she* obviously wanted it from Beppe AND/OR Sandro, was giving both of them the come-on throughout) and of course Flossy and I went up the wall, calling him a macho idiot, her an ignorant so and so, etc. etc. He was quite hurt, but surprised more than anything else. Not used to English feminists. Marina was catty. Sandro said if anybody bothered him, he'd say he'd got AIDS.

So to cool down we went to look at Beppe's dogs. We found out that not only does Beppe work 12 hours a day for the shop, he also teaches karate in a gym in town (he's a black belt) and breeds Belgian shepherd dogs in these kennels he's built illegally at the bottom of the patch of land he has and is fighting a neighbour over. Flossy didn't believe it, about the karate; she has a theory that ninety percent of what men say is bullshit to impress other men; so Beppe demonstrated. He went and got his baggy white outfit and did a 'concentration session' on a patch of stony gravel, barefoot! It really was most impressive, all these rigid, tense, trance-like positions, and then sudden, violent movements. The hilarious thing was that while he was doing it, he kept making barking sounds – 'hoi, ji, lin!' – and said they were Japanese; apparently he always gives commands to his class in Japanese. Then when we got to the kennels he talked to the dogs in German, 'Raus, Sitz, Heil Hitler!' and so on. They were black, rather ugly-looking creatures that he sells at £200 apiece. Sandro asked him what language he talked to women in, but he said he hadn't found anything that worked yet, and Flossy called him a chauvinist pig. She said she'd like one of the dogs though, if he'd give her a big enough discount. Poor Flossy, she's streaming hayfever. I've never seen anyone use so many Kleenex. Probably if she got a dog she'd turn out to be allergic to it.

So there you are; a slice of my life. I must be settling in. The people I know seem to be becoming a group of friends, more or less. I'm not sure if I'm happy or sad. Probably both.

Give my best to Stuart. I'll be at the wedding; so see you

soon. (I'll stay with my mother, but as soon as I arrive I'll phone to sort out what sort of dress I'm expected to wear as B.M., etc. etc.)

Bestest.

JULIA

PS. I just re-read this and thought how boring it must be for you, telling you about all these people you don't know. But I couldn't think what else to write. Short of exposing one's soul every letter (and I refuse to think about L), what can one do but say what happened the day before?

Please write and tell me what's happening that end. You are a meany not writing.

———◦◦◦———

It is curious how some people are always imagining doing certain things, embarking on certain adventures, and never do so, how others never imagine doing those things, and yet at the first material prompting will act at once and with determination, as if the past had never been and the future anyway must be different, and there was nothing anywhere to lose.

Amongst the things that Alan imagined with a certain regularity, were his leaving his wife, his falling in love with another woman, with many women, his participation in erotic games, etc. It was not that he fantasized or masturbated over these possibilities, or not often, just that he liked to think of the different courses life might take (in fact he prided himself on the way in which he wouldn't allow such thoughts to pollute his relations with his wife – and in particular on the way he never allowed images of other women to cross his mind while they were making love).

And then he did have other imaginings of a non-sexual nature which he found equally intriguing: how he would behave on TV interviews were he ever successful; a possible return to England, inheritance of his father's spacious house in Dorset, life as a small-town schoolteacher. Or he imagined throwing himself into some business (father had good contacts in stock-broking); or, since the accident (for which he would never forgive himself), he imagined giving everything to charity and working for the disabled (the grand expiatory gesture).

Another fertile subject for daydreaming was how life would be if Elaine died; how he would bring up the children alone, winning respect, establishing a deep, blood understanding with them (whereas at the moment there was only the tedium of unpaid babysitting); how he would negotiate a decent path through regret of her to a new love with somebody else; what kind of somebody else he would choose (and how different it would be choosing now, with the experience one had, free of the traumas post-Mary). This particular line of thought, for example, had occupied him for upwards of half an hour around dawn of the day Margaret was born. Elaine had been leaning on his shoulders going through the most racking labour pains, when over her tousled hair, through a grimy window, he had spied, almost simultaneously, in the grey light of the street below, first a crow sitting on the bare branches of a tree, and then, to the left, four men in overalls carrying a coffin out of the main entrance of the hospital. The omen was so trite as to be laughable (who would believe it in a book?), and yet despite this, his mind, half in fear and half in the relish of rich thoughts to pick over in the long hours ahead, had been unable to deny its potency, had accepted the crow as a harbinger of death. Yes, Elaine would die now, in childbirth; he would bring up the kids, bravely, marrying, after a respectable year or so, the midwife, a delightful, dark-eyed young girl who came in at regular intervals to listen to the baby's heartbeat and check the dilation of the uterus.

In much the same way, some three months later, he had foreseen his own funeral quite clearly when they had given him bed number thirteen in a provincial hospital where he had gone to have his appendix out; and on this occasion he had imagined Elaine bringing up the kids, while his own photograph, the one with the wind blowing his slightly over-exposed hair at the rail of a Dover ferry (he'd had a moustache then), smiled down from the mantelpiece at where another man (Sandro?) would be kissing her on the couch.

And instead it was neither he nor Elaine who had died, but a child; a child he had never known nor dreamt of: Giordano Fontolan. Because life never never never went the way you, the way he, imagined it.

Again, the pleasure he took, or used to, over such morbid daydreaming was not so very unlike the pleasure he derived from contemplating the outcome of certain particularly dramatic football matches. Could Inter defend a slender two-goal lead in the cauldron of San Bernabeu, Madrid? Would Rummenigge be fit for the game? Was it possible that Barcelona could really dismiss Juventus? Alan read all the pre-match speculation in *Corriere della Sera*, and all the post-match self-congratulation, dismay or protest likewise, and he loved to let his mind dwell on those heroes and their matador lives, on how they must feel the last hours before the big game, how their lungs and legs must strain through the final minutes of extra time, Platini with his socks rolled down, his shirt untucked; Hernandez, Archibald.

But he didn't watch the game itself on television. Because he refused to have a television in the house. Television mesmerized the kids and wasted aeons of time that would better be spent reading or writing or in company; or, as far as the kids were concerned, playing, so that they wouldn't simply turn into passive cathode-irradiated lumps (he was responsible for their future, was he not?). And hence, in what was really a sacrifice at the altar of the dying god of his ambition (or was it just that any self-respect he had derived from repression?), Alan missed the big matches, and they remained entirely in the realm of fantasy, in that area of his brain where he might, alternately, return to England to embark on a business career, or desert his family to bum his way across the Hindu Kush, where Elaine might die and Brighton win the European Cup.

And perhaps it was precisely due to this indiscriminate relegation to the status of daydreaming of both the probable and improbable alike, the conscious decision (*Guardian* jobs) and the fatal wrench (Elaine's demise), that there could never really be any question of Alan's ever acting at all, of his ever finding and forcing a direction. All change was daydream and what there was now was all there ever would be. So that if he had made the move of coming to Italy it was only because the job had been directly offered to him (through an old tutor who had had a homosexual relationship with Scudellotti), and then because Mary had started bothering him on the phone again, because the BBC had turned down his play, and perhaps above all because Elaine had been so captivated by the idea of Italian sunshine, the thought of leaving her boring secretarial job, and the financial advantages to be accrued from letting their Hampstead flat while they lived in much cheaper accommodation abroad – so altogether enchanted, that she had gone out to buy bucketshop tickets before he had even made up his mind. And despite the ensuing argument, he had secretly thanked her for this. And could remind her of it forcibly when it was she who began to yearn to go home.

But in the period following the accident and Elaine's confession of unfaithfulness, Alan began to lose his grip. The lack of decision in his life (rebounded into marriage, spirited to Italy, tricked – there was no other word for it – into children) had always been finely balanced, justified, made acceptable, by the thrust and steadiness of his ambition, an ambition which reduced everything else to secondary importance, an ambition which, delightfully at first, but then more and more disturbingly, had no effect on anyone, didn't involve action, could be undertaken anywhere, living with anybody, and thus left him free to be pushed around, not to have to resist ('open to experience' as he put it to himself). He could fluster about, insist he needed time, give the impression of fighting to get somewhere, without going anywhere at all, without doing or deciding anything. He was running (scribbling) on the spot. Killing time.

But how, after such an accident, after doing something so

truly awful, which again hadn't been the result of a decision, but the product of a fatuous and superfluous tension – how could he concentrate on such fooleries now? How could he write about guilt and regeneration for BBC Radio Three (the play version was looking rather more promising at the moment), when this was just a slot his mind had fitted (squeezed) the story into, as they, if he were lucky, would slot it into the interminable schedule the media is. Where was the reality in that? And how could he write about rekindled love for his wife, when the accident had had no such effect on him, when all he could think of was her pretty body in the arms of that smarmy sod, Sandro? Yet if he didn't sit at his screen every day, then what was he to do with himself? The university was only 12 hours a week, the kids bored him (though he did love them, though he felt acutely it was wrong to be bored by one's children); inevitably they gave him the impression they were stealing time from somewhere else (but where, when he had nowhere to go, when time itself, in a way, seemed to have stopped?).

Elaine was her usual pixyish clean-limbed practical self. Yes, she had confessed her unfaithfulness, but it wasn't the end of the world, was it? She didn't seem to appreciate how that betrayal had destroyed an idea he had of his life, a whole *Weltanschauung*. She didn't appear to share his sense of the importance of having something sacred, something safe, to be handled with care, despite destructive impulses, maintained through healthy repression (because if it took ambition to make marriage acceptable, still marriage, family, could make failure bearable). No, she simply shrugged the whole thing off. It had been a moment's distraction, an unfortunate accident. She smiled her girlish smile, pouted her practical pout. (The obvious came to him now after five years of marriage, she had no imagination.) And in the same way, she said, it was sheer bad luck that that bike had swung out like that just as he was overtaking, and it was a tragedy the child had died (appalling for the mother), but there was nothing anyone could do about it and no point in dwelling (Alan's tendency was to dwell precisely because there was nothing one could do about it). The trial, she said, would almost certainly result in a suspended sentence (they had checked out similar cases), after which they would go straight home to England, sell the Hampstead flat, buy a bigger one further out of town and settle down to the London suburban life for which, when all was said and done, they were so well equipped.

And in the meantime could he please stop moping and drinking so heavily and generally making a fool of himself, when there was so much to be done about the house.

It did seem, Alan felt, that at some point during the two pregnancies and the difficult nights that followed, waking at intervals, her sleeping on the couch, rarely making love, they had lost touch with each other; they played their little love games – piggies in the trough, the minstrel hedgehogs – less often and with a rather unpleasant sniff of poignancy (this is empty now, only a rehearsal); their arguments (always over practical problems, attitudes to the children, division of duties) had taken on a ritual feel, created no sense of urgency or laceration, and the making-up afterwards was likewise cere-monial; the olive branch (once so fragrant, so sweet) had taken on a plasticky feel. And now even her unfaithfulness was being rather cursorily papered over in the daily routine, when it should have been the occasion for wrath and breakdown, tears and promises. Elaine simply carried on; she busied herself about the house; she taught her two hours a day at the Cambridge; she wanted to drive out to the lake on sunny afternoons to get a tan; she never missed her three sessions a week at the gym; she hired and fired babysitters, prepared meals for the children, stacked Tupperware in the freezebox. There was something disturbingly robust in her slenderness, in the neat jeans, small bras, in the ever complacent femininity that had once seemed the natural refuge after Mary's demanding and unpredictable passions; there was something slightly sarcastic now too in what he had always thought of as a twinkling little-girl's smile. What did Alan expect, this smile appeared to ask, life to end? Or even to change?

For this?

Or even this? (At least Mary had suffered with you.)

And yet it did change: it changed in the sense that he had changed, was paralysed, in the sense that the balance between disciplined routine and daydream was breaking down, in the sense that the whisky bottle in the thirties drinks cabinet and the beers in the fridge loomed larger and larger, until he just couldn't see his way round them anymore.

On May 15th, evening of the European Cup Final, Alan broke his rule and went to watch the game at Flossy and Julia's. Already in a state of some drunkenness, he sat on the sofa with Sandro and repeated, like an excited child, all the things he had read in *Corriere della Sera*, sucking one of Julia's gin and tonics through crushed ice. And while he was away, Elaine, who had never imagined she would, took the opportunity to walk out on him. Her action was so instinctive and unreasoned that when it came to writing a note, no explanation came to mind. After a flicker of hesitation, she wrote: 'Alan, I've had enough, I'm going back to England with the kids. Don't try to do anything about it. ELAINE.'

Part Two

HOME
AND BACK

'............... five beetles,
   Blind and green, they grope
Amongst the honey meal.'

Two in the Campagna
Robert Browning (1855)

June 29th   *Piazza degli Inculati*
                                               Quinzano

Dear Julia,

I'm writing to <u>warn</u> you! The day after you left, <u>the very next day</u>, Marina arrived. And I mean arrived to <u>stay</u>!!!

With <u>Snake Sandro</u>!

I don't want to offend, but it was quite clear they had been fucking already. I am sorry to use a word like that, but any other would be an insult to the act itself.

She brought Baby Janet and they have been making me babysit while they. . . .

She bosses him around. I don't think he asked her to come and stay <u>at all</u>. He just suffers it. He was/is too weak spirited to tell her to <u>piss off</u>. With me he tries to act as if this were all <u>perfectly normal</u>. But then perhaps it is for him. He didn't even ask me not to tell you.

I wouldn't say any of this to you if you hadn't been such a good <u>amica</u> to me. If I didn't think you <u>deserved</u> to know. Thank God you didn't really care about him!

In this given period I am doing all the dishes and the wash. I am being exploited as always. The people who don't want to live in a pigsty always are. They won't hear of a rota. Marina has obviously got it into her head she's on a extended holiday.

What do you plan to do? If you are coming back soon and we can kick them <u>both</u> out and return to our <u>feminist haven</u> well and good. I was very much enjoying living with you as I'm sure you know. If not, I'm getting out.

They haven't even made any mention of paying their shares of the rent yet. <u>Us muggins are paying for them</u>!

Of course I can understand a woman leaving her husband. I think Elaine did the right thing getting away from Alan, because he's such a <u>pompous prick</u> always wrapped up in himself, fussing over his soul and his manuscripts and wondering why they aren't giving him the Nobel Prize (he's started 'researching' for a TV script on Pasolini now. Talk about pie in the outer atmosphere!). No, Elaine did the right thing, even if I could never put up with that smug little-girl, madonna-knows-all smile she had. But why does Marina have to leave Colin only to swop him for <u>Snake Sandro</u>?

The truth is she is one of those women who only feel content when they have a man under their thumb – or rather between their legs. She doesn't realize she's a <u>slave to traditional conditioning</u>.

I tried to talk to her about it, but she just went on clipping her toe-nails (which she paints green) and letting the parings whizz off where they would. We're having a real hot spell right now and she walks round the flat in just knickers and a shirt that she leaves <u>unbuttoned</u> at the front. Which is partly to provoke Sandro with her slinky doll's publicity-bred body, and partly because <u>she's in love with herself</u>. She said – get this – she said she left Colin because Aquarians are too demanding, whereas Sagittarians are more accommodating!! No comment.

The only thing that makes me <u>laugh</u> is she insists Janet sleeps with them and this morning, woken as ever by our maniac bell ringer, I found Sandro snoring on the couch in the sitting room in his yankee boxer shorts. She spoils the child silly and seems determined to turn her into a moron like herself.

I'm sorry if this isn't splendidly edifying, but it is better that you know, isn't it? Especially if you weren't sure about whether to come back or not, though I hope you do.

I also hope things at home weren't so bad as the telegram suggested.

Remember to bring me back 144 Typhoo Tea Bags and a few assorted jars of Sharwoods Mango Chutney.

Yours in Sisterhood.

FLOSSY.

PS. Napoleon is fine. I'm doing your students to keep them in training, though it's a <u>bit difficult</u> explaining the bras and underwear SHE leaves lying all over the place, not to mention the <u>four</u> suitcases open in the hall.

PPS. Apparently Alan and Colin are to be found hashing up tagliatelle and apple crumble evening times for Colin's kids, then drinking heavily and playing chess with Beppe. Perhaps if they drink heavily enough he'll win a game. I'm not losing *any* sleep over them. The only person I feel sorry for is <u>you</u>.

PPPSOS. I'm going to Beppe's KARATE CLASSES – Rape Defence!

PPPPSUPERTRIUMPH!! I weighed in at 9st 13.

———— •◦• ————

July 12   *Hawaii*

Dear July-poo,

I am so sorry about what happened. I rang up a few times but you were always at the hospital. I managed to get hold of Mike once and he said you were very upset. I hope things are looking up now.

The wedding went off marvellously. First time I've been to church in years. Lenny and Barry were ushers and had actually dug out suits from somewhere (perhaps you've spoken to him about it. I always have the impression you're probably thick as thieves still, whatever you both tell me – 'For old love will still to . . .') All the old gang were there and did all the old corny things – shaving foam, and tin cans attached to the car – which was very sweet really, seeing them so happy to play their silly roles for me. Even dour old Do-Leave-Off did us the honour and read out a long celebratory poem in Czech which I then had to translate on the spot – the first thing he's ever done that hasn't been desperate and suicidal. It went like this:

'Dawn skies: don't you though
   Have to hope. Why is it misery
You poets must predict, when all her flesh is radiant.
   Her eyes are radiant
   And the sun only rising.'

Ten very flattering verses of it (it sounded rather better in Czech, though people never believe you when you tell them). Anyway, everybody applauded politely and Stuart announced a special toast for 'Our poet Laureate', though I don't suppose he'd mind me telling you he couldn't tell the difference between King Lear and Edward Lear if he tried (and he wouldn't). About half-way through the reception I had to dash to the loo to take off a girdle (yes, a girdle!!!) dear mumsy had insisted I wear to reduce the evidence of junior – amazing what one succumbs to for the sake of respectability, and especially amazing when everybody knew anyway. In fact, when we went to see the vicar to arrange about the church, he said very coyly, but determined to be modern: 'Is there already a joyous event to look forward to?' And Stuart said, 'the gynaecologist tells us October.' The BBC boys underrate Stuart. Jealousy is the key (not of me – it's his looks and salary). The truth is, he's very bright when he wants to be. He's like one of those jolly swains in Renaissance plays who turn out to be intelligent princes in disguise.

So, honeymooning in Hawaii. The place is exactly as you imagine it and wonderful the first few days, but then progressively more boring. I'm rather wishing we'd gone to Czechoslovakia so I could have got some language practice in.

Now Julia, dear heart, do us all a thundering great favour and don't hurry off back to Italy, however this awful business at home turns out. Frankly I could never quite understand why you went and even less could I understand why you stayed after losing the job. You obviously don't get on with the Spare Rib, nor the improbable Harrison-Ford cardboard cutout; and then for all your talk about a clean break with Lenny I know you've been writing regularly, because he told me so; in fact, when I told him about you having a boyfriend there, I did it on purpose to try and make something happen between you. But no. All goes on as before. So why not just accept that and stay in London and make the best of it. You're simply not cut out for karate-chopping greengrocers, freezing canaries, Scottish communists and manslaughtering failed writers. What a riff-raff! Stay in London, still 'flour of Citys all', despite the demise of your beloved GLC. Stuart and I will be leaving the flat soon – it's too small for the two of us with junior as well – and I think we could work it so that you got back in there if you found a friend to share the rent (maybe your brother would be interested). You could inherit all the bottles in the famous cabinet and decide all on your own who to invite to parties. How about that? We were, as you say, such a happy group of friends. Why shouldn't it go on being that way? And then, I'm really not up to filling all this stationery you've sent; actually it seems rather too nice for my scrawl (it's funny how everybody takes me for such a literary creature, yet setting pen to paper is really almost more than I can manage.)

Well, Stuart sends his love, and I do hope your mother is better.

Love

Your DI-PIE.

———— ◦◦◦ ————

July 30th   *SWIFTAIR*   *Kilburn*

Dear Sis,

Safely back?

Just to say we've got an offer on the house. Ninety thou. This man Mowbray says if we invest through a trust we can get 18% p.a. (£16,200). The home costs £800 a month (£9,600 p.a.), so if we get through the sale fast (and the estate agent says the price is okay if not terrif), then we should manage, though I'm not quite clear about the tax situation yet (maybe it was a good

113

job I did some economics after all). Everybody I meet says we're mad selling up when neither of us has our own place here, which is a bit unnerving, but I can't imagine any other way of paying for Mum, if that's where we want to put her. And then I think I'd feel like a ghost of myself in Friern Park.

So the guy came for the furniture, which he took for a measly 300 quid ('robbin meself, guv, robbin meself, never unload this stuff'), which I'm presently living on. Brünhilde bagged the knitting machine, which I must admit came as rather a surprise, and the first thing she turned out was a baby jacket. Alarm bells!! (she said it was just practice). Her idea now is to turn out sweaters for the local shops (or was that already under discussion when you were here?). Oh, I kept the car, but may have to sell it when the tax runs out.

What else. Nothing. We went to see Mum yesterday, but she's still not recognizing anybody. She kept calling Brünhilde 'nurse' and asking for an extra cardigan, though the day was sweltering. Her speech was still slurred and the left arm completely limp.

About the future. Are you quite sure about your decision to go back? I mean you seemed in a bit of a daze when you left, like you didn't know what you were doing. Especially after saying every day for a week that you'd stay and look after her. Look, if you do think you'd rather do it that way after all, just phone as soon as you get this (I'm sending it Swiftair) and I won't exchange contracts. We can always get some different furniture in the house. The other stuff made me vomit anyway. Obviously for me this would be the ideal solution, a weight off the old shoulders, but far be it from me to push you either way. . . .

Phew, I feel so surprisingly R for responsible. I quite miss my old self, never mind Mum. See how my style's changed!

Best love, BRUV.

Oh, I forgot. Your man Lenny was at the flat here when I got back from Gatwick, arguing with Lance and Brünhilde about homosexual marriage. He seemed very upset he'd missed you. I'd say you'd got that guy on one hell of a long string. Can't understand why you don't just wind him in, freckles n'all. He's alright. Invited us to a party at a place in Ladbroke Grove. We'll go. It's all free grub. And at least we've got the car to get back in now.

———◆◆◆———

August 5th   *Fortis Green*

Dear Julia

I heard about your poor mother. You have my deepest sympathy. These things are so distressing. I lost my own mother last year and found it very difficult to adjust. I am sure, though, that you are taking it well. You are such a tough person emotionally, as we all know.

Presumably you are aware that Lenny and I are divorcing. Personally, I wouldn't wish him on anybody, but I know you may feel differently.

Very best wishes. Do feel you can write if you'd like.

LIZ.

———◆◆◆———

August 6th   *Shepherd's Bushed*
                                          (and so am I)

Julia love, sorry about your mum and all that. We missed you at the wedding, we really did. I go to so many these days, yet can never persuade Kat-Kat to put me in the protagonist's role (despite a glorious victory in the BBC squash finals).

Presumably you know all about Liz and Lenny divorcing. It now seems she wants to marry that American bloke Curtis she screws at the Adelphi. Anyway, this is just to say that I get the feeling Lenny's going to need his hand holding. He's been looking pretty beat up at the studios. It's the prospect of parting with the kids I suppose (apparently Curtis is mad on kids, a great source of dramatic inspiration or something).

I say no more. I just thought you might like to get the picture from an independent source as it were. I don't know what communication there might or might not be between you two, but it would be great to see you back together.

Love,

BARRY

◆◇◆

Dear Julia,

I'm leaving this note for you in case you come back. Do check that THE FUCKERS haven't gone and opened it! (Yes, they really are <u>that</u> bad, or at least she is. She's <u>abominable</u>! He probably couldn't care less).

Anyway, the fact is, I'm <u>getting out</u>. I'm not going to be exploited any more here (why do I always end up playing slave to heterosexual couples?!). The stories I could tell. They've been expecting ME to look after the little girl almost full time; I took her to the paediatrician the other day because of some nasty-looking spots she'd got, and I've been taking her to the children's park to play every afternoon because otherwise she'd never get any fresh air at all. They even got me to pretend they weren't in when Colin came round (he stayed an hour drinking your gin – neat – and swearing and saying in the end perhaps it was all for the best!!!). PLUS I've paid the gas and electricity bills, AND I had to pay for the plumber when the loo got <u>blocked</u>!!!

And you know what Mr Plumber said?

He said: 'DON'T FLUSH ANY MORE OF THOSE RUB-BER THINGS DOWN THE TOILET.' and because I'm a foreigner he felt obliged to repeat it (in capital letters every time) while standing in the stairway scratching his concrete block of a head, so that our dear stroke victim downstairs got to hear and will probably start lecturing me soon on encyclical whatever number it is that expounds the immorality of CON-DOMS.

THEY were out of course. Janet went and pissed on the couch because she was scared of saying she wanted a 'pi pi' in front of hunk plumber.

Marina was talking about divorcing Colin to marry SNAKE SANDRO a couple of days ago. He just said: 'Yaaas, yaaas,' at his most drawling and kept on eating ice-cream watching car-racing on the box. (Is there anything more stupid than car-racing? Anything more male than three million macho horse-power going round and round in circles?) She buys him ice-cream and strawberries and cherries and other goodies every day. Quite with whose money it isn't at all clear. Not, as I said before, because she cares for him, but because she wants to get her teeth into him. It's maddening. When will we women realize our security doesn't lie with men?!!! And especially not spineless souls like Sandro. Still, he laps up his strawberries and cream and cherries while the going's good.

One detail to sum up her character. Yesterday morning, coming back from picking up the milk, I found her fussing in the freezer compartment in just her slip, obviously still half asleep. When I asked her what she wanted, she explained that she rubs ice on her nipples for ten minutes every morning to keep her tits firm. She recommended I do the same. She puts a couple of blocks in each cup of an old bra and straps it on tight. Aaaagh!

So, I'm getting the hell out. You can find me at Beppe's place out in the country. Remember? I'm looking after his house and dogs in return for a room and vast amounts of fresh fruit and veg. He only comes up at the weekends, so I'm sure you could come too if you want. I'm thinking of getting him to give me a small patch of his land to farm on. Want to join me? The events of the last month have convinced me that women living and working together in harmony is the only solution.

IN SISTERHOOD
FLOSSY.

PS. If you don't want to stay here with them at all (I can't imagine you will), you could always stop over at Alan's for a night before coming out to me.

———◦◦◦———

Having picked up her post and Napoleon, Julia crossed to the bus-stop and stood in the meagre shade of a balcony. The sun, directly above, divided the space into blinding glare and dense shadow. The sky was not blue, but an intense, luminous, unpleasant grey; the air droned with insects. She thought, the only person she would like to write to was her mother, who most probably would never read a letter again. She thought she could happily have strangled Liz and Barry, and Lenny. Especially Lenny. With wire flex twisted round her wrists. She would rather enjoy filling the columns of the cheaper Sunday newspapers. But how could one ever explain? She thought, as it turned out they had been right not to buy a new cover for the sofa. Quite right. It had made a big impression that, picking out her things from the confusion poor Marina was living in, sorting out underwear, finding her make-up pencils in the carton that served as Janet's toybox. One did live so much with others (for brief periods), amongst others, and presumably one was like others (God knows one was substituted by them often enough) yet she didn't feel so. She didn't feel she was quite like Diana or Flossy or Marina. Diana was so light, so bright, so sudden and serene in her loves and dismissals, her poetry and predictable unpredictability; and then Flossy so sure, almost manic in her prejudices and miserableness, her interminable cold and aggressive friendship; Marina so vain and childish with that unforgivably radiant skin, green toe-nails, erect nipples. She didn't feel like her mother either with her prayers and fuss (in retrospect so lovable); nor anything at all like the Teutonic Brünhilde, camped amidst queers, with her impossible schemes for making money.

This feeling of difference, Julia reflected at the bus-stop with

Napoleon hopping from perch to perch in his cage, should have created a strong sense of identity, purpose, destiny even (not that, nor that, nor that, but *this, me!*) – yet she really couldn't feel it at the moment; at the moment all she felt was lost, a little tired and most of all overwhelmed by everybody else's clutter, physical and emotional: Lenny's, Marina's, Alan's, Mother's. Her identity seemed only a perception of all the difficulties and complications ahead.

Or rather, if she did have any identity at all, it was the one she hated so much she had left England to try and shake it from her back, as an insect shakes itself out of its cocoon. Yes, she had wanted to metamorphose perhaps, was that it? Not to be herself, not to have her past, her future. She had imagined the hot Italian sun would turn her sluggish, blind burrowing caterpillar into a dazzling butterfly. That her life would come together in the fulfilment she (perversely? miraculously?) had always kept before her, had always measured her failures by. If so, the first attempt to fly had crashlanded rather pathetically in Piazza dei Caduti. Or perhaps the name wasn't really so apt; perhaps the whole thing had never got off the ground at all: she was still the same old grub, just a little lost out of her favourite cabbage patch.

She had wanted a metamorphosis. Yet everybody back home appeared rather to have liked that old caterpillar. They had liked the occasionally grumpy, commonsense Julia with her angry sadness and determined dreams. They had liked her bitter humour and the drinks she mixed, the parties she organized; they had liked her too, of course, why not? for the long saga with Lenny, the human interest it gave them – as one likes page 3 of the *Telegraph*, or *Dynasty* – or perhaps more aptly, *Soap*. And so when she had wanted the serial to end, to change her part, they had all protested. They liked her like that. She was a staple of their lives. Which at least was something. Quite a lot in fact. And she could still go back. The warm cocoon dark of Khan's was still available. More than ever so.

Or better still, this might just be the moment when Lenny

would metamorphose, the frog become a prince to kiss his Sleeping (with the aid sometimes of pills) Beauty (as it were). Julia smiled to herself, smoking a cigarette in dense heat. She hitched up a bra-strap, remembering how Barry had once remembered that.

Most probably she would simply end up nursing a mother who no longer recognized her: 'Dear Mum, If I hadn't left, perhaps you'd never have had that stroke. . . .'

———◦◦———

August 21st   Via Quattro Novembre

Dear Sandro,

I'm writing to you so as not to write to other people. The letters I have to write to other people now are full of consequence. I have to tell my brother whether I agree to sell my mother's house and therefore whether she should finish her life in a home. I have to write to Lenny to explain why I left England so abruptly and most of all whether I intend to go back to him now he and his wife are splitting up. I have to write to Diana to say whether I want to move back into the flat in Kensington, since she's leaving it. Terrible letters to have to write, even if they need be only a couple of lines long. But I can write a few pages to you and none of it need be of consequence, nor could be. I realize now in fact, Sandro, that nothing said or written to you would or could ever be of consequence, since you are so determined to be of no consequence yourself, nor to have any in anybody else's life.

When we first met at that pathetic party in the faculty (remember? Manwearing and Habershom were trying to arrange a cricket match) almost the first thing you said was that you weren't married. I can't remember quite how the subject came up, but in my leaving-England-and-everything euphoria I somehow latched onto the words as if they were an omen. You were my age, attractive (very), unattached; I was free as the air myself

(I thought), and so immediately there I was imagining an attachment, cultivating a crush, as if I were an adolescent all over again (do people really grow out of adolescence, or do they just learn to disguise it better, until it pops out and betrays them). And the laughable part of it is that the only thing that worried me was that perhaps you weren't telling the truth, that perhaps you'd left a wife in Canada who would come over to claim you. Something like that. When what I should have seen was your glowing self-satisfaction at not being married (that's right: Colin said, anybody over 30 with any self-respect had been married and divorced at least once, and you said, 'Not me, buddy, I've got a clean sheet,' and Alan said, 'You don't have to be married to stain the sheets.' The usual banter – why do we all try so hard to be witty all the time?). I should have seen that you were saying, 'I'm not married and I never shall be because I have no intention of tangling my life with other people's, I'm too smart for that kind of thing (look how self-contained I am); so smart in fact that I'm going to be the one who gets the permanent contract here, ahead of all of you.' Or perhaps I <u>did</u> see it. I'm not sure, but sitting here writing this I realize that probably I always knew you had no time for anyone, let alone me; what I mean is that I always knew <u>who you were</u>. So that my decision to get involved seems to have been consciously stupid. I suppose it's just that one simply goes on hoping willy-nilly that people will fall in love with you (why shouldn't they?) and you with them; that one insists on ignoring the obvious; and then again, with leaving England, I did feel suddenly young and rather silly and ready to believe all sorts of unusual things might happen. That is the fun of life after all. I felt very excited and bright about everything.

So we became lovers. Because you came over to talk about the problem of the university and suddenly got the hots to go to bed with me. At first I liked to think it was the other way round, the university an alibi and me the object (if only subconsciously), but then I realized that any and every time you meet a woman you get the hots to go to bed with her, and seeing as you're so handsome and charming, walk so tall, speak so smoothly and rap your comb in such earnest rhythms on your knee, you fairly often manage it. Don't you?

You have an odd way of making love, Sandro. You're not passionate, nor hurried, nor callous, nor naughty, nor imaginative, nor exactly tender. Careful is the only word I can think of, the same way you're so careful making the coffee you drink with your after-dinner TV, so careful with your clothes and hair and university diplomacy, so careful with whatever it was kept you half an hour in the bathroom every morning while Flossy went up the wall. I'm always nervous about taking my clothes off with a new man (always! about five times in my life), so that making love the first time for me involves as much fear as it does pleasure (what will he think of my breasts, what will he think of my thighs? Adolescence coming out again). But you didn't seem particularly interested in discovering my body. Ever. It was the act itself interested you, getting everything perfectly timed and enjoyable (like making sure meat and veggies reach perfection simultaneously and on the nail for dinner). You never tried to undress me sexily, or make any of the text-book explorations. No, instead you let me undress you, me admire you, so that I would be sufficiently roused to slot into your infallibly timed routine: the well-paced start to warm up, the long slow tantalising plateau, acceleration and sprint to finish. Wasn't it always like that? You just like fucking, I suppose. And who could blame you? Certainly it took a lot of pressure off me.

But what were we doing together? You didn't want any contact that wasn't to do with cooked meals, accommodation and a well-paced orgasm. You didn't want to know about anything that wasn't absolutely convenient. Whereas for me, sex on its own is just boring in the end, even with someone who's good at it. For me – get ready to laugh – for me the only thing that makes getting up in the morning and going to bed in the evening and all the attrition between bearable – the only thing that changes anything and everything, is partnership, is permanence, is love. And despite a couple of very determined efforts I found it impossible to be in love with you. In fact I doubt really, Sandro, whether you will be able to understand what I mean.

Still, the funny thing is that once I'd got used to the idea that we weren't going to love each other, I quite enjoyed living with you. Or at least part of me did (the cowardly, hedonist part). I enjoyed the humdrum feel of your always being around and lazy and predictable and making love in the same way every other day more or less. I enjoyed the fact that we never argued (was there anything to argue about, given the minimal requirements?). I enjoyed how undemanding you were, and light-hearted and unashamed of all your scheming. I enjoyed the way your being there bothered Flossy and enhanced people's image of me and I enjoyed the strange fact that I was never jealous, as I have always been so painfully jealous with my one or two other loves, perhaps because in your case the relationship always seemed to be on a rental rather than have-and-hold basis. It was a sort of emotional hibernation for me, I suppose, a rejection of all my hopes in a parody of what I'd always wanted, which is again, companionship, partnership, home. And perhaps if I hadn't gone away it would have stayed like that, I would have hibernated with you a lifetime. Or perhaps not. Perhaps you were only waiting till the holidays to ditch me, as you did Marina, as doubtless you have done others.

Poor Marina, when I went to pick up my things she asked me if I wanted to stay and share the rent. She said she never wanted to see you again, even if you came back and begged. A healthy enough attitude. And she was right (it isn't usually the case) about there being no need for hard feelings. But the girl's too neurotic and spoilt to live with. I don't know how you put up with her even for a couple of weeks. In fact I've giggled to myself once or twice thinking of you trying to sleep with Janet in your bed and put up with all the fuss over what the child should wear and what she should eat (my advice was asked at length when I went over for my stuff). Presumably when she runs out of money for the rent she'll go back to Colin or to her family. I hope it won't be difficult for her.

When we next meet, Sandro, if I decide to stay that is, perhaps you could let me know whether you don't ever feel just a teensy bit guilty.

I am now staying with Alan Bexley who seems determined to rub in your unfaithfulness to me as if it were some consolation for his wife's desertion of him. (How you figure in both our lives, I discover now.) He also seems determined to drink himself to death just to show he really is upset about Elaine and guilty about his accident. Not awesomely original, though I do feel sorry for him. At least in his fucked-up way, he does want to be a man. I'm sleeping in what was the kids' bedroom with a frieze of picture-book animals and a mobile of huge bees hanging from the lampshade. If I reach up and wind it up I can tinkle myself to sleep with Brahms' lullaby over and over. If that doesn't work there are always pills. I have so many BIG DECISIONS to make and I just can't do it. I want to come out of my hibernation, but what does one wake up to? Unlike you, I would like to do the grand, the courageous thing: except that I can't see what it is: looking after a mother who has lost her wits? going back to an old lover? staying here without career or prospects (and with a drunk depressive flatmate into the bargain)?

If you should ever feel so generous as to put pen to paper, perhaps with all the philosophy you've been reading you could help me out. (Do you think I'm being funny?)

I hope you have enjoyed my letter of no consequence.

I also hope that living with Bertelli is proving perfectly convenient for you and that she doesn't start accusing you of putting powder in her eyes (perhaps I shall be complaining of that soon: I sometimes feel like a younger version of Bertelli). I can see you on the veranda overlooking the lake, sipping gin and pretending to concentrate on her silly book. I can see you pausing over the chest of drawers she will have given you, wondering which colour T-shirt would be best for a stroll on the waterfront. I can see your sunglasses pushed back in your hair as you look down from the drop at San Zeno. Will you get a will made out in your favour before pushing her? You'd better destroy this letter, hadn't you?

JULIA.

And what was wrong with Flossy? Were you afraid you'd catch a cold. Or was she allergic to you?

Did she go chop chop?

And do you simply jerk off now, having no-one for the moment to screw. I don't imagine the difference will be so great. Though I do still like you, Sandro.

—◦◦—

Alan couldn't have pleaded more guiltily at the trial. And he was feeling guilty; in part because he had spent so much time dressing for the occasion, seeking the combination of clothes that would give an impression of respect for the court without seeming arrogant or flashy; in part because he had for days been forming the guilty words he would address to the parents if he should get a chance to speak to them. As it turned out, none of his shirts was washed or ironed, since he had consistently rejected Julia's offer to do his wash along with hers (why?). And now he couldn't decide whether his crumpled, slightly scruffy look, even in shirt and tie, would be interpreted as an insult or merely an indication of the kind of slovenly careless character that had led him to overtake so wildly. He was irritated too by the way part of his mind was calmly and irrelevantly reflecting on this obsession with self-presentation and observing that it was impossible simply to go as one was, because when one put on clothes (just as when one picked up a pen) one had to choose who one wanted to be. And the more styles there were, the more images and permutations, so the more difficult it became, and especially for someone like himself who had no idea what he might be if not guilty. Guilty above all of letting his mind get short-circuited into these unproductive, tiresome, narcissistic reflections. And why – perhaps it was this that was bothering him most – why was he unable to write to Elaine at her parents' (she must be there or in touch with them) and beg her to put things back together? Which would be the obvious sensible thing (otherwise there would be all the financial problem of the flat to settle). Was it pride or inertia? Why did part of him cherish the liberty he was squandering in this theatrical fiasco with the whisky bottle (unless all alcoholics were theatrical, addicted to their parts and assiduous as self-audiences). Why – and this was quite simply criminal – did his children, his lovely children, have so little leverage over him, despite the modern father he'd been, nappy-changing, nail-clipping and nose-wiping; why did the tabloid tug-of-love hold no attraction for him at all? He felt really quite relieved not to have to bother with the million chores being a self-respecting modern dad involved. That was the truth. So was it possible in the end that the only thing he missed in being left alone was sex, the only thing that hurt the loss of self-esteem? He'd pontificated so often on the virtues of faithfulness. How they must be laughing.

And why was it that Alan Bexley saw with such clarity the person he ought to be, the feelings he ought to have, the actions he ought to take, and yet wasn't, hadn't and didn't?

The judge asked the questions advanced by the prosecution. Alan declined the services of an interpreter and answered that he had acted like a fool, irresponsibly, and could claim no mitigating circumstances. In the shabby room with its rows of plastic chairs he was unable to imagine who the parents might be. He was upset too to find himself deliberately biting his lip (was he trying to arouse sympathy – how should one behave, how should one ever behave? his face he knew was so forceful and proud, the straight fleshy nose, powerful forehead, one had to do something to tone down these features). The judge anyway was not looking at him. For all the interest he showed he might have been working alone in an empty office. Would Alan himself ever learn to be so professional? Rather modestly the prosecution asked for a two-year suspended sentence and got it.

Outside in the courtyard, Flossy, Colin and Julia obviously felt the outcome was cause for celebration; his own feeling, though vague, was that another occasion had slipped through his fingers, gone ungrasped, misunderstood. He would, he foresaw with resigned weariness, think over and over it for days, realizing too late what he should have said, what he should have done. His freedom, drinking sparkling prosecco at a table in Piazza Erbe not fifty metres from the court, seemed unreal.

'Ter-rrific,' Colin was saying, 'Fucking terrific man! Got to fucking-well celebrate this one.'

Because once again all that tension and self hatred had simply come to nothing. Another non-event.

———◦◦◦———

October 1st   *St Mary's Maternity*
                                                      Kensington

Dear Julia,

I know I said I'd get cross if you didn't stay back (and I am!), but it's no reason for not writing for so long (it's April since I heard from you!). Not that I can talk really I know, but I'm quite missing your missives (as it were). I even want to know what's happened to Flossy and Sandro and Beppe and the rest, not to mention the diet. The fact is, Julia love, that you are a letter writer and I'm not (it must be genetic, they'll find the gene one day), so that when you stop writing, it's serious, it worries people. By the way I hope that now I'm married I'm not going to lose all my old friends or anything. It's not as if I'd disappeared entirely from circulation.

On top of which, I just can't understand you and Lenny. What a whining Werther he's become, a truly atrocious Tristan. For the best part of 10 years he's done nothing but bitch about Liz and how badly she treats him and flaunt the fact that he goes out with you. And now she finally does the selfish and sensible thing and leaves him, what does he do? He goes round bursting into tears at everybody's parties, saying how he won't survive it and how much he misses seeing the kids and giving them a kiss while they're asleep (which was the only time he ever saw them probably with his social life), pretending he's auditioning for the next Terms of Endearment no less, etc. etc. ('Lenny, A Different Love') Then, worst of all (angels and ministers of grace defend us!) he starts apologizing for being such a sop, and we have to say, 'Lenny, but we understand,' when we most definitely don't. He was round the other night (he's grown a rather ugly, straggly red beard by the way) telling us how lucky we are and how much he envies us our relationship and wishes he could go back to the beginning, and how wonderful it is having a baby when both of you support each other. I could have throttled him. Stuart of course is too kind. He listens to all his troubles for hours and hours and never seems to mind (they have lunch together sometimes and argue over whose expense account to put it on – modern generosity).

Yes, so why aren't you here to put the man back on his feet? This is the other insoluble mystery. You were always saying how much you wanted to look after him. You remember our giggly serious pre-sleep conversations when we still shared the bedroom before the argument about the curtains. Well, during one of them you definitely said (and I quote from a perfect memory): 'I want to save that man. He'd be so fine in the right hands.' (Funny how I remember even the tone of your voice disembodied in the dark, sometimes words just stick for some reason, God knows what the criteria might be.) So this is your big chance. I never saw a man who had more need of being saved. And you love him if ever anybody loved anyone. You've been writing to him all along (you sneak you!). Then brother Mike told me this bloke Sandro had walked out on you while you were back here, so what on earth's to lose? I must confess at this point I simply don't understand either of you at all (and everybody's always saying I'm unpredictable). Your Mikey, by the way, seems to be the centre of attention at every party one goes to these days; a great social future, especially with Brünhilde playing magnificent straight-man to his delightful camp. They'll be in the gossip columns soon.

Anyway, I haven't mentioned it yet, but I'm lying in a hospital bed at the moment, St Mary's. My silly gynaecologist got it into his head that junior's head (pretty heady sentence this) was too big and what's more 'ossified' to boot; so they brought me in for scans and tests and all their other modern barbarisms and it turns out that everything is perfectly normal. In other words I've been reduced to a terrified trembling jelly for nothing (Stuart's been super though). Fingers crossed is the order of the day. You should be an honorary aunt on October 12th (surely worth a visit, you could be godmother – yes, family pressure strikes again, there's to be a baptism).

Do write, July-poo. Otherwise I'll have to be sending fancy notepaper.

Wish me luck. If you knew how terrified I am.
DIANA

Into the breach . . . but I am the breach!

———◦◦———

Undated. Delivered via Beppe.

Flossy, can you get over to Borgo Trento hospital as soon as possible. General Surgery 6th floor. Alan cut his wrists last night and I've been here all day. They're keeping him under sedation.
JULIA

The luxuries men do allow themselves!

———◦◦———

October 20th   *Kilburn*

Dear Sis,

You could at least have written. What the hell's going on? I was waiting to hear what you thought, holding off and off and

129

off and driving the estate agent and the prospective buyer round the bend. These people live such ordered lives (as someone else used to, if I remember rightly) they just can't understand when you don't do things their way. Anyway, we made a thousand squideroolies out of your lying doggo because in desperation the buyer upped his bid and gave me 24 hours to exchange contracts, so I did it. (I tried phoning the University of Verona to see if anybody knew where you were, but nobody spoke English). You do realize the responsibilities you've just plonked on my far from well-developed shoulders. I have never felt so nervous in my life. I, Michael Rhodes Delaforce (shall I ever forgive father that Rhodes? – he must have been National Cunt at heart), at I suppose the not terribly tender age of 28, utterly poundless and penniless, negotiated a sale of 91 grand, thus deciding to stick my mother (poor Mum) in a home for life (call it that). I suppose this kind of activity is what people refer to as growing up, something that friends never cease to remind me I'm not very good at. Given the agonies of the decision-making I've been through I felt it was only fair that I hang onto the extra 1000 quid myself to keep body and soul music together a while longer (all of a sudden Brünhilde is into Aretha Franklin and co. and we're spending a fortune on records).

What's happened to you, Sis? You give me all that crap about responsibilities and obligations, you spend two weeks bustling about trying to find some way of saving Mum from the dreaded home, offering to sacrifice yourself, weeping in the hospital waiting room, and then all of a sudden, no, you have to think it over, off we go to Gatwick, and you disappear into thin air (it usually is), without a trace, so that I'm not even sure if this is the right address. I'd imagine you'd been kidnapped if I wasn't fairly sure that Italian kidnappers probably do their homework rather carefully before bothering to fork out room and board for someone for a couple of months. No, but really. . . . I met your friends Barry and Kat the other night (they're moving into Diana's old flat by the way) and they were all for dispatching a posse to bring you back by brute force. Lenny was there (party in Notting Hill) and bored the pants, if not the very undies off Brünhilde, moping about his love life (death) again (the whole story has finally been explained to me – very odd learning about one's sister from others). Anyway Barry is running a sweepstake on which day you come back to claim Lenny the lonely lion, and I'd be a few quid better off if you made it December 18th (nothing like betting on one's birthday – remember when all the aunts and uncs used to give us ten bob notes for our birthdays? You used to save and I squandered on lollies and gobstoppers.) Actually this brings to mind something I'd forgotten for years. I must have been around seven or eightish, after Christmas, and I asked you what on earth you were saving for and Dad said, 'She's saving for a rainy day, my lad, and you'd be very well advised to do the same,' you know how he used to speak, and in a moment of inspiration I said, 'but it's rained every bloody day for a month, what's the point of waiting?' and of course Dad belted me for swearing, but didn't take the money off me interestingly enough. Property was sacred even then. Perhaps you've finally realized that it does in fact rain every day and are squandering everything right now. I'd be tickled stink to hear that. I'd love to get a card from you from Monte Carlo or something, sweating over a hot roulette wheel. In the end I'm less pissed off by your not writing as intrigued. Do I mean jealous? Our roles seem to have changed.

Hum hum, what next on the agenda? Disorganized aren't I? But now I'm at it I may as well get through everything. Yes, I'm seeing Mum twice a week. She's driving the nurses crazy, insists on wearing her shoes in bed, keeps saying she'll be late for church, tried to climb out of the window the other day, etc. etc. I am told this is perfectly normal. Nothing like normality to put one at one's ease of course: 'He's dying in agony' 'Oh it's perfectly normal.' Anyway there are obviously whole areas of normality that have hitherto been hidden from me. Brünhilde has stopped coming because she argued with the head sister about the quality of the food given the price of the place. I've asked her to marry me by the way (Brünhilde, not the head sister). The truth is, I suppose, that I have come to luvvy dove her. Anyway, it seems the only chance I've got to stop people thinking I'm homosexual, living with Trev and Lance. I've also been given the commission to paint the Pears' Soap Girl of the year!! No less. Two thousand green ones! (Somebody even interviewed me in a pub in Maida Vale but then spent more time talking about their own love lives than any aesthetic secrets I might have – when it was published I discovered I had opinions I'd never even dreamt of.) Anyway, Pears give me a delectable little girl and I just have to do a painting of her in some position that evokes her innocence and soapy soft skin. Why not? What better subject could one have? Trev and Lance insist that I break with tradition, surprise 'em all, and unveil a little boy, but they don't have 2000 pounds at stake; nothing worse than social revolutionaries with good jobs. Lance is at the *Guardian* now, guarding socialist ideals and an overly generous salary with drawn sword.

Lots of love, Sis. Do come out with it and spill the butter beans. Remember my birthday is December 18th (we could split the takings).

MIKE.

PS. You will have heard presumably about Diana's baby. And she seemed such a lucky girl. Life is so unfair sometimes. You hear news like that and it feels like an arrow just whistled by your ear.

———•◦•———

'Sure she's got the hots for him. She's always gone for big hunky men. I think she went through a period of wanting to be a lesbian. That is, discovering men were not interested in her she tried to get into all sorts of alternatives, Buddhism, the peace movement, feminism. She convinced herself men were inferior beings and that one should sleep with women. It was in vogue. But then women weren't interested in her either. So now her real nature comes out and she chases Beppe. Who, after all, is a big attractive man. I wonder if she writes a rota for him.'

'Maybe she just likes dogs and fresh air.'

'And karate into the bargain?'

'Rape defence, she says.'

'Who's queueing up to rape her?'

And Alan said: 'I am a pig talking about my sister like this, aren't I? The problem is, she's so easy to run down, but at the same time really quite lovable. So that you have a good bitch about her, but then feel guilty about it.'

'You could say that about all of us. She runs you down all the time too.'

'But probably doesn't feel guilty about it afterwards.'

'Maybe because there's nothing lovable about you to make her regret it.'

'You don't find anything lovable about me?'

'Don't fish for compliments,' Julia said sharply, but then after a moment added, without looking up from the table she was wiping after dinner: 'I do sometimes wonder whether we won't end up going to bed together though.'

Alan watched her cupped hand by the table's edge as she pushed crumbs into it. He opened another beer.

'Yes, so do I.'

'But then I think' – she walked away from him into the kitchen – 'I should have learnt by now not to rush into things, not to end up in bed with somebody just because they happened to have a spare room when I got back from London and needed one, because we both happen to be rather lost souls at the moment. To say the least.'

'And then I am married of course.'

Julia didn't say the obvious. There was something of a pause while she played with the taps to get the right temperature for washing up.

'No, even now she's gone,' Alan began, 'I still feel amazingly moral about it. I suppose I rabbited on about faithfulness so long to convince myself marriage was the right thing, and only then perhaps because it seemed other people weren't going to let me escape it, that now it's hard to leave be. I feel a kind of virgin again. I mean, I get that slight shudder at the thought of going to bed with someone new.'

He might have been soliloquizing, the way she went on busying herself with what were after all only a couple of dinner plates, saucepan, cutlery. Perhaps he should have gone over to Colin's.

'However attractive.'

Julia said nothing to that.

'I feel totally paralysed.'

He didn't hear with the banging of dishes, but she said, 'Snap.'

'I was thinking about this: you talk yourself into being things over the years, you see your life a certain way, you settle for it; and then when something changes, something major, it takes a while to talk yourself out of being these things again, a while to realize that you could be anything really, whatever, whoever you want, it's all a question of will. You have to change character almost, if you don't your life just stops with that change, that disaster. You're paralysed. You try and kill yourself. I was married and expected to stay married, so I preached the social virtues and practicality of faithfulness. To convince myself more than anyone else probably. I was scared of ruining everything with the way I couldn't help looking at women, but then who can? I also expected to be something of a success, which isn't going to happen now either. So I shall simply have to talk myself out of being faithful and married, then talk myself out of being ambitious and successful, and finally talk myself into being happy with my lot and getting on with it. After which, it's merely a question of destroying the old photographs and any other evidence and quite serenely I rise from the grave and start again. Perhaps I'll even get something done at last.'

Rinsing, she said: 'Unfortunately it's impossible to talk oneself out of being the age one is.'

'But we're not old.'

'Hardly young though.'

'Oh, you mean menopause again.' Alan laughed, tipping his beer. 'You are a killjoy, Julia.'

Julia said with abrupt unpleasantness: 'Perhaps it would be better if you talked and drank a lot less and opened your bedroom window from time to time. At least your sister doesn't let herself go to pieces, whatever problems she may have.'

Alan said, 'Fuck off, Julia.'

Then, rather curiously, after only a moment's ritually observed tension, the conversation seemed to start again from scratch.

'Anyway, I think she's doing the right thing. She's in the fresh air all the time, she grows her own vegetables, she runs the dogs, her Italian is improving with speaking no English and she has all the time she needs for her meditation. Then if she has got a crush on Beppe, she has that too. Even if it doesn't actually get her anywhere.'

'So why not join her?'

'I may yet. I wouldn't mind flinging my cap at Beppe either. I admire optimists.'

'Look, all I was trying to tell her was, it's not her life. She's marking time. She went to an English girls' public school and to Oxford, she defined her whole character by a fairly stereotyped rebellion against the school, the university, my parents' way of life and authority in general. So her main interests are feminism and the Labour Party; she never misses a single episode of *People and Politics* and *This Week in Parliament*, she holds a subscription to the *Guardian Weekly* and *Marxism Today*, so why the hell doesn't she go back and get on with it? She only came here because she fell out with the group she was with at Greenham and had nowhere else to go, and I said we could give her food and board if she helped with the kids. Now it's time she went back.'

'Shouldn't we all?'

It annoyed Julia how he would keep upending the empty can to chase a last few drops into his glass. And his voice too annoyed her, its plummy self-assurance, pontificating over other people's lives, when it was only a month odd since he had tried to take his own.

'No, the point is that I can write my crap anywhere, but the particular kind of mentality she's developed only has an outlet in Britain.'

There was a brief silence. But it was so fascinating this talking about the others that there was no question of the conversation's ending. Indeed, for all the reciprocal irritation, Julia and Alan were particularly fond of this kind of exchange, as if searching in Flossy and Colin and the others for an explanation of their own sense of displacement. Explanations bringing as they will an illusion of control. So that sometimes it would seem this same conversation had been going on for hours, days, weeks.

Julia said: 'I know what you mean. But probably the truth is when one leaves one's familiar environment for any length of time, one begins to lose interest, like when you miss a soap opera for a few weeks or some news story you were following. I used to have quite wild set-to's about approaches to education; I used to shout at the television; I even threw an orange at one of my room-mate's boyfriends once when he said teachers were nothing more than overpaid babysitters. But I couldn't care less now. They can say and do what they like. In fact it seems rather incredible that I ever did care.

'Though I'm not sure,' she added after a moment, 'whether that's a good thing or not.'

Alan watched her across the table. She was not a beautiful woman, except perhaps for a certain handsome harried stubbornness about forehead, eyes, cheek and jaw. A rather touching stubbornness. Because curiously, for all her affected bluntness and less than perfect features (the mouth was the real problem), she had an aura that was more feminine than the catty practicality of Elaine's last days. He drank and watched and listened, the other novelty with Julia of course being how strange it was (and what a relief) not to hear oneself doing all the talking all the time.

'And you're thrown back on yourself,' she was saying. 'There are none of the old sides to take. So that until you've built up a similar series of relationships and interests, like someone like Colin has, you're at a bit of a loss. And then he overdoes it really with all his freemasonry and astrology conferences.'

'Much as when you split up with someone,' Alan began. But Julia was fed up with hearing about this.

'The fact about Flossy though,' she steamrollered, 'as about everybody else really, is that we simply don't know what she thinks or who she is or what she should do. Most probably, having left her regular haunts and activities behind she doesn't even know herself. Maybe she does have a crush on Beppe. And it doesn't matter what she tells us, we'll never know. Perhaps people are only what they are to themselves in the end.' And she added: 'I'm not sure what I mean by that though.'

'And what they do,' Alan said.

'Or don't do.'

'Touché,' and he added, 'Yes, I suppose everything else is what we invent about them.'

'And about ourselves.'

'Although at the same time Flossy is such a definite character. I mean, you could never mistake her for anybody else. You could always say how she was different from them, unlike Habershom and Manwearing, for example, who I sometimes find myself thinking of as interchangeable. And yet, as you say, she really is quite inscrutable at the same time. Like Elaine' – he was suddenly melodramatic – 'you know I never imagined she would go until she already had. I supposed she was in love with me, that the thing with Sandro was just a bad joke. . . .'

But even as he spoke, he knew he couldn't care less now one way or another, physically, mentally couldn't. His whole marriage, kids; nothing; a blank. Which seemed rather to confirm Julia's theory. Once you were out, you were out, you stopped caring. You tried to give an impression of caring to attract attention, and because you were scared of not doing so. But you didn't really. Not any more. You were a creature of the moment, shedding selves. That was the truth. And so maybe for safety's sake, for the sake of any continuity at all, they should all just go back to where they had a place in the grand social bagatelle, where they had a vote and knew who to vote for, or who not to, where they had a class, where they could label most of the people they met (was that what home meant?), so that they didn't simply seem extraordinary, like Beppe with his dogs and karate, or Professoressa Bertelli, daughter of a fascist mayor who, with all her wealth and three or four villas, insisted, despite severe mental disturbances, on teaching in a third-rate English faculty, and now shared her home with an amorphous, smooth-talking, horny Canadian.

'Oh God,' he said.

'What?'

'I just had a vision of Sandro humping old Bertelli.'

For a while then Alan and Julia talked about Sandro and how infuriating it was that he appeared to enjoy himself so much and at the same time set such a steady course in life, how he never seemed to waver or have unsatisfied emotional needs, or lose his grip, or be at a loose end, while other people's lives shattered in fragments about him, as if thrown into confusion by his stupid cheap film-star grin. And Alan said of course even if it was the most sensible thing, he couldn't go back to London now, because it would be awful having to deal with all his old friends who had known Elaine too, not to mention the general sense of failure, the let-down applying for jobs in marketing and advertising, or crawling, most probably unsuccessfully, to old friends in the BBC, licking arse. Julia told him not to be ridiculous; she had never heard of anything more ridiculous; but then she was aware it was her mother's voice speaking, or her own wishes; and after a moment she changed her mind and agreed it was terrible the way a group of old friends could be so wonderful, and at the same time such an awful barrier, the way the past would so insist on being the past, as if one were forbidden by some curse from ever going back to it. And yet if one did, everything would probably be all right.

'There's optimism,' Alan said.

'Never forget,' Julia announced, quite consciously making an effort to be the person she wanted to be, 'Never forget life can be a lot of fun,' and standing abruptly to snap on the week's *Letter from England* she unexpectedly jabbed Alan Bexley in the ribs.

———— ◆◇◆ ————

Colin had come to see a client about a translation. In Domegliara, he said. One had to keep one's contacts up. Almost at once, however, he asked Flossy if she was happy here in the back of beyond. Flossy was fighting out a shrub root with her fork and had to be asked again.

'Why shouldn't I be?'

'Just wondered.'

She grunted.

'That's a fucking lot of hard work,' he said.

They talked about Kinnock purging Militant and she showed him the Brussels sprouts she had planted which were doing surprisingly well, despite Beppe's headshaking.

Because if she wanted, he said, offering Merit, which she declined (socialists shouldn't smoke; it was a bad example, an anachronism), she could always stay at his place in town in return for a bit of help with the kids.

He scratched at his beard, looking at her muddy boots in the earth. She stood up and rather theatrically pressed a hand into the small of her sweatshirt. The sky over Rivoli was dull with cloud and winter twilight, making her eyes more colourless than ever.

She explained that Julia would be coming out to live with her soon here. So the answer was probably no.

'I thought she was shacking up with Alan.'

'No, she isn't.'

'Oh. I saw them out buying a carpet together just a few days ago. They were trying to get it into somebody's van they'd borrowed.'

Flossy had to suck in snot: 'Look, I happen to know that Julia is not shacking up with anyone. She's coming out here. Anyway, nobody in their right mind would shack up with my pig of a brother.'

'It's not such a large proportion of the population to exclude,' he suggested, but she didn't seem to catch this.

'Why don't you get back together with Marina? I saw her recently and she was saying how terrified she was at night being on her own. She's spending her evenings watching television with the stroke victim downstairs.'

Colin said if Marina wanted to come back, all she had to do was pack her bags and come. But he wasn't going to go on his hands and knees and beg her. Was he?

'Oh don't give me that male pride crap. You're such a conservative under the surface.'

'I'll leave you to dig your grave,' Colin said, 'I've got to be home for when the kids get back from school.' And walking back to his car he was muttering: 'Sometimes it seems I'm the only person around here who has responsibilities and recognizes them.' He tried to stamp mud from his shoes. 'Sometimes it seems I'm the only person I know who's grown up, for fuck's fucking sake.' He slammed the door of the Cinquecento which caused the window to fall rather abruptly. 'Sometimes,' he rolled the car down the hill, surprising it with a violent clutch release in second, 'it seems I'm the only person in the whole world with any fucking sense of self-sacrifice.'

Because he had already tried Julia and a nice Aries at the translation agency. And drawn the same blank with both. 'Sassenachs!'

———— •◦• ————

December 18th   *Via Quattro Novembre*

Dear Lenny,

Age 34 and still writing to you. Just. This will be my last letter. I write in tears because I feel a massive chunk of my life has been thrown away, is gone and dead and will never come back. I don't know why this has caught up with me today in particular, but caught up with me it most certainly has. Let's recap one last time. (I'm being romantic, I know, but when you've finally, awesomely, plucked up the courage it takes to write, to believe, 'last time', you can be permitted a bit of romanticism, can't you, especially with a sentimental old fraud like Lenny McDowell.)

Let's recap: December '73, we meet (amazingly I can't remember where, a Homerton freshman's party?) and I fall in love. I don't know about you. I never shall. I suspect not. And God knows why I should have fallen in love with someone as wiry and freckly as you. But I did. I liked the way you talked, your jokes, your shambling walk. I liked your nervousness. I liked your eyes.

March '75: I find I'm pregnant. Your offer to marry me is so half-hearted that I decide (because in a strange mad way it has become the done thing) to have an abortion, which I do in April. This is the turning point, the point in my life at which the past becomes more attractive than the future, the point beyond which fantasy is always for another parallel life which branched off from mine at that crucial forking of the ways. A sort of suicide, if you like. Though I don't realize this at the time.

After Part I exams in May you depart for your 'all-young-men-need-experience' American working holiday, and then take the following year off. Your intention is clear: you want me to finish and get out before you come back. Which I duly do in a flurry of career determination. The year of the application form and the interview board.

December '77: you marry Liz Jarret, a silly, eyelash-batting, casting-couch Sloane who immediately accepted your dutiful and doubtless once again half-hearted (but there were her roof-tiles) offer to wed her deliberate pregnancy.

'75–79; I go through three boyfriends, Barry, Rod and Ken, all of whom I am mean and unpleasant to, often against my will it seems; I sense that my character has changed, that an acid bitterness has eaten into my soul, or rather that a source of joy has been hacked out, as if I had aborted the life impulse, vitality itself, but I disguise this, successfully, even with myself, as a fashionable feminist cynicism towards all and everything (and am actually liked for it!).

Finding me depressed – this was before I moved in with Diana – my mother tells me I am suffering from a 'God-shaped hole', and occasionally, in desperation, I am half-persuaded. Matins at Christ Church, Friern Barnet, however, can usually be relied upon to convince me to the contrary. In fact, not until I arrive in Italy and your letter about the abortion coincides with a friend's running over and killing a young boy, will I appreciate what has really happened to me.

Summer '79: Thatcher time. We meet again by pure chance at Kat-Kat's party. Barry had come across you at the BBC and pulled you back into the fold of old friends. Nobody told me you would be there. Nobody told you I would be there. Perhaps they had half-forgotten we'd ever had an affair and anyway never knew how important it had been. Only Diana knew of the abortion and she was in Czechoslovakia, spending government grants. Otherwise one of us might have had the good sense to avoid such a meeting. You spotted me first and you came up and whispered in my ear from behind: 'Hi Delaforce, how's tricks!' It's touching and infuriating how at crucial moments your inadequacy prompts you to ape Americanisms or make puns, as when, returning to your wife after our lovemaking, you'd say, 'so long, hon,' or at Gatwick Airport when you kissed me over the passport control barrier and said, 'may the force in Delaforce be with you.' No comment.

So you whisper in my ear and I decide, in the space of an evening, that my problem is not a God-shaped hole, nor a hole of a job; my problem is I still love you. It's a functional alibi, in the sense that I believe it; in the sense that your determination (despite my begging) to stay with Liz allows me to imagine that my own prolonged unhappiness must be due to this; in the sense that our untidy, hole-and-corner, after-hours affair fills up my life sufficiently for me to ignore things I might otherwise, sooner or later have been forced to face. In short, I have a problem that has an obvious if obstinate solution and can thus dream as long as I like of its one day being resolved.

What's more, I am now living with Diana of course, which accounts for the *Rhoda/Liverbirds* feeling I like to think my life has. Diana has millions of affairs with all kinds of men and seems totally, delightfully carefree. I, with my long affair with you, my grumpy cynicism, my apparent worldly wisdom am able to feel more mature than her while at the same time admiring her, as one does a brilliant pupil at school. She has a soft spot for us and is always saying how wonderful we are together; this support has a totally disproportionate effect on me, makes me determined to stay with you at all costs. The truth is I adore Diana, I am almost, without knowing it, in love with her. It is the most satisfying relationship of my life and remains so. Diana's smile, her clean limbs, bright face, her fun, her blasé, misapplied intellectuality, the sense of security and belief in life I used to have when I was around her – these things were really, truly wonderful. They gave me a feeling of contentment that was quite physical, a glow that, remembering, comes back even now, makes me smile just thinking of her.

Anyway, my life at this point appears to consist of you and Diana and the way each relationship supports the other. But all the same I am quite blind to the real reason I'm staying with you, which, as I say, I stumbled across recently here: I cling to you because somehow I believe that you, and only you, can take me back to the time before I made the fatal decision to kill that baby, that with you I can somehow regain purpose and innocence, recover the past, the time when, even if only very slightly, I was like Diana. Because Diana is all potential.

This goes on five, six years. You have no intention of doing anything about anything. Despite your protests you are of course perfectly content to remain with your wife. We both, in our different ways, savour our emotional confusions. No comment again.

1985: A number of things come to a head. My father has died and every weekend my mother piles on the pressure to go and live with her. She insinuates that I'm more or less over the hill as far as marriage and family are concerned, that my place is by her side, that I will save tons of rent and that this will give me security, seeing as I lack the security of a man's salary. I even remember the line. 'What you're paying for a room in Kensington would give you a handy pension with the Prudential.' (Perhaps my mother should have worked for Saatchi and Saatchi.) Obviously the cynical, modern, feminist Julia rejects this conventionally and rather tastelessly baited hook, but other people's visions do have a way of superimposing themselves on one's own. There are moments when your thoughts, my thoughts, uncontrollably, fall into quite different patterns (as when you rearrange the letters in a game of Boggle, or look into a kaleidoscope) – and you catch yourself afraid. So just as I once half-believed in the God-shaped hole, I now half-accept the tall story of Prudential security for a middle-aged spinster under her mother's roof.

At the same time everything goes wrong at school where arch-enemy and ponce George Drummond has been promoted ahead of me, where the kids are suddenly calling me 'ma'am' instead of 'miss'.

My 33rd birthday doesn't help. The mighty M begins to loom. One jokes, but this is serious. No, for me this is everything. I am a woman. I make no apologies for wanting children, and all the more so to relieve my conscience of the child I killed.

I try to talk to you about it all, but you feel threatened. According to you I'm being too dramatic, too all-or-nothing. I should 'accept life's half-truths, its compromises, its complicated at once poignant and delightful cadences' (I believe I'm quoting, though it sounds like a bad book jacket; but we have all read enough bad book jackets to talk like them sometimes, I suppose).

Anyway, you have persuaded yourself that this pseuds' corner, arts programme crap is 'an intelligent response' (how the old phrases come back) to life. We go on making love as tenderly as ever (right from the start you always had a magnificently wistful line in lovemaking, a sort of 'Oh-how-marvellous-it-would-be-if-I-could-commit-myself-but-I've-no-intention-of-doing-so' approach; so that every fuck was supposed to take on the deliciousness of relished impossibility – I'm not quite sure what I mean myself here, only that what I say is true. And forgive me all these parentheses, but there is so much to say, and one feels it all has to be said simultaneously somehow, if one's not to give the wrong impression – have you never had the feeling that to say what one really means one would have to say in a single phrase, 'I love you' and 'I hate you', 'I adore you' and 'I despise you'?).

We make love in Kensington, in Studio B when you're working late, and sometimes, I don't know why, we go for weekends to a bed and breakfast in Hendon that you obviously got to know with a previous acquaintance or acquaintances. The landlady gives you such a smirk that I can't help feeling you are taking somebody else there. Your eyes do stray so frequently when we walk down the street; you have a new attractive-young-thing secretary, Elsa, who accompanies you on all your mysterious and convenient trips. I get paranoid. I am not beautiful, I know, nice eyes, but a little plain, patches of cellulitis, etc. etc. (though I have learnt not to bore people running myself down); what hold have I got on my Lenny who I love? With feminist discipline I practise reversing this question, asking, what hold has Lenny got on me? No sooner reversed, however, than the question infuriatingly becomes rhetorical. Every hold.

And I throw the whole pack of cards up in the air. I look for a different job away from education. I'm constantly turned down (which gives me plenty to bitch about – I have begun to cultivate my bitterness quite consciously as a defence, a social style). If I can't change to commerce, I can at least change schools and get away from George Drummond's smirk. I open the *Ed. Supp.*, thinking of Chelsea or Fulham, and instead, immediately, there it is, the job in Italy. I go.

One is such a coward. One is interminably such a coward. I tell Diana this is it, the complete break. I tell myself this is a test; deprived of me we'll see if he really loves me. It's so <u>tiresome</u> to find myself hanging on like this, but over the years, all my self-esteem has somehow come to hang on the question, did he/does he really care for me? Does he love me enough to take me back to the crossroads where I made my great mistake, walked away from life. I don't know how much sense there is, or was, in this, but this is how my mind was really subterraneously working beneath all the intelligent argument I'd deploy to discuss teaching methods, government support of the arts, the licensing fee, education cuts, etc. etc., beneath all the happy gossip with Barry, Kat, Rob and Sally – did he/does he love me, will I have a child?

In one of your letters you said how differently you thought of me, or indeed of any other person when you weren't meeting them day by day, how you saw their lives, their stories as a whole. And it's true of one's own past too, I mean of a period of your life when you leave it behind you. No sooner was I away than I began to see my London life as a kind of aerial photograph, the contours stripped of details (they come back only when one is nostalgic). I saw the alluring, exhilarating peaks of Diana's glittering life; I saw the long, dull infertile marshes of our directionlessness with, deep below, the way they photograph for archaeological remains, a tiny buried corpse.

Waxing lyrical seems to help. You'll be glad you're not here. I've been kicking the cupboards. Old habits – don't we know – die hard and long (there should be euthanasia for old habits). The flat, fortunately, is rented furnished.

October '85: I arrive in Italy. Almost immediately I plunge into a relationship with Sandro. I do this to be like Diana, and partly because Sandro, just at the very first two or three meetings, seems carefree as Diana, beautiful as Diana, and even, in flashes, intelligent as Diana. I do it to tell her, so she'll tell you, so you'll come back to me. I do it on impulse. I do it because I'm terrific at cocking up my life. I don't know why I do it. One does so many things. Sandro turns out to be thoroughly mediocre, utterly selfish, infinitely predictable and not a bad bloke if that's what you're looking for, the kind you won't have any trouble with until he decides he won't take any more trouble with you; and at least there's no danger of regretting him (though sometimes I have managed even that). Still, I wouldn't have agreed to actually living with him so soon, if I hadn't been unnerved by some lesbian advances on the part of the unfortunate girl I'd again hastily and on impulse, chosen to share a flat with, a girl even more bitter than myself to whose Julia I imagined I was playing a Diana. Advances I might conceivably have accepted from another quarter (one is once again appalled – I mean that – by the all determining importance of that random factor, beauty. If life has been less than lavish with me, it was downright cruel to poor, allergic, broad-beamed, thick-ankled Flossy). No, I wouldn't have asked Sandro to live with me right away. I was still vaguely hoping on you, on your reaction to the realization that I had well and truly escaped you.

(I stop and wonder sometimes if my own account bears any relation whatsoever to the way other people see events. Do you know what I mean? I'm referring to that word 'escape' – I sometimes fear it wasn't like this at all.)

But in the meantime what I had so often dreaded in the past, happens. Dear Diana is pregnant, is going to marry. Marry one of the idiots it was fun to watch her tease, but very rum to think of her spending her life with. I phone and offer to go back and help with the baby if she doesn't want to marry the bloke, but she says, no, she does want to marry, really does. This affects me more profoundly than I could have imagined. There is less and less to go back to, my boats are burning behind me and I haven't even the meagre satisfaction of having lit the match myself. So despite losing my job at the university, I decide to stay put. I hunt around for casual work and draw on my savings. I try to make Diana write to me, by writing long, long, remember-this, remember-that letters. 'Remember Raunchy Ronnie? Remember our plants, our parties. Remember our LIFE?' Or again by trying to entertain her with slightly exaggerated stories about the new people I've met here. When finally, after the wedding, she starts writing, I don't want to write to her any more. Perhaps I don't want to write because I realize that Stuart must be a lovely man, and she loves him and is calm and happy and not going to do anything unpredictable any more. Because I realize that she is making, with her ever ineffable serenity, the transition from potential to realization, and my jealousy knows no bounds (and yet we all know that I am a nice person).

But I've jumped ahead of myself. June '86: I receive a telegram, 'MOTHER SERIOUS, COME NOW.' I go back to London. I am in fact there the Saturday of the wedding and could perfectly well get the train down to Lewes if I wanted. But I don't. I also ask Mike to say I'm out if anybody wants me on the telephone. It suddenly seems so pointless getting in touch with you all again, though it would be wonderful. I don't know if you can really understand this. I don't know if I can myself. I just know there is this insurmountable psychological barrier which prevents me picking up a phone and getting in touch. A sort of stubbornness about my self-exile. Sometimes it's as if phonecalls can only work one way, as if boats, trains, coaches and planes, like time, can only travel one way: away from home. There is no point in trying to reverse the direction. So even back in London I feel I am an ex-pat, I am not at home, I am the living dead, a ghost of myself, walking streets I know so well but can't be bothered to shop in or really take seriously. Unless perhaps this is just the typical traveller's conceit on returning home. The desire to feel one is still different when one most definitely isn't. But enough of explanations: who the hell knows or cares what or why it is, but this was how I felt on my return.

By the way, I am swatting winter flies now as I write – they hang on long past their season here, buzzing round your hair – and this seems peculiarly appropriate somehow.

So. My mother has had a stroke. Every day I go to stand by her bedside where she sleeps, mutters and doesn't recognize me. Despite the doctors telling me that with the extent of the damage she is 99% unlikely to recover her faculties I am sorely tempted to make this my mission in life, just so that mission there should be. I sit on the plastic visiting chair, staring at her, trying to come to terms with her combined presence and absence, with the blank in front of me lifewise.

Which is where you find me one afternoon to cart me off to the old Hendon Way B&B, where the landlady salutes you as if you'd spoken the day before. Had you?

It is very curious about you Lenny, how despite the fact that you never knelt at my feet to offer me your life, so to speak, you nevertheless find yourself incapable of leaving me alone. I suspect this is because you want to live three or four different lives simultaneously, you can't accept that you be limited to one life, you can't let anything die. With the result perhaps that you have lived no life fully at all. And perhaps this is why you proved such an avid and faithful correspondent: because there is nothing easier than living one life (or lie) while keeping another going on paper. I should know.

But then we are all so chameleon, so inexhaustibly chameleon, and life is a constant updating. There I am kissing you in the car a very short while after having decided not to.

We climb the stairs to the room on the second floor at the back with its view over garden and toolshed. When I look out of the window a moment, the landlady, bent over her radishes, looks up and waves. I draw the curtains. Dear Lenny, what sad lovemaking! Nothing seems to be different. You might be slipping back into an old raincoat you couldn't quite decide to take to the Oxfam shop, partly out of affection, partly because there's still some wear in it yet, a jingle of change in the pockets, a mess of old bus tickets, the destination always the same. I tell you Sandro has left me for someone else. I tell you about mother (you have her polo-neck on, which is actually and unusually quite nice). You begin to tell me how marvellous it will be if I come back to look after her. Seeing as she's out of her mind she won't be able to object to your staying the night now and then. And Liz is out late almost every night these days. It's all working out, you tell me enthusiastically, while I am lying there in amazement at the thought that nine months' separation should collapse to nothing at all. I have made no progress. My aerial view had shown this was all marshland and yet I've wilfully crash-landed here, and very near the site of that buried corpse. The details crowd back, your eyes, your bony body, your tweed jacket, Rothmans King Size and the rotating flick of your wrist when you strip the cellophane off a new pack. I lose all perspective. I don't know if I'm euphoric or aghast.

Next morning I tell Mike I've decided to stay and look after mother, but I'm in a state of such agitation I can't face the hospital. Mike goes off to college for a few hours where they're still letting him use some studio space. Trevor and Lance are away. To calm down, I do the washing up for them all, because they live in complete chaos, and take the opportunity of having a long talk with Brünhilde who comes down in what was once (and this is disturbing) my father's dressing gown. She is prettier than I remember her, though the nose is a bit hard to take. She has that fresh if wearisome confidence of a teenage boy and she spends a long time explaining exactly what I should do with my life. I should come back and look after mother; she will persuade Mike to live with me in Friern Barnet and she and I can get into turning out fancy knitwear for the local shops. Some of the new German patterns are magnificent. The British are incredibly stupid the way they go on ignoring German fashion. She had an argument only the other day with a shopkeeper who pooh-poohed the samples she brought. Mike, she says, will have to be persuaded to do some commercial art work to balance the budget, and not keep thinking he's Leonardo da Vinci. I mention you, Lenny (I can't remember why), and she asks, did I know you were getting divorced? She gives me all the details. Liz and this bloke Curtis, what you plan to do with the children. She seems remarkably well informed. But then I hadn't realized she was babysitting for you sometimes. How one's social life short-circuits. I was on the seven o'clock flight that evening.

I was on the seven o'clock flight that evening, thinking, he's getting divorced and he didn't even tell me. Brünhilde knew, but not me. He made love to me in the Hendon B & B, but he didn't say, this is it, now we can be together. He was thinking, should I tell her, or shouldn't I? Like a juggler, he still had all the balls in the air; his three or four lives, turn and turn about. He was still saying, 'I can stop over at your mother's (now she's a paralysed mental wreck). Liz is always out late and can't object.'

Lenny, Lenny, Lenny.

You could still have retrieved it, of course, with a letter. 'I'm getting divorced; come back and live with me.' But you didn't. You came round the evening I left, presumably to take me back to Hendon again – to pop the question? But then you didn't write to me here to tell me about the divorce. You must have realized everybody else would tell me about it, but you didn't have the courage to face a decision now the moment had come. You haven't written for four months, knowing I was waiting here. I hear you have been crying on the shoulders of half London, but you didn't write to me.

What am I supposed to salvage from all the time we were together, Lenny? I feel torn between fond farewells, generous memories, and simply calling you names. I still feel somehow the abortion was the key to everything that happened afterwards, to all our wistful tenderness and ultimately sterile sex. But I know I haven't quite understood it yet. I haven't understood why, having rejected your offer of marriage and killed the baby, I remained paralysed there, constantly dreaming what I had so determinedly refused, fantasizing a parallel life that led the other way from that turning point. And you, Lenny? Can you see us photographed in front of our commuter-belt house with three children? Can you? Does it wake you at night, just sometimes?

However. For the first time now I pluck up courage to tell you that even if the urge should come you must never get in touch with me again. Never. Enough is enough.

I am living here with a guy called Alan Bexley, perhaps I mentioned him in earlier letters. His wife walked out on him, though he was faithful to her. He's a bit pompous, pontificates and takes himself rather seriously (he talks to himself), but he has something pleasant about him, and he's attractive. I've decided to go to bed with him if he makes a move. Why not? We may even have a lot of fun. But I'm not in a hurry. He wanted to be a writer, but doesn't seem to be getting anywhere and is always saying the important thing in life is to learn how to fail gracefully. I feel I could do with a lesson or two myself.

What a dying fall! I've made it a long goodbye, so long I'll have to get it weighed. Or shall I put on a regular stamp and have you pay the postage due? That seems apt.

Goodbye Lenny.

JULIA.

No PS.

———— ◆○◆ ————

Enclosed in a Christmas Card produced by the Spina Bifida Foundation.

December 21st   *17 Sheldon Ave.*
                                                  Highgate

Dear Julia,

You haven't written for quite some time, though I suppose you must have heard the news. We have had a baby girl, Joyce, but she is severely handicapped. They have now identified the problem as something called Larsen's syndrome, which is apparently extremely rare and explains why they didn't pick it up on the scans. It seems to entail every kind of handicap, mental and physical, though the extent of the damage is unclear as yet. My impression from the doctors is that there is not a great chance of recovery.

Diana has been most upset and under sedation for the last month or so, but she is picking up now. I have been encouraging her to write to you, as I know you were her closest friend, but she is giving all her time to the baby and doesn't want to contact anybody.

Could you write to her, or better still, though I appreciate it may not be possible, come and visit? We have a new place in Highgate (see above address) and there's plenty of room to stay. We would be so grateful.

I hope all is well with you.

Best regards,

STUART.

Oh, I forgot to say, if you should write to your brother, could you please tell him how grateful we have been for all his visits. He seems to be the only person capable of cheering Di up just now and we couldn't have expected it of him since we hardly really knew him.

Best again, STUART.

———•◦•———

Sandro has observed a considerable improvement in Professoressa Bertelli since he became her unpaying lodger. She suffers less from, or at least speaks less about, the powder her enemies put in her eyes, and her contributions to the book they have now almost finished and will publish with the Verona University Press are definitely less bizarre than they were and more easily adapted into something manageable. If he could only sort out the dialogues that introduce the chapters (Bertelli's real genius would seem to have lain in the theatre of the absurd) he would be quite happy to have his own name added to hers on the cover and to include the publication in his curriculum along with the translation of a series of art catalogues he has done through Errico (though not to say a word to Colin) and along too with the title of 'Assistant Faculty Librarian' which comes from having spent a few voluntary hours each week recataloguing the English faculty's books by period and subject, as required by

Scudellotti, rather than merely alphabetically. In fact, Sandro reflects, his curriculum is beginning to look rather promising.

Smoking a cigarette, sipping orange juice, drumming a pencil on the wickerwork table, Sandro stares at Chapter 17: THERE IS GRANDFATHER, while Professoressa Bertelli (far too casually wrapped in a light dressing gown) fondles the head of an ageing terrier and stares, smiling maternally, gratefully, condescendingly, across the humid space at his naked torso. They are surrounded in this expensively heated terrace-cum-conservatory, by tropical plants. Sandro reads the dialogue for at least the tenth time, though still not without a certain residual fascination:

CHAPTER 17

THERE IS GRANDFATHER

Mary: There is a man.

Jane: Where?

Mary: There is a man at the door. There he is!

Jane: Oh! He's my grandfather. He was away for a long time and there was a lot of foolish talk about him. But he's really a very good person.

Mary: What shall I do?

Jane: There can be no question about it: let him in of course.

Mary: There's a cat on the sofa. What am I to do?

Jane: The only important thing for you to do is to let Grandfather in. He may be tired and anxious to see me. It was he who helped me when I was in trouble two years ago. He always gives a hand to everybody.

Mary: All right, the door isn't far away: he'll soon be in.

The intention of this dialogue, Sandro notes on the opposite page, is to teach 'verb pattern 2A1 THERE + NOTIONAL 'BE' + LOGICAL SUBJECT, INDEFINITE NOUN OR PRONOUN + ADVERBIAL ADJUNCT OF PLACE, DURATION OF TIME, etc., *which is a prepositional phrase*, OR ADVERB.' As well, the book goes on to explain, as 'verb pattern 2A2, SUBJECT + NOTIONAL 'BE' + ADVERBIAL ADJUNCT OF PLACE OR DIRECTION OR DURATION etc. OR ADVERB.'

Well, there must be more sensible ways, Sandro thinks, avoiding the glance that would take his eye directly to Professoressa Bertelli's wrinkled right breast, carelessly, or perhaps most carefully displayed as she bends down to rub doggy's rump. Should one bother to change this drivel? Does it matter? It is co-authorship on the curriculum that counts, not the quality of the material. And then aren't all language books of necessity ridiculous in the end, removing language from the contexts that give it meaning (when it has any)? Still, there is ridiculous and ridiculous. No, perhaps an interesting way to get round the problem would be to put in an exercise inviting the students to suggest, in English, situations, contexts, which would make this dialogue feasible (if not exactly meaningful). Bertelli would never notice the addition of just a single sentence. At which point the passage's very idiocy becomes a deliberate challenge to the student, its vagaries nothing short of genius.

But is it possible? Isn't it asking too much? Sandro tries to imagine a scene where such a conversation as THERE IS GRANDFATHER could actually take place. Difficult. Think. His own grandchild, for example, in years to come, call her Jane (always assuming that Christine has in fact gone through with it and had the baby and that this same baby will go through with it him/herself some day and have another) – yes, his own grand-daughter, or rather no, her cousin Mary, sees him, Sandro, old Sandro, standing at the (glass?) door of grand-daughter Jane's large suburban Winnipeg house (because Christine will of course have run back to her family the moment he left). It's a start. Jane and Mary are out back on the patio, which explains the passage's curious sense of distance from the door (unless they are looking down from a balcony, but this seems unlikely in Winnipeg). They spy him, grandfather, then, through a screen window, across the house and through the glass front-door, though he doesn't see them, nor, apparently, does he ring the bell. Perhaps he is uncertain as to what to say, uncertain as to whether to bother, or perhaps he does ring, has rung, the bell, but it isn't working. Hence the first thing the two women (girls?) know of his presence is Mary's glimpse of him, despondent? diffident? outside the door.

So far so good. In fact, Sandro thinks, this is rather a splendid exercise for encouraging class participation.

To continue then. Mary, rather sadly, must be a half-wit. How else can one explain her sudden and most poignant loss of attention (so convenient for the grammar teacher of there + notional be's) when, on the point apparently of letting the old man in, she exclaims: 'There's a cat (why "a" cat? Isn't it theirs? Shouldn't it be "the" cat? Or is the area infested with cats? Come on students, let's have some ideas) – There's a cat on the sofa. What am I to do?' Given the money lavished on the expensive living-room suite, poor Mary has obviously been instructed, had it drummed into her no less, to keep all animals off it, and in her half-wit's brain, deprived of a normal sense of priorities, a normal attention span and normal independence of action, she allows the arrival of 'the', or 'a', cat to throw her totally, to constitute a real dilemma – Grandfather in or the cat out.

And it is again because Mary is a half-wit that Jane is not going to give her the whole horrible truth about her dear grandfather: 'He was away for a long time (Italy, that fits) and there was a lot of foolish talk about him,' i.e. 'People spoke rather badly of his having deserted my pregnant grandmother rather than marrying her' – but this would be too much for Mary's precarious mental balance and inadequate grasp of basic human relationships. Good, good, good. All fits. Yet what about, 'He may be tired and anxious to see me,' and, 'It was he who helped me when I was in trouble two years ago.' Does this denote an ageing, repentant Sandro, who, after Christine's death, along, why not, with her son or daughter plus appropriate in-law in a highway pile-up, or air crash, chooses to make amends to his long lost family by helping out grand-daughter Jane with the crippling death duties. Just feasible, even if, 'He always gives a hand to everybody,' does seem a little over the top as a description of himself, would require a road to Damascus, no less (the point being how very few people are actually worth giving a helping hand to, even should he have one). But times do change, and there's no denying that it is a sad and decrepit Sandro that a young half-wit has to hurry to the door for, while a/the pussy-cat – Sandro has always admired cats – snuggles into the sofa despite cousin Jane's ban.

But why doesn't Jane herself displace the cat while Mary opens up for Grandfather? Or vice versa. Why, in short, the poignant necessity, all the more poignant because of her psychiatric condition, for Mary to choose between letting the old man in and chasing off the cat? And again, why that: 'the door isn't far away: he'll soon be in'? (How far away could a door be?) No, only a moment's reflection and the answer is obvious, inevitable: because (this is really a much easier game than he imagined) – because Jane, of course, is a cripple (both legs lost in that same tragic highway/airplane crash), and it really is rather a neat arrangement to have the family half-wit wheel out the family cripple onto the patio to get some post-winter, battery-charging Winnipeg sunshine, while all the fit folks are out to work or off on vacation. So Jane can't answer the door. She can't get her wheelchair over the back step. But for Mary the door is near enough.

There remains only to explain this anxiousness of Sandro's to see the rather peremptory Jane, an unfortunate wheelchair-bound grand-daughter with no legs. But the reason here is surely that it is half-wit Mary he is really anxious to see; because for all her lack of wits, and quite apart from the fact that she's always forgetting from one moment to the next who he is, dear Mary is one of those young girls older men are only too anxious to get a load of (she's been sunbathing on the patio in whatever costumes are in fashion in – when, the 2020s? – or have we got, and not before time, to total nudity now?), yes, just as he himself is the kind of young man older women like to get a load of as he sits in only bermudas with March sunshine gleaming through the panes of Bertelli's lavishly heated glass-covered terrace. And being a half-wit, naturally enough, Mary may be willing, when Jane on her wheelchair is not in a position to see, to allow certain caresses from an old man that a more sensible girl. . . . Now now students! Students!

Because life is so fecund of situations. And so of course this dialogue is okay, perfectly within the realms of possibility, and, 'I think,' Sandro says, snapping out of a trance, 'that if we just make the indefinite article in front of "cat" definite, then it will do. We can get it off to the setters.'

Professoressa Bertelli comes to stand over him, an old bizarre woman for whom something at some point in her life has gone drastically wrong, but that is not his fault. She lays a hand on his shoulder and considers. He knows she likes this physical proximity and reflects that he is in fact doing her a favour, living in her house, letting her touch him – very few men would, her breath is appalling – as, come to think of it, he did Julia a massive favour saving her from Flossy's lesbian clutches and keeping her from moping over her inept pig of an ex-boyfriend, did Colin a fantastic favour getting Janet out of his bed, did Elaine a favour showing her what a sop she was, repeating what her husband said all the time, even did Alan a favour, since all he wanted was to get on with his masturbatory books and have wifey and kids out of the way; and above all did Christine the most marvellous favour of all, giving her a child, his image, which was all she wanted in the end, the husband bit being just family pressure, she herself couldn't have cared less. So that perhaps, he reflects with a sudden grin, perhaps grand-daughter Jane is right, albeit a shade ironic, when she refers to grandfather as always having a helping hand to lend (perhaps she means a 'helping gland . . .'). Since in an unfathomably curious way, he thinks, quickly recovering the sober, I'm-pondering-over-your-book face which so impresses Professoressa Bertelli and makes her feel secure and unthreatened – something no doctor has yet managed – yes, in an unfathomably curious way, he, or his dick, functions as a kind of catalyst for helping others sort out their lives. In a very complicated manner, for example, it was he who was responsible for bringing Alan and Julia together, which is a good match if ever there was one, between two, large ego-ed, innately depressive, impractical and idealistic souls.

Perhaps it is his role in life.

'Yes,' Professoressa Bertelli says, 'Good.' She is indulging in that awful habit of chewing at nothing in her mouth, though at least she has her false teeth in. 'One thing, Sandro, I meant to tell you: next week we shall be considering applications for the permanent post of research assistant and I thought you ought to know that I shall be veto-ing any name but yours. I feel you've done a lot of hard work and deserve to become permanent. So many of the others give the impression that they are just birds of passage and have better things to do than really commit themselves to the faculty.'

Sandro says: 'Sorry, I was just checking though this section on demonstrative pronouns, I didn't catch that.'

She puts her other hand on his other shoulder and begins to massage his neck.

———◆◦◆———

In her dream, Julia and a boyfriend, who is alternately Lenny, Sandro, her brother, are going to her mother's to eat.

They are standing at a bus-stop in Hammersmith waiting for the 260, because Lenny likes to sit on the top of a bus on a Sunday morning. She is smoking the morning's first cigarette and in her hand she holds her tennis bag, because Mother is ill and they promised to cook lunch and take it. She has cooked chicken. It's in the bag. Lenny, for some reason, is speaking fluent Veronese dialect, complaining about Liz never cleaning the bathroom. There is a sense, and this is characteristic of Julia's dreams, of nothing being more than a yard or two away, and yet for all this proximity, blurred, oddly distorted, oddly coloured. The sky, for example, is indigo only a foot or so above her head. The bus-shelter is twisted into a geometric puzzle.

And every time she turns, she is disconcertingly aware that what was there before has undergone a transformation, though it would be hard to say exactly how. It is still Hammersmith, still morning. Unless Lenny has become Sandro? Anyway, the bus-stop has certainly changed, and likewise the faces in the queue, one of whom now appears to be the balding stroke victim of Piazza dei Caduti. There is an unpleasant feeling of swirl, transformation and distortion together, which is making her tense and anxious, though she knows it's only a dream. Nothing to lose one's head about. She hitches up her bra-strap.

Or perhaps it's just the nausea of that first cigarette.

Or even morning sickness? Could it be? Her brain is suddenly feverish, counting days.

Then on the bus – they are sitting at the front on the right by the driver's periscope, Lenny's favourite seat – on the bus, she is suddenly appalled by what she has done. Disguising the foetus as a chicken like that, and just to save money. She is invaded, almost choked, by a dark suffocating fear of that bag. Lying there on her knee, on her nice grey wool dress. Is she going to be sick? Is it going to spring to life?

And she hears herself saying that they'll have to throw it away. They can't possibly eat it. It's all been an awful mistake. Get off right here, where were they? Harlesden? Get off and throw it away. It will probably go in one of those bus-stop bins if she takes it out of the bag. Or somebody's dustbin. They'll never notice.

'But then we won't have anything to take to Mum's,' Mike says, 'and I'm famished.'

'Lenny! Lenny!' Where in heaven's name has Lenny got to? 'Lenny!' He hasn't left her, surely.

Mike is sitting rather primly, hands entwined on crossed legs, handsome profile watching out of the window, lips pursed, rather camp.

'We can buy something.' She's feeling calm again. She can breathe. She can handle it.

'Where? It's Sunday.'

'There's an Indian shop on the High Road if we get off a stop early.'

'I don't have any money. Anyway, what's wrong with the chicken?'

'It's not cooked properly,' she says cunningly. If it was Lenny, she'd tell him. But not Mike, she doesn't want Mike to know.

And now here she is by an orange-painted bin on a pole near Friern Barnet church, alone. Mike seems to have gone on ahead, to arrange the funeral. Whose? Just unzip the bag and stuff it in. It will be a tight fit, but not recognizable as a foetus because of the way she trussed it up, cooking it. She isn't so stupid as to arrive at Mother's funeral party with a foetus that looks like a foetus. And she was only trying to save money. Such a bad habit.

There. Except that the bag is dripping blood! It's soaked in it. But that's impossible. She cooked the thing at 350, didn't she? And she's soaked in it too. Hot warm blood. The bag begins to shriek as she pounds it into the bin and runs.

As she came back from the bathroom, Alan's voice asked:

'Julia?'

'Who else?'

'Can't sleep?'

'Had a Hammer Horror nightmare. Got my period into the bargain.'

She picked her way through the shadows across the room.

'I suppose a man should feel grateful for mere insomnia. Want to talk?'

'Okay.'

And a few moments later she was telling him her dream, which came back now, as dreams will sometimes, with the clarity of vivid film, so that she could remember the angles she had seen everything from, could remember Lenny's bony face, sense Mike's characteristic complacency, the jerky ride of the London bus, her own hysteria. And the more she told, the more she remembered and the longer and longer she found she could go on talking about it, pushing the dream back and back to when she had been preparing that chicken (she had been sure it was a chicken then); she remembered the cookbook she had used, she remembered not letting Lenny hold the bag when he offered, in case he banged it against his legs, like he would. She remembered so much she began to wonder if she wasn't inventing.

'Only I realized I just wasn't getting any further away. Like my legs were too weak, wouldn't carry me. Or like I was trying to run in inches of mud, quicksand, and I was paralysed there. With the bag screaming and shrieking and calling me back.'

Alan said if there was one thing he'd learnt from all the turns his life had taken, it was that dreams didn't mean anything at all, and the best thing you could do was to forget about them right away, especially if they were unpleasant.

'Do you mind if I roll a fag?'

'Not at all,' Alan said. 'Elaine always did.'

March 10th   *Rivoli Veronese*

Dear Julia,

Long time no see. I thought I'd write, seeing as I can never be bothered to come back to town. Why should I? I like living out here. The city pollution cycling in is the last thing I need. When I cycle I go up to the mountains, or to the lake. It would be much more sensible if you came out here.

So, Beppe, in case you hadn't noticed, is a PRICK. And I mean a really <u>ginormous humongous PRICK</u>! He is more than mildly convinced he is <u>God</u>, with his super karate body and BMW Series whatever. To say nothing of the PORNOGRAPHY in the house! A <u>century</u> of *Playboy*s. When he's losing in an argument, which is all the time, he has a way of tapping his forehead and saying: 'I know what I know,' or 'It's all in there.' What the 'it' might be or how it changes things remains unclear.

Still, at least you know where you are with him. Not like blokes who pretend to 'understand' women and be 'sympathetic to our cause', like someone we both know! (Why are you staying there? What's the attraction?)

Anyway, guess who he brought up at the weekend? MA-RINA. Yes, the identical selfsame Marina in the identical self-same horny spirits as the creature who arrived in Quinzano. With Janet of course. I must say, I don't envy these people their sex lives.

I was treated as housekeeper, inevitably enough. I won't list my various chores, but you can imagine. Still, THE REAL FUN came at beddy bed time when Beppe REFUSED to have Janet in his bed. Now, I had taken her, Janet, out with the dogs in the afternoon, so one would presume they had DONE THEIR SQUALID BUSINESS then (as had the dogs). I don't know. Or maybe Beppe was playing Mr Macho Insatiable. Anyway, around midnight (I am presently having a love affair with the Upanishads, you must read them, as they do put one's trials and tribulations into a rather clear perspective), yes, around midnight, there was the most furious argument with little Janet howling and wailing and them both shouting insults, pretty-well Neapolitan fashion, at the tops of their voices: obscenities, threats, even spitting on her part I got the impression, the works. (Of course they don't give a fleeting damn about the little girl's psycho-emotive development.) Bang, slam go the doors and Marina is screaming that she's going straight back to Verona and never wants to see the filthy pig again. She'll have to fucking-well walk then, porca troia, he says, as there are no buses and he's not taking her. In fact, as soon as she's out of the door, he'll bolt it so she can't get back in, stronza di merda.

Such, apparently, is heterosexual love.

Anyway, I got up and went downstairs to do a little marriage guidance counselling, like I used to with Elaine and Alan when he used to skive off the housework, or with Marina and Sandro when she started weeping about him not showing her any affection (a certain behavioural pattern does emerge, does it not?) You'd think I'd have learnt not to bother by now for all the good it does. I went down in my dressing gown and offered to have Janet in my bed if only they'd shut up rowing and let me get some sleep. Beppe said he didn't want to see her with or without the baby and she said she didn't want to see him ever and anyway Janet would never feel safe with anybody but her and most certainly never with an English strega like me. And she sets off into the night to walk thirty kilometres to Verona with a three-year-old. And good riddance.

I'd been back in bed about five minutes, Upanishadding, when Brainless, Balls & Brawn Beppe comes stomping into my room without so much as a by your leave, rails about Marina and women in general (we're so irrational) for about fifteen minutes, and then asks me if I want to go and sleep with him. (Men, of course, have a monopoly on rationality!) I say, no thank you very much, and he grins and says okay, not to worry (the vanity, who's worrying?), and goes off to bed. About half an hour later I hear him go downstairs and start up the BMW (Big Man's Wankmobile) – rev, rev, rev, roar, roar, roar, bye-bye Beppe in the night.

And of course Sunday morning hey presto back they come together towards twelvish, all smiles, a positively honeymoon couple with him bouncing Janet up and down on his he-man's apple-crate shoulders, her smacking sloshy kisses on his watermelon biceps, and they start telling me how they spent the night (what was left of it) in a five star hotel by the lake, and how luxurious it was, and how good the showers were and the breakfast, and how angry the receptionist was to be woken at 1.30, even though presumably she was being paid for the privilege, and how good Janet had been sleeping right through in an excellent cot that was the hotel's only one, but just happened to be available, and how they haven't slept a wink themselves, yawn, yawn, etc. etc. (they had stolen towels naturally), and all this as if the squalid escapade were some kind of monumental achievement to be eternally proud of. I, surprise, surprise, am enlisted to cook lunch while they go out to the shed to see if there's any wood to make Spoilt Brat a doll's house. Beppe's Daddy Day it seems.

It will end badly of course. Doesn't it always?

As for me, I am beginning to feel I've made all the right choices in life. I have never felt so calm as I do now, living alone and growing my greens and fruit (Beppe is going to buy some off me and sell it at a high price as 100% organic). Of course, it would be even better if someone like you were to come out and live with me. But I'm beginning to realize that perhaps I'm best with people when I have some simple working relationship with them, and not when trying to become their close friend. I don't know, I just get on with them better (I really get along fine with Beppe, oddly enough). Perhaps after a while I'll return to England and become a woman exec and boss people around.

Do come and visit.

My love.

FLOSSY

PS. I told Marina, just to warn the poor girl, about Beppe asking me to bed, and she said something that sounded like the Italian equivalent of, 'that'll be the day.' She obviously felt she was so much prettier than me, I must be inventing. You can see why so many men hate women.

PPS. I don't know if I really mean that about close friends. What do you think? I'd like to be able to talk it through with you as it's obviously an important aspect of one's psyche. Too bad there's no phone here. I really thought WE were becoming close till we got split up like that. I mean, I would like to be a good friend of yours and I feel quite upset about your not coming out here. I thought we had some kind of pact together. Anyway, I do hope you're not just staying with Alan because of his attempted suicide (I must admit I don't know what the relationship with you two is). That wrist-cutting was the merest exhibitionism. He's far too intelligent to think he could really kill himself like that. Everybody knows you have to do it in a warm bath.

PPPS. Weighed in at 10 stone – but there's been a lot of fat-to-muscle transformation. How about you?

———— •◦• ————

June 2nd   *Christ Church Comprehensive*
                                              Borough of Westminster

Dear Julia,

This letter may come as something of a surprise, but I met someone at a party recently who told me you had lost your job in Italy. Liz, I seem to recall her name was. She gave me your address.

Be that as it may, this is just the briefest of notes to say that the girl who substituted for you is leaving at the end of this term since she's pregnant and apparently she doesn't want the job back afterwards (though frankly I can't understand why she applied at all if she was intending to get pregnant so soon).

Harrington and I have decided to place an insertion for the appointment in the T.E.S. the penultimate week of this month (June), interviewing toward the end of July, but we both felt that if you should want to return and can get in touch with us to that effect before then, the job is yours. Your reappointment would obviously be the most practical solution for everybody, since you know the system here and we all know each other and that we can get on together very efficiently. I should be particularly glad if you chose to come back as I always found your company as a colleague highly stimulating and your approach reassuringly professional (whereas the new girl was something of a scatterbrain and rather a misjudgement on my part I must admit). I am not sure what effect your 18 months' absence would have on your pay grading, but if you do decide to take up the offer, I shall look into the matter and get back to you at once.

Be that as it may, you will no doubt be pleased to hear that

everything at Christ Church marches on exactly as before.
Best regards,
GEORGE DRUMMOND

———◆◇◆———

Dear Julia,

It's more than a year since you last wrote to anyone here as far as I can make out. We none of us are even sure we have the right address and I know Mike is thinking of coming out to try and track you down. I do hope this letter reaches you, and, assuming it does, that you will be glad to receive it. It has taken me a long time to decide whether to write. At first I thought you had stopped writing because of our handicapped child. Many people did stop seeing us around then. Lenny for one. I find this incomprehensible, as it's obviously just the moment when one needs company and support most, though I do remember you telling me how Lenny ran off to Nigeria when his mother was dying because he couldn't face it emotionally. I suppose I can half-way see that. I also suppose it was this business with him and Brünhilde that decided you not to come back. Frankly, seeing how he's behaved, I think you had a lucky escape. Mike, I know, was awfully upset, especially as it turned out it had been going on for quite some time. (How depressing all this inconstancy is, it makes you feel uncertain even of yourself, though I have been so blessed in Stuart. He has been more and better to me than I could ever have imagined.)

Our life has changed a great deal since I last wrote, mainly because of the baby. Poor Joycie. She is 10 months now and can't even control her head movements, never mind sit or crawl. She has constant ear infections which have kept us up the best part of many nights and the antibiotics they give her for them don't exactly help. But she is holding her food down better than she used to and we are hoping and praying that when we get this new special chair that Help the Handicapped are making for us, she'll be able to sit up and take an interest. Every tiny progress is so precious, makes life worth while. Fortunately Joyce has no facial deformity and is really a delightfully pretty girl with a beautiful smile and giggle. Which is so important of course.

I know you won't think it's quite me, but we're both getting very involved in the whole business of the problems for handicapped children and their parents. I'm sitting on the local NCT committee and have special responsibility for the handicapped, which means I go round all the hospitals 'counselling' mothers and fathers who've just had handicapped children and need help to overcome the shock. It's not much fun, but it does seem so much more relevant than Czech poetry and interminable programmes about how bad things are in Eastern Europe. Some of the women are so relieved to talk to someone who actually has a handicapped child themselves, especially because so many of the doctors (like Lenny) are such awful cowards and just try to avoid seeing them.

So that's me. Stuart is soon going to be leaving Cornhill to take over the finances at the Spina Bifida Foundation. Apparently they need someone of his experience. It's going to be something of a come-down salarywise, but we both feel it's the right thing for him to do.

All a far cry from Raunchie Ronnie's pyjama parties, no? and the would-be Nobel, Do-Leave-Off, another person I haven't seen since lightning struck (I shall never forget when you threw an orange at him, though I can't remember why you did it – anyway, you were right not to like him. In the end he just had the hots for me – he was always trying to look in the top of my blouse – but not the courage to up and say it. How I <u>hate</u> weak men; they are a curse).

Which brings me really to why I finally decided to write this letter: I just can't believe that two people who were as good friends as we were could really have lost touch; I can't believe

– because I know you loved me in a way – that you stopped writing simply because you didn't know what to say about the baby; I've always thought you an exquisitely delicate person beneath your gruffness (do you mind me saying that?). So that all I can imagine is that something has happened to you, that things have gone wrong in some way; do write and tell, July-poo. Don't you let me down.

I still have all kinds of things of yours here. Your green-and-orange sombreros are in Joyce's room (she loves colours), and Stuart has been using your tennis racket, which I somehow always forgot to send, because he says it's better than his. (I was telling him what a hilarious grunt you used to make when you served and how I'd be so in stitches I wouldn't be able to return, and you got furious, though it meant you always won, of course, because I never broke service.) What else? The green curtains you made for our bedroom are in the study room. And then there are a few boxes of your stuff that Mike couldn't find space for when he closed down the house in Friern Barnet. They appear to contain all your teenage memorabilia by the looks of it, so you'll have to come back one day to sort it out.

Anyway, if you don't write soon, I'll get them to put out an emergency call on the World Service. What's it there for after all (the 60,000 dollar question!)?

Best luck, dear Julia, wherever you are and whatever you're doing.

And God Bless.

Your DI PI.

Julia, I had already sealed and stamped this letter, when at the last minute, in the post office, it occurred to me that you won't have heard the awful news about Barry. He and Kat had finally agreed to get married, after a trial period living together in our old flat. It was so ironic. They threw a big party and just before eleven Rob knocked over the whisky bottle, so he and Barry decided to make a mad rush to The Grenadier to get another before closing. Rob drove and ran into a lamp post taking the corner out of Peel Street. Barry was killed instantly. He'd forgotten to put his belt on it seems. I wasn't there because of Joyce, but I heard the whole thing from Mike. It seems so awfully bald and prosaic writing it like this. Barry was such a lovely idiot, and so happy that they were finally going to marry, because he was a romantic conservative at heart for all his non-conformist posing – one of the only men I know who has always outspokenly wanted to marry and always wanted children (remember how we used to tease him), so it seemed really such a great moment for rejoicing when Kat-Kat at last caved in. And then that. They cremated him and Kat spread his ashes in the Thames at Kew where they used to go (to have their arguments, she says!) when they lived round there. Because she says she'd never be able to bear going to visit a cemetery or anything. And I think I know what she means.

So, no more charades, no more clowning. The whole clan really does seem to have had nothing but bad luck since you left, love.

D.

———◆◇◆———

'I can't fucking well believe that Sandro,' Colin said. 'The cunt. I can't understand how someone could be such a cunt.'

The rather petite, dark girl at his side smiled, understanding nothing. Alan thought, watching her T-shirt, that here was yet another girl with better nipples than Julia. And he thought he had all the time in the world to make his announcement. He didn't want to give the impression he was dying to come out with it.

'While he's a lettore, it's a strike issue and he's going to fight to the death, and then as soon as he's permanent, it isn't, he goes in to teach just the same, he doesn't give a twopenny fuck about the others.'

Because if he just jumped in with it, it would seem arrogant, insensitive, and especially considering what a loser poor Colin was: because for all his fighting talk about never being settled, about courage and socialism, about every frontier being open, about a fight to the death with the authorities, it was patently clear that he was bound and shackled by the mouths he had to feed, to the extent that he was forced to repeat now exactly the mistake he'd made with Marina, taking this girl on just to help with the kids. Though she did seem rather more serious. He liked to think of himself as the kind of patriarch who magnetizes women, with his big beard and Scottish accent, his battered flamboyance (Alpine hat, red blazer), his mysterious freemasons' talk, astrology (mixed with Marxism?), his putting 'Professor' in front of his name in the phone book and on his business card that he never forgot to carry around with him. He liked to play twice-your-age big daddy with the students, with the other lettori too for that matter, the elder statesman of the ex-pats. He liked to look after people if they'd let him. ('All Brits together. Help each other out in a squeeze.') But the simple fact was that his five-year-contract was over. They were chucking him out. He would have to make money sweating over his typewriter, translating specification sheets for local industry, quarrying equipment, tourist brochures, the financial reports of internationally owned companies: he was a good translator and the work was there; he would make enough to pay rent and keep his three children by the first wife, plus, who knew, another, the fifth, by this little girl. But it was lonely work as every ex-pat knew: the footwarmer in winter, the fan in summer, a set of dictionaries, bottles of white-out (if he insisted on not going video); and he would have lost his forum for intrigue, crusading speeches, his sense of valiant social conflict. He would no longer be able to feel magnanimous by being generous with his time with the students, which was also a way of escaping the claustrophobia at home. The normal day-to-day business would give him nobody to dress up for. He would start going out and getting drunk with anyone who could bear listening to his permanent sense of outrage. He would find other protégés like Beppe, though perhaps ones less likely to ogle his new girlfriend (was he good in bed? What was she doing with a man twice her age, and ageing badly too?). Perhaps he would join clubs, or more likely start them. In any event, his grammatically perfect Italian, which you had to admire, would always be Clydeside, always scream his foreignness.

'The kids,' Colin was saying, 'need encouragement, not punishing. They need continuity, man. The more experienced you are, the better you get, the better the service you can give.'

He was out. His time was up. They were firing him. He hadn't got the permanent post he'd been relying on Errico to get for him. Sandro had got it. Sandro had played his cards better. More quietly, with less noise, more diplomatically. You had to hand it to Sandro.

'You must have felt yourself, Al, the way one improves with time. These are the things they've just got to understand. Anybody'd think we were just reading from the course books, for fuck's sake. Otherwise. . . .'

Maria Teresa, tiny chin on cupped hands, was gazing about the square. Her nose was small, perfectly cut, her mouth likewise, definite, delicate, done in miniature (to Colin's rough burliness) – and there was something sensual about that smallness, those tiny sharp teeth. Her eyes were her real glory though, quite disproportionately large, great shining wide windows on her girlishness, and with the attractive vulnerability of short-sightedness too, which somehow, Alan thought, was not unlike the marvellously femine vulnerability of nipples. Losing track, he followed the girl's gaze. The light was dying, draining the colours from pink and baize stucco, from a faded fresco over the café opposite; white neon flashed out from a restaurant, reducing the building above to a silhouetted skyline. The spring evening took on a liquid velvety feel, on which the voices of the passeggiata crowd seemed to float, disembodied, unreal.

An unreality which wasn't surprising really, given that the scene was 1000 miles removed from the West End of London, where Alan Bexley had already returned in spirit.

'Published,' he said.

'What?'

Yes. Incredibly. And just when he had learnt to be resigned. So that there was no point in his staying to fight the fight. He was returning. From exile.

And Alan was touched to see how Colin was capable of switching from outrage to warm congratulations, touched by his genuine interest in the publisher, the plot, the print run, by his immediate switch to Italian to explain to Maria Teresa (though one called her Esa apparently – she smiled), touched by his prompt ordering of another and more expensive drink, when, with the way the wind was blowing, he might have done well to save his lire.

They got nicely drunk on rum and grapefruit juice. They both regretted Alan wouldn't be there to see the great battle through. And when the plot had been explained and all the details, Colin made the banal reflection (and Alan agreed) that in novels everything and everybody seemed obliged to come together and climax and abruptly stop, whereas in life they were more likely to drift apart and lose touch, with just a few wet squibs going off here and there before everybody knuckled under and sorted out their pensions in case the world didn't end before they were sixty-five.

Alan began to say that nevertheless he did feel that the novel, within the limitations of its representational nature and its obligation to entertain, could offer a metaphor for life that. . . .

Colin said, 'Give us a break,' rather brusquely, and despite Maria Teresa's pleading little tugs at his sleeve, ordered yet more drinks. If there was one thing he had learnt it was that metaphors, symbols, emblems and the like were all sheer crap. There were just people living. Nothing else. And he said: 'So what's going to happen with Julia, if you're going back?' And Alan said he would think about this when the time came. He hadn't told her just as yet.

Colin grinned: 'Play it by ear,' enjoying, Alan thought, in his mind's eye, the comparison between bulky Julia and this lithe young girl.

'I will,' Alan said. And added: 'Now everything is going my way.'

Colin grunted. He launched into a long account of a reference book he was translating for an international finance organization. He had to phone America daily, reverse charge, and was constantly going to freebie lunches in Milan. One of the Italian directors involved was a freemason in the same order as the President of the University of Verona and what he hoped was to bring pressure to bear on him through. . . .

As Maria Teresa's tugs became more insistent, Alan could hear Flossy saying, 'Bullshit.'

Though fleetingly he did hope for Colin's sake it was true.

———◆◇◆———

'Sandro!' Flossy swung a thick thigh in elasticated black biking pants over the crossbar of a 15-speed men's racing bike. Her complexion was patchy with exertion, nostrils flaring. As she dismounted, her breasts moved apparently independently of each other under a thick sweatshirt.

Like guinea pigs beneath a blanket. Bertelli's were firmer!

'What a surprise! How's things? Long time no see, eh?'

Sandro wore bermudas and a tank top. His symmetrical, well-made face grinned a crooked grin, one corner of his mouth turned up; his eyes were hidden behind sunglasses that reflected Flossy's moon-round face to her twice in a sort of greasy quicksilver.

'Fine. Want a cappuccino? Ice-cream?'

She joined him at a bright red table at the water's edge. The lake sparkled and winked away as it always would: ruffled surface, hints of transparency. Sandro had been reading, Flossy noticed, a commentary on Jung. In Italian. He set the book, title up, on the table, slithered down in his seat and ploughed a hand into glossy hair swept back.

Some minutes later, she asked: 'Seen Julia at all?'

'No. You?'

'No. I refuse to go and visit them. She's sleeping with Alan, you know.'

'So I gathered.'

They watched erect Sunday-best Italians passeggiata by along the lakeside.

'It was really ridiculous; she was planning to come out to Rivoli to live with me, only he, my fraud of a brother, said he'd kill himself if he didn't have someone with him. He even made a pathetic attempt to cut his wrists, patently fake, and she like an idiot went and stayed. To look after him.'

'Is that the story?'

'Oh way back.' And Flossy said: 'It'll end badly, of course. Doesn't it always?'

'Cassandra.'

She grinned, rather monkeyishly, her face creasing up around the broad nose, the rather glassy, allergy-ridden eyes. Not an unpleasant smile, quite endearing even. 'Oh I know what I know,' she said, and tapped her temple where short bangs hung sweatily, a gesture he couldn't remember her making before. Very Italian.

'How come alone?' she said then. 'No girlfriend?'

Sandro seemed to think a moment. He was obviously enjoying a feeling of complete relaxation and well-being. He breathed deeply through his nose filling out the chest and raising the shoulders that muscled attractively out of his tank top. 'Look,' he said at last, breathing out, smiling – he sat forward, took a comb from his pocket, flexed it this way and that, and tapped it experimentally on the metal bracket that held the tablecloth – 'fundamentally, Flossy, there are two types of people: the ones who crave company, like Julia, like Colin, like Alan. And others who like to be left alone, like me.' He raced the comb from table to knee in a sudden swift rhythm. Then stopped and sat back, relaxed again, smiling broadly.

'Oh come on, I never heard of anybody have so many girl-friends as you.'

'Right. But I'm just the poor prey. I didn't put the make on any of them.'

'Oh bullshit!'

'Did I ever make a pass at you?'

'No-o, but that's. . . .'

'So?'

She frowned. The air was so fresh here by the water, the morning so bright, buzzing with people, and at the same time so peaceful, so relaxed, it really felt as though they were happy to see each other, happy to spar, as though they were having a good time. She watched him.

'And the people,' he went on, 'who crave company, are always moving around to get it, or to get a more satisfying version of it, while the people who like to be left alone are always moving around to escape it. It all keeps society in motion and generates a sort of dynamic tension.'

'Bullshit,' she said again, but asked, 'And what about me, what category do I come into?' She squinted at him, inquisitively, balefully, head cocked, one hand on the saddle of her bike beside her chair.

'You,' Sandro said, he smiled, 'you, Flossy my sweet, are the perfectly balanced personality, both seeking and escaping, attracted and repelled. My warmest congratulations.'

Throwing her leg over the saddle some ten minutes later, Flossy asked: 'Do you mind if I tell you something?' But obviously she wasn't going to wait for his answer. 'I don't know what they all see in you.'

'Neither,' said Sandro, after a moment's thought, 'do I.' And there was his infuriating smile again. You could never get away from it.

---·◦•◦·---

Given the announcement of a two-hour delay, Alan thought he might as well do it now. It seemed appropriate in this moment, as he perceived it, between two lives, to settle as far as one ever could, the outstanding problems of the last. Added to which he felt vaguely guilty, and he knew there was nothing assuaged guilt more than exposing it. He bought a beer and opened a notepad on the bar. Though oddly enough, he reflected now, there was no cause for guilt, as there had been no cause for guilt with Elaine, he having limited any betrayal on his part to the imagination, the spirit, while she . . . but women were so secretive! so mysterious!

He had limited his betrayal to the imagination, it suddenly came to him, out of fear in the end; indeed, all his action and inaction (this was intriguing), could probably be attributed to fear. As for example, glancing backward through his life, he hadn't betrayed Elaine despite the come-on from a couple of very attractive students, because even given that their relationship didn't seem, and perhaps for him never had been, anything terribly special (was that really true?), he had nevertheless been afraid of life without a family, without a home, he had been scared of upheaval, he had been scared of how he, Alan Bexley, might feel about himself the morning after the betrayal. Afraid of the unknown. Then again, he had chosen to write of course, because he had been afraid of being a nobody, of not existing (why so, when nobody – ha ha – else was? Wasn't non-existence inevitable in the end?). And to bring things more up to date, he had chosen to slash his wrists, if one could really speak of that awful moment as a choice, rather than an illness, a fever, a nausea, perhaps less out of a desire to die, than out of the immediate fear of facing, of having to go on facing, other people, himself, the meaningless passing of time, the frustration of all that rage and self-contempt coming to nothing, finding no outlet.

So there, in a couple of minutes, was another theory to explain his less than honourable life. Fear.

And such a square jaw in the mirror behind the bottles on the bar! Such a sensual, purposeful mouth! Such a fine figure of a man! He was going to look really something at 40-ish.

And guilt? Guilt had become a habit of mind, a simple reaction of Alan Bexley to Alan Bexley's own quite lucid perception of Alan Bexley (for which he should congratulate himself?). He had tried of course, with what was after all the accidental death of that child, to trick himself into believing that the guilt he felt was a direct response to that crime of carelessness. That all he had to do was to suffer for that. But this patently wasn't true. He felt guilty, here was the crux, for no other reason than for being himself, Alan Bexley.

These traits, he reflected, guilt, fear (guilty of his fear, afraid of his guilt?) – these traits must be the things that *were* you, things one could perhaps limit and modify, but never eliminate (despite all Julia's plans). So that in the end he had been wrong in the past to suggest that you could choose to be who you were; more accurately, one might choose, just perhaps, in very lucid moments, what to do with the self one indisputably was.

But this was tail-chasing.

Flicking to the back of his notebook, he scribbled: 'Curious element of self-congratulation whilst indulging in self-destructive analysis.'

Alan drank his beer. He grinned at his own square face. In any event, both fear and guilt were clearly part of a failure mentality which a successful young man, as it suddenly appeared he was going to be, could and should do without.

'And that settles that,' he mouthed to the mirror, savouring his own smile.

Except that today's guilt of course was *because* of his success, his escape, was because, in the end, he had always in his inner soul hoped for, and then been relieved at, the failure of her crazy idea, yet could never be blamed for not having agreed to it, nor, now, for being released from her despair, since it was she had done the releasing, she who had decided not to come.

Or was it much simpler than that? He felt guilty because he knew that the reason why he hadn't been able to cheer Julia, or to make her come with him, or to love her in the way one should (yes, should!), was because her body was not beautiful, or rather because he could not find it so. And because of that, because, to put it bluntly, of her flat nipples and heavy hips, he hadn't tried as hard as he might to persuade her to come with him, he hadn't saved her.

Or was that arrogance? Who was he to save people?

And that whole explanation rather too simple? He had loved, did love J, loved her for her personality, for her endearing irrational doggedness (so different from Elaine's bright, off-the-cuff, prissy practicality), for her intelligence, for her outbursts of determined, hard-earned joyfulness, for her bright green eyes, her broad smile. And he *had* asked her back with him, damn it, he *had*, and albeit relieved that she didn't accept, he would nevertheless have been the best of men to her if she had. He really would. Would have repressed his doubts, played respectable lover, respectable husband ultimately, when things sorted themselves out. Because he was monogamous at heart, that was the truth of the matter, wherever his eyes might rove. He had never had more than one girl at once. Out of principle. And that must be a virtue of some kind. Mustn't it? He couldn't be considered all bad.

The problem was the way the truth seemed to be something different from one moment to the next.

But he should have got used to that by now.

Alan looked around the grubby airport where holidaymakers were making themselves comfortable for the delay. God knew, and only God could or would want to know, what mightn't be going on in all those busy heads. He only hoped they had a clearer grasp of themselves than he did. Otherwise the whole of humanity was just a seething amorphous mass of temporary roles, casually assumed, casually thrown off, carelessly filed for improbable future reference.

He wrote:

September 20th   *Milan, Malpensa*

Dear Michael,
    I don't know if your sister ever spoke of me to you. My name

is Alan Bexley. Anyway, I have been living with Julia for some time and felt I should write to you about her. I don't know if she has been keeping in touch herself, I suspect not, but in any case I thought I should write and I took the liberty of getting your address from her address book without asking her. The simple fact is that I am afraid she is in rather a bad way and that somebody who is capable of influencing her should really come out to Verona and help, if possible take her home. I tried to persuade her myself as I am presently returning to England, but without success. . . .

It occurred to Alan here, and not for the first time, that the more obvious thing to do would be simply to go to her brother's place when he got back to London and talk to him directly. But he wanted to avoid such personal contact. He didn't want to mix up his two lives; he didn't want to be drawn into deeper and deeper explanations: and then a letter could be cooler, more clinical, and, in its own way, more romantic and portentous too. Added to which, something remained with a letter, something made. Anyway, he'd had a few phrases going through his head for some time now and he rather wanted to use them. He was a writer after all (a published – about to be – writer). Plus there was the advantage that one could say all that needed to be said in a letter and leave no address. Though it might look odd if he didn't offer some reasonable explanation as to why he was leaving no address. But then when had there ever been any lack of reasonable explanations in this world, however wide of the mark? Life teemed with explanations for those who felt consoled by them.

. . . Julia came to stay in my flat something over a year ago. She had lost her own flat and needed somewhere to go and I had a spare room. We were both, to be quite frank – I feel I should tell you this so that you get some idea of the present situation – in a fairly sorry state at that point. My wife had recently left me and I had been involved in a road accident, for which I shall never forgive myself, in which a young boy on a bicycle was killed. Julia was very depressed about your mother having had a stroke and about having been left (though I never quite understood all this) by an old boyfriend back in London. But the thing that seemed to be upsetting her most of all, and this you may not know about, was the fact that some ten odd years ago she had had an abortion. I don't know why this had suddenly surfaced and was disturbing her so much (my sister, who lived with her before me said she had never mentioned it to her), but she used to cry about it a great deal with me and would often say that she thought of herself as a murderer. We were also both pretty depressed, I suppose, about our situations here in Italy, which seemed to have no particular future. . . .

But was he really going to write all this down in a letter? The whole thing? So embarrassing. And especially given that (you never know) people might be writing biographies of him one day. The phrases that echoed in his mind were for fiction, surely, not for Michael Delaforce, nor any future researcher. Or would they applaud his candidness, his compassion, would they say here was proof he had really lived, been through things, knew the world, had the authority to write, to expound the wisdom accruing from such a difficult passage? And then of course the story did take on a certain poignancy when told in this spare, straightforward style, which wasn't his at all, a quality which would be entirely lost in the spilling and spluttering of facts that conversation was, or again in the stylishness of modern narrative. The bathos, for example, of that stuff about her thinking of herself as a murderer being followed by the, in comparison apparently inconsequent, 'We were also both pretty depressed, I suppose, about our situations here in Italy . . .', was marvellous! Because despite its seeming banality, that sentence was so true, reflected how difficult it was to give centrality to those momentous things, abortion, manslaughter, when the rest of life, like the steady current beneath the tossing waves, sucked one so interminably in and on. Yes, if he had been working at the processor, he might have gone and altered that or shifted it around the text, before realizing how haunting it was; and not only because of that bathos, but quite simply for its eloquent ineptitude, its woeful inability to come to terms with, to engage in what had been weeks of unrelieved, stifling, self-induced despair, extreme mental discomfort. The straightforward understatement in fact served to indicate a need on the part of the writer to distance himself from, not to return to, that period of extraordinary bleakness they had passed through: the oppressively hot, humid weather, the sense of utter directionlessness, of hating life to the very core, of complete waste. And the reader, even without knowing it, would sense this, would sense in that understatement the fear of touching a wound that hadn't yet healed; and might thus be spurred to imagine the whole thing rather better than if he, the narrator, were to tell, as he might some day in a book, how he had leaned out of their window and declaimed, screamed, bellowed Empson's lines: 'Slowly the poison the whole blood stream fills . . . The waste remains, the waste remains and kills' to a black stifling street at three in the morning, and how Julia hadn't even woken up with all the pills she was taking. (What a literary sufferer he was. How trite!)

No, the letter gave you, in that formal reserve towards the reader, the chance to have him imagine all the things you were hiding behind your simple words, if for no other reason than that letters were rarely more than a few pages long; whereas in a novel you might be rather crassly obliged to tell all.

And then he did have an hour to kill.

Alan made a few notes at the back of his notebook again: 'Epistolary novel? Cut you down on action and dialogue. Your strong points. Then people tend to think of Richardson and groan before even looking at it. Probably a no-no.'

(Hadn't Julia once said something about killing time? Yes: 'We can't go on killing time' – she had been talking about her idea – 'it's a non-replaceable resource.' Quite undoubtedly Julia was the cleverest girl he'd ever known, the only one who had shared his sense of what it was like being alive, what it involved.)

Anyway, and to keep things as short as possible. . . .

But go easy: with the first-person letter style the important thing was not to give an impression that one was at all conscious of what one was doing.

. . . she became obsessed by the idea that in order to expiate . . .

Or if he was going for the simplistic approach, shouldn't he rather write, 'make up for'? But there was a delicious charm about the notion that what was written was written and couldn't be changed; pen and paper; write the word and stand by it, my good man; a kind of honesty; whereas the word processor was the prevaricator's tool par excellence. Leave it, expiate.

. . . for the fact that we had both destroyed life, we must create new life, have a baby.

Re-read. Yes, but this gave the impression that Julia had been/ was suffering from deep guilt feelings over that obscure abortion of so many years before, her murder, whereas living with her, this was clearly not the case. Or not exactly. The driving force was more desire for the future, mingled with nostalgia for the past, or, to put it more succinctly, desire/nostalgia for a lost future, which she was determined, for all apparent cynicism, to recover. In a way it was really herself she thought of as having murdered and was now trying to resurrect. Lost time, lost opportunities.

So that to the extent that there was any guilt involved in the affair, it was her playing on his so as to get her own way. 'It's got to be better than cutting your wrists . . .' was a salient phrase that came to mind. Because there were times, now he thought about it, when Julia had been more the manipulator than the victim.

Or wasn't this again rather too schematic, as if one day she had suddenly said, A + B = C = Create. Whereas in the event it had had more to do with their living together as flatmates for a few months, their getting used to each other, confessing each other bit by bit, so that as he got himself off the drink, as they ended up, very compatibly as it turned out, and rather sweetly, in bed together, the whole idea had slowly begun to seem the obvious thing, or at least it had for her. Not so much a brainwave as a discovery. Light, quite plausibly, at the end (it seemed) of a tunnel.

But these kind of motivational details were not what was required in this letter. And anyway, the truth was (and wasn't this always the way) that he couldn't quite remember how it had all come about.

So what was required? Details of the pact? Hardly. And had they ever been clearly articulated? (She had written up 'The Pact' once – 'We, the undersigned, do hereby solemnly swear . . .' – but was that it? Hadn't that been a bit of a joke? Hadn't there always been a tone of private banter when they used refer to 'the pact'.) Just the bare bones then.

. . . We were, as I said, both extremely depressed about the breakdown of any stability in our lives, and so in the end we agreed that as a purely rational act we would have a baby, a family, and create a stable social unit, living together and sharing domestic chores, even if we weren't actually in love. Julia's line was that seeing as so many arranged marriages in the past had ended in love there was no reason why ours shouldn't too, and at least we wouldn't be subject to the disillusionment of discovering the bankruptcy of an initial passion, nor to the blindness that such passion can generate. . . .

Come to think of it, the schematic approach did have a certain eloquent romanticism about it. We did this because of that, that because of this; as if life, however painful, was a doddle decisionwise.

Anyway, it should at least serve to wake the lad up over his muesli. Even if she had never said anything of the kind, or not in so many words.

Though haggle as one might, the naked and very banal core of the thing was, she wanted a kid; it seemed for her the only way of demonstrating that her whole life hadn't been just an awful mistake; and he had been in a condition of such snivelling wretchedness he had felt that only a strong (as she had seemed) personality could save him from ending up the wreck that deep down so far he had been carefully managing not quite to become. It was curious though, in retrospect, how, being given, with Elaine's departure, the freedom he had so often longed for, he had done nothing with it; his plans to become a world traveller, a seducer of beautiful young women, had not materialized. Nor had there been the careful choosing of a new partner he had sometimes fantasized in the unlikely event of Ellie's death. No, insecure, he had merely clutched at Julia's safe solidness. Because she happened to be there. A total failure, morally unchanged, unreformed, unhelped by that terrible accident, bewildered at finding himself still who he was, he had longed for the minimal success of that same family unit that he had previously found so tame and disappointing (the culminating irony in his book of course).

Unless he was being too crude again, too unkind to both himself and Julia (was there any limit to how often the facts could be turned inside out? how many different ways the prism of his mind could split the light of experience? – that was good); for apart from the morbid side, craving security, craving family, there was a sense in which they had both seen it as a bizarre adventure – yes, adventure – this setting up house with a person they barely knew; it was a way of filling in time, filling life, like any other, and laudable for its cold-blooded honesty, for the impertinent way they were taking their destinies into their hands, the way they had admitted to each other that practical need, not love (whatever that might be – and this was *not* a disingenuous aside), was the driving force behind their 'union'; not saying, 'you and nobody else,' but, 'you, since you're here and no worse than anybody else.' Indeed it might have been, come to think of it, the only time in his life when, briefly, he had been emotionally honest.

Anyway, they had both derived a strong sense of fun, of freedom, of confidence, from this straightforward, over-the-counter bargain approach, which augured well, had a positive feel to it, although Julia's determination to take things to the limit, to buy new furniture, carpets, pictures, not to 'camp in other people's detritus,' ergo to purchase baby-clothes, dish-towels, oven cloths and gloves, all with little regard for their financial resources (officially pooled, though he had kept a separate account, thank God, otherwise he'd be hitchhiking now) – all this had unnerved him, since Alan never had a clearer sense of life's awful, ordinary, drip-by-drip reality and irreversibility than when money was being spent and was gone and the shops were offering no refunds (was it this that had saved him from an alcoholic's fate?). Still, he had been game; he was fed up with Elaine's and his own past miserliness, material and emotional, and he did see Julia's point about creating, in a quite literal sense, the world around one, and not just being forced into the shape and state of mind that other people's flotsam and jetsam impressed upon you. How delightful when one particularly miserable day, shortly after Christmas, she had declared with that ludicrous, overacted determination of hers, which was also the ironic veneer she drew over God knew what secrets and sadnesses (or simply across nothing, the most awful secret of all – she was always careful never to tell him more than so much about herself) – how delightful when she had declared that the problem with them was not so much their actual selves as that hideous mock gloom-and-doom, Gods-and-ghosts, pre-tentious, portentous, crappy, impractical, dark, depressing, last century, provincial, wop furniture! not to mention the painted contusions of Santo Stefano and the tears of the tomb-weeper. Announcing which, she gave the living-room table such a kick that they had both wondered for a while, between howls of pain and bursts of laughter, whether she mightn't have broken a toe.

Yes, he had been game for this adventure; he had spent, albeit with his heart in his mouth, money, real money, on bookshelves, armchairs, table lamps, pots and pans, plates, mugs, cutlery, a wall-hanging (showing brightly coloured hats and scarves), knick-knacks, clothes, baby equipment, wool (she was learning how to knit). He had even got an initial high from the whole thing which lifted him out of what had seemed, until then, a terminal depression (spending and accumulating were exhilarating as well as unnerving). Seeing what taste she had, what simple flair, the way the bookshelf projected from the wall, instead of standing against it, decorated with painted pots and plants and a beautiful marble ball, transformed the living room; the way even the washing up was more bearable with nice cutlery and the bright clean lines of modern-design earthenware; or again seeing the way an expensive quilt on the bed spread its own sense of luxury and well-being, made you want to relax, make love, he had begun to believe in the whole project, their pact, was rather annoyed in fact by her desire to keep their actual relationship secret until she was pregnant (who was playing ifs and ans now?), became, in short, and something he hadn't been in years, positively enthusiastic. He got into D.I.Y., finally oiled the doors after years of creaking, added a few strategic plug sockets, solved the problem of the dripping loo. He pottered and enjoyed pottering, captured and convinced by her vision of how they might make their own life, their home. No, there could be no doubt about it, it was this surge of purpose that had saved him, got him back on his feet, given him the energy, as if by direct transfusion from her, finally to mine that novel out of the computer's memory (in a remarkably short time as it turned out). Yes, in a modern and rather domestic version of the Promethean gesture, Julia Delaforce and Alan Bexley had saved themselves.

So why had it all folded?

Was it that he had never realized until too late how much of his ability to maintain a relationship with a woman depended on her physical beauty? So that while the excitement of a new body, new ways of doing things, the extraordinariness of this whole adventure, the escape from a suicidal dead end, had been enough at first (when there was nothing to lose), later on, as he began to view her more coldly and carefully, as quiet observation replaced the stimulated confusion of early contact (of life rediscovered, for heaven's sake!), he had found the slightly fallen breasts, the just a little thick stomach, for all the clothes she so carefully chose to hide them, depressing. Self-pity, having passed through excitement and salvation, turned to pity of the other, the worst (even though betrayal wasn't planned). And she sensed it of course.

Though that was only half the story.

And definitely not the half for this letter.

What happened, very simply . . .

But wasn't he saying that rather too often? Unless of course his unconscious intention was to have the reader decode it into the obvious realization that none of this was simple, but that the only way to write letters to each other was to pretend it was.

. . . was that she proved unable to have a child, the result, her gynaecologist said, of damage done by the earlier abortion, and this threw her into such a deep depression that I am afraid she may have lost her reason.

How Dr Johnsonish! One did come out with things from time to time. And it felt so odd having to leave it there, rather than marking it off with the cursor and cancelling. There it was, the unwieldy, unexpected thing that was an expression of oneself – 'I am afraid she may have lost her reason.' Indeed!

I tried for a long time to comfort her and made it clear that her not having a baby didn't affect my plans in any way . . .

!!!

. . . but there was nothing I could do.

So should he give the gory details? Best not. His purpose was just to get someone to go out and help Julia, a letter of compassion, of conscience salving. And in itself, the fact that anyone had bothered to write, would be enough to transmit that urgency. There was no point recalling lines like: 'You're glad, you fucking shit' – smashing one of the expensive mugs depicting Castelvecchio against the wall – 'you're glad because now you can piss off to London with your piddling novel and piddling future and piddling success and not have to worry about me.' 'But I'm inviting you to come, aren't I? for Christ's fucking sake! I'm not leaving you.' 'Even a rat would know how to make an invitation more inviting. "You can come"' – she mimicked – '"if you want, Julia." If you want! You're glad' – picking up her plate with the copied deco design and breaking it on the edge of the table – 'because you haven't had a baby from a woman you don't find physically attractive any more, if you ever did. You feel like you'd won at Russian roulette, you shit!' – bringing her own head down hard on the same table. 'And the last thing I need' – screaming now – 'is half-bloody-hearted wimpy invitations, a half-bloody-hearted life with someone who can take me or leave me now he's got his book published.' (Did she want him to go down on his knees? Wasn't their whole relationship supposed to rest on the cornerstone of mutual practical need? Or didn't she want him to be successful at all? Did she want him always a failure and attached to her because of that?) 'But isn't the truth, Julia' – later now, in the bathroom, helping her to sponge her forehead where the skin was split, putting on a sad voice he more than half felt – 'that really it was only ever the baby you cared about, not me, and that's why you don't want to come.' 'No, it fucking well isn't. Get out of here. Get off me. Don't touch me. Leave me alone and piss off to your piddling computer!'

No, lines like this wouldn't help, and perhaps anyway were more a demonstration of her perception than real mental distraction. Or were they? Did he have to run himself down so badly? Was he necessarily responsible? Had he actually done anything wrong? And wasn't it interesting that it was she who had apologized later that evening, in tears, hugging him tight in the bed they had ceased some weeks back (after the verdict) to make love in, murmuring over and over, 'My nice plates, my nice mugs, I was so happy when I bought them. I'm sorry, Alan. I'm so disgustingly sorry. It was meant to work out so well. Our home. What an idiot! My nice plates.' 'And when you think,' she said later, half-laughing, blowing her nose, 'of all the years of contraceptives. I'm so sorry, Alan.'

No, in the end even this sad scene hadn't given him any inkling of anything more than life's ordinary unpleasantness (on the contrary, it had reminded him of Mary, who actually it might be quite fun to get in touch with now he was going back. See what she was up to).

It was what came after that period that decided him to write.

. . . She went through a period of hysterical fits (this would be July), then seemed to recover. Or at least I thought she had. She became quiet and even and it was a while before I realized that she was simply withdrawing totally. She stopped teaching her lessons, stopped listening to the radio, refused to talk except in monosyllables and recently not even that. In the last couple of weeks she has eaten next to nothing and rarely comes out of her room. When people visit she refuses to see them. Hence my fear she may need psychiatric help. . . .

Curious this change-over. At the beginning him morose, suicidal. At the end, her. Though one had to admit in a more dignified way. And without the drink.

. . . I should explain that my teaching contract at the University of Verona recently terminated, so that I am more or less obliged to return to England . . .

Hardly the right moment to mention personal triumphs, though the temptation was there, and resistance a sacrifice.

. . . I did, as I said, try to persuade Julia to come back with me, but she refused.

I would come over to speak to you personally, except that immediately on return I shall have to go up to Edinburgh about a new job. As soon as I have a permanent address I shall be in touch again.

Sincerely

ALAN BEXLEY

He read it over. Of course the business of why he had written, rather than visiting (and why he didn't even mention phoning), had a somewhat contrived feel; but then the thing to remember was that people were not as a rule looking for lies and contrivances and so could generally be expected to take things at face value. Her brother would be so concerned by what he was reading about Julia that he would have little mental energy to waste on the true genesis of the text and exact location of its at once confessional and yet mysteriously reticent propagator. He rather liked that line: 'Hence my fear she may need psychiatric help.'

Poor Julia.

Oh Christ, what for fuck's sake was he doing, gloating over drivel like this when the poor woman was heading for a total breakdown! (And after she had rushed him to the hospital, sleeves drenched in blood.) Get back, post the letter at once to someone who could help her. Alan, Alan, Alan!

It certainly didn't get any easier living with oneself.

Nevertheless, on the plane, Alan explained the plot of his novel to a young nurse complete with hennaed blow-wave and pearly teeth, and surprised himself by arranging to meet her for dinner the following evening at a restaurant he knew of old on Old Compton Street.

———◆◇◆———

Dear Di & Stu,

Still haven't found the old girl, though I have tracked down where she was living with this Alan. But first things first.

After phoning you – that was the night before last – I went back to the old address we had and simply hung around – there was a bar open across the square that didn't seem to want to close and I just kept saying 'Bardolino' and they just kept filling my glass, which I then tipped up in my inimitable style (I don't suppose more than 300 billion other people share it). Who would ever have guessed, seeing me Soavely knocking back my Bardo, that it was my first ever evening out of Inghilterra (quite embarrassing actually, I missed out on the whole post-adolescent de-anglicization process for lack of funds)? Anyway, around midnight, when I went to ring the bell for the N-to-the-nth time, the door finally springs open with a frightful electronic buzz – even the most ancient places seem to have them here, can you imagine in Kilburn? the Paddies'd think they were being shot at – and it was a girl, dressed in a skimpy, hello-milkman kind of slip, more or less justified, I suppose, by the weather which is remarkably warm even at night and all in all a far cry from the coldest whatever London's having on record.

So I explained who I was (she seemed a delicate shade disappointed on my opening the door, as if she could have thought of other people she would rather have had hanging around for her when she got back at midnight) and explained about the letter and its not saying exactly where Julia was living, and she told me (she speaks a deliciously broken English) that her name was Marina and that she'd taken the Quinzano place over from Julia and knew her quite well and would give me her address with pleasure (turns out she was a little annoyed about getting so much mail for J and having to forward it). She also gave me the addresses of those other people you said I should go and see if there was any problem, Sandro, Flossy and Colin. She knew everybody.

Boy, it does take an awfully long time just actually physically writing everything down, doesn't it? Never mind the style! (I don't as you see).

So, thinks Mikey, somewhat prematurely as it turned out, got the address, that settles that.

First problem: it was already too late for a bus back into town. Marina said I could stay with her; she was rather pushy actually, saying how impossible it would be for me to walk the three or four kilometres it was in the dark and how I'd never find the place. So I accepted. She rustled me up a meal from a bombsite of a kitchen and then, despite having (I don't know how I forgot to mention it) an incredibly ill-behaved little girl with her who she had no intention of packing off to bed, and despite looking, when you saw her in profile, just a teensy bit pregnant, she made a pass at me – very blatant. She sat herself by my feet on the floor, dressed as I said in the skimpiest slip (which I could now see down), put her head on my knee – me slithering and floundering with my midnight spaghetti! – and said there was only one bed but it was big enough to share (I should have said, she's quite attractive actually, in a banal, dyed magazine blonde, foxy-faced way). So it really is true, thinks Mikey, about Latins being hot as their chillypeppers – and I told her I was gay. She didn't understand, so I said ho-mo-sex-u-al very slowly, and that seemed to sort that out. (As Lance was remarking only the other night, women do seem rather less eager to reform even the handsomest of gays since the AIDS scare began.)

After which remarkable declaration of identity (a first point-blank, I think), and despite my being tired and already half-drunk on the Bardo, she insisted on plying me with some sickly fruit liqueur and kept me up half the night to hear her life's long disaster story, which appeared to have a great deal to do with being a Pisces and having been briefly married to an Aquarius. I could hardly get a word in edgeways about Julia, but when I did, she told me rather scornfully that I was blowing the thing up unnecessarily and it was just the regular splitting up depression everybody had. I like 'regular' after what I've been through recently! Anyway, Marina is the only person I've ever met who twitches both big toes in unison when she's excited, which unfortunately is the kind of detail that's no use at all to a painter, though she does daub the nails a nice grass green I wouldn't mind mixing (sorry, am I boring you, folks? I'm sitting in my pensione here with zilch to do for a while but write – maybe I'll do you a sketch of her if I can find a good pencil. Wait a minute).

SKETCH OF MARINA

So the following morning (after a few hours' sleep on a couch with a suspiciously stained, itchy, dried-vomit cover, and after washing what must have been a week's worth of dishes to show gratitude) I took the bus to town and found Alan's/Julia's address. It's in a six-floor pre-war block on a busy street about half a mile from the centre proper. One of the twenty-odd bells had Bexley/Delaforce on (strange running across your name in this foreign country next to Bernardino, Dordenone, Dagodago, Wopwopwop, etc.) and I rang and rang, but nothing. I spent all day walking round the centre and going back there at hourly intervals, but to no avail. Between visits I found a room in a pensione at a reasonable price and did a sketch of a place called Castel San Pietro, but it really is all rather too picture-booky for my style, not real somehow; I mean, I really go for those chimneypot Kilburn skylines, damp brickwork, sodium lamp-light on wet asphalt, etc. My territory. I've been trying to imagine Julia walking around these postcard streets and being her busybody, sisterly, teacherly self here, but I can't. It's like trying to picture Edgware Road acquaintances in some exotic tourist-brochure snap, impossible unless they happen to look good in a bathing suit and regularly use a sun lamp, and Julia never did either. No, if I try to picture her, the clearest image I have of Julia goes back to a time I saw her before she first left (funny how the mind stacks untaken photographs, rather than simply seeing the face as it is – if it can really be said to be any one thing, that is. They'll give me a teaching post yet). I was in town and walked all the way from Covent Garden to Victoria to wait for her at her school-gate and ask if she could lend me some money (the penniless days seem so romantic in retrospect, they suited my character. I loved feeling totally irresponsible, and one knew one's place in the world so well). Anyway, she came hurrying and bustling out, the way she does, bent slightly forward, the usual busy, worried look, gripping her old brief-case, and when she spotted me, she just lit up with one of those bright cynical pally smiles, and without any greeting (we couldn't have seen each other for weeks) said, 'How much this time, brother mine?' which I must admit I found quite hurtful and so didn't ask for any money at all. We went to the Bag O'Nails where she bought me a couple of pints and then quite off her own bat, just as we were saying goodbye and I was racking my brains for what on earth to say to Lance about rent, she gave me forty quid, which was all she had in her purse. T for touching, n'est-ce-pas? Though she never invited me to any of those famous parties I hear so much about.

Yes, anyway, when I was still getting no answer at the flat at sixish, I managed to call Colin on the phone (the only one of them here who actually has a phone) and he came and talked to neighbours and things and they said they hadn't seen anybody around for quite a while. So he found out who the landlord was and we drove out to his place, a modern architect's sore thumb on the hills to the north of the city. He, the landlord – squat, cropped white bristle, apopleptic complexion, talkative, flat snout – said Julia had left the keys in the mail box at the bottom of his drive a week or so ago without leaving a forwarding address and without paying the last month's rent; he kept insisting how odd it was that she should have bothered to trek out all that way to leave the keys when she was in fact doing a flit. Which is true. It is odd. I wouldn't have. Anyway, I settled up the month's rent in return for a chance to see the flat this lunchtime. I'm hoping she'll have left something there that'll give an idea of where she is. How ironic though, me paying Sis's rent! What a reversal of fortunes!

After which I spent the evening with Colin. He's a big, tallish, paunchy, slobby kind of bloke, with a big slobby beard, long conk-ord-take-off, beaky nose and lots of I-want-to-be-weird-even-though-I'm-middle-aged clothes – oh and very Scottish. I made the goof of telling him about this girl Marina trying to seduce me and he burst out laughing and said she was his ex-wife (which meant he was the ex-husband she'd been maligning for hours and referring to as Lino). Anyway, I suspect that despite the laughter he was feeling pretty depressed about life, because he insisted on our spending the whole evening together and getting hopelessly drunk (between phone calls home to check that the kids were behaving themselves). His line on this Alan was that he's a rather aloof, intellectual type, typical Oxbridge snob, never wanted to really get involved in all the strike problems they have at the university, a self-important bastard with delusions of artistic grandeur, who, he was sure, had just used Julia sexually to get over his wife leaving him, and then dumped her as soon as he heard his novel was going to be published. He didn't seem to know anything about the baby thing as reported by Alan in his letter, so I didn't enlighten him. It's rather humbling, isn't it, the way our opinions of other people would change so radically, if only we had just one small, crucial piece of information (Alas, fair Brünhilde!), and then perhaps so radically again if we had just one more. This Colin kept coming on very Scottish strong about having Julia entirely sussed out, about her being on the look-out for a male figure to dominate her own too easily explosive character, about how it suited her zodiac sign to the ground (ha ha) (did he get it from Marina or she from him?) and I was just soaking up this excellent stuff they call prosecco (a dry sparkler with a real kick) and thinking, no, my nice old tartan fart, you don't know my sister at all, and neither do I for that matter, because if we did, we'd most likely know where she is right now.

Dear friends, I've broken off for a day or so, partly because I was interrupted last time by the arrival of Flossy, partly because I was hoping to be able to report something definite, though I'm afraid I'm going to have to disappoint you again there. (Unless J's already back in London and you're all giggling together over my letter. But something tells me not somehow).

Yes, Flossy arrived, Alan's sister. Colin had told her I was here and she wanted to go and see the flat with me. It turns out she is a close friend of Julia's and they had been planning to live together out at this farm she lives on in the country; she'd imagined J would be coming to her more or less as soon as Alan left, so she was obviously surprised and a bit upset to hear she'd simply gone off without saying a word to anybody. She's quite a noble-looking girl, though rather solid and squarely built, not the modern type at all, more Victorian, with an endearingly earnest, perfectly rectangular, take-everything-serious face that somehow looked more serious still as a result of heavy cold with consequent bleary eyes. Wore tight trousers on big horseriding thighs, which in this weather seems, nay is, nothing short of masochism. Ultra-concerned about Julia though, which was touching, and anyway I thought I could use the linguistic support if I had to deal with the landlord over anything missing.

So, the flat. A simple, two-bedroom job on the first floor with pull-down slat shutters, green-tiled floor, white walls: very tastefully furnished given that it was rented, tall windows looking down over the main street, bags of bright light boiling about with dust, birdcage, but no bird (very apt), a nice colourful wall-hanging in the bedroom, a low modern double bed, etc. etc. It reminded me rather of your place in Kensington. But after much searching in cupboards, through drawers, wardrobes, absolutely nothing of Julia's excepting an empty bottle of Rive Gauche in the bathroom waste bin. I pressed the top and it let out the faintest breath of something recognizable. Everything was very tidy (that at least was typical Julia), but nothing to give any hint of where she might be or how she passed the time here: books, records, etc. I kept nosing about while the others sat on the sofa, the squash-snouted landlord half-heartedly chatting up Flossy (hand casually falling on her shoulder) and her coming out with the most gruesome hypotheses of kidnap and rape and saying how she was learning karate herself against just such eventualities (hand withdrawn from shoulder).

Anyway – and just for the record – it occurred to me, rooting about that flat, how strange it was that my sister had been living here until only a few days ago and yet had left no trace. I suppose you get to expect places to be haunted, to hold an after-image of people (you think of people and places together, of one giving a clue to the other), and then when they don't it comes as a surprise and disappointment, or in some cases a relief. I don't think I mentioned it at the time, but a couple of weeks back, while I was going up West Bend Lane, I couldn't resist turning off a mo, to look at our old place in Quex Road. The main door was open and I nudged in and looked up the stairwell, expecting visions of B in ersatz Patricia Roberts sweaters to come floating down, or at least a glimpse of Lance and Trev, linking limp arms. But nothing, not the haziest image; no presence or echo at all, no ghosts. I thought (Mikey putting on his thinking cap), haunting is wishful thinking, I thought; places are no more nor less than what they are, they take no imprint from us and we impress nothing on them, otherwise the whole world would be thronged with ghosts. A room is just a room, a stairwell just a stairwell. Bear that in mind for your painting, Michael my lad (you see, I am a real artist, I do fudge around with aesthetic considerations from time to time!).

Anyway, there we are, not only no Julia, but my mind couldn't even fish up a Julia to stick in this flat. It was spacious and nicely furnished and she hadn't left a note or anything, just on the table in the hall there was a gas bill which the landlord surprisingly made no comment on. Outside Flossy said he must have had a brainstorm or reformed or something, because he'd changed half the furniture and nobody had mentioned anything to her. Apparently J used to visit Flossy, rather than vice versa, because she, Flossy, doesn't get on with her brother.

So, no Sis. For the first time I got nervous that maybe something serious had happened. We went to the police and reported her missing, but they weren't very impressed – foreigners always moving in and out of Verona without informing the authorities, no time to hunt them all down, bound to turn up in the next week or so, etc. etc. fob, fob. The relief was, though, no accidents or anything with her involved – that they knew of. And anyway, if she had wanted to do anything drastic she wouldn't have gone to all the trouble to take the keys back and clear away her stuff, would she?

Sitting outside a bar in the centre – again too picturesque to really be true: the vines, the billowy figures frescoed on the walls, the cobbles, the belltowers – Flossy asks, has it ever occurred to me Julia might be a lesbian? I do a double take. No it hasn't. And she begins to explain the whole thing, Julia's story, in terms of her being a latent lesbian. The Lenny relationship was a classic feint, allowing her a boyfriend she can never move in with, under cover of which she ogles you, Diana (Flossy knew all about you, seemed quite jealous). Then she leaves England so that her personality/sexuality can develop away from the criticism of friends and family, and promptly moves in with her, Flossy. Except that at this point, nervous of her own tendencies, she dives into a meaningless relationship with Sandro, then the same thing with Alan, thus denying herself the chance to find herself.

She was all very serious about this and kept batting her eyelids and wiping her nose like a Sloane at a funeral (what a silly description! Julia always said I had an unbearable epistolary manner).

Anyway, I ask her if she's a lesbian and she says, sort of, she isn't sure.

I tell her I'm sort of gay, but even less sure.

That was the first proper smile I got out of her. She says in the end a lot of ex-pats come over chiefly so as come out of the closet one way or another, away from home criticism. It being easier to be who you are away from home.

If you know who you are to begin with, I tell her.

You find out by doing what you want, she says; which, as I point out, is classically unhelpful when you don't know what you want.

It sounds rather like the discussions we had when Brünhilde left me, doesn't it? Still, we became quite good friends arguing about it. Vive la discussion!

I decided to tell her what it said in Alan's letter. She hardly took a moment to assimilate it. It obviously proved her previous argument. Julia wanted to have a baby, something essentially female, part of being a woman, but she didn't want the conventional trappings of heterosexual marriage. The fact that she hadn't bothered going with him when he went back proved it was the baby not the man she wanted.

So what is she doing? I ask. Where is she?

Flossy has no idea.

I ask about her brother and she breaks out into the most incredible invective. Imagine an ego, she says, about as high as the Barbican and twice as black, priggish, opinionated, totally vain, totally dedicated to himself, his career, so much so that when things are going badly he tries to commit suicide because life isn't worth living if he can't think of himself as God (at this point it emerges that Julia twice rushed Alan off to hospital, the first time when he cut his wrists, the second when he put his head in the oven). She, Flossy, has no sympathy with him at all. It seems she found his notebooks once and read through them and they were full of obscene things he'd like to do with his little girl students. She said he masturbated a lot as a boy and put her off men forever asking her to wank him off once in the garden shed when she was only nine.

A bright life and no mistake, eh? The amazing thing is how people'll tell you anything, and when they do you get the distinct impression that your own experience you thought was so agonizing is all pretty B for banal.

Spent the rest of the afternoon going round all the language schools to ask if Julia had been looking for work, but zero again. Unless you count a couple of job offers for myself (now that I don't need them of course)!

I'll try and pick up an envelope for this and get it mailed tomorrow morning.

October 7th

As you see, I didn't. Laziness. Or no, the truth is I really want to put a proper finish to this letter (not quite sure what Mikey might mean by that). Just to report, I've now left the pensione and come to stay with Flossy in this rather bare old farmhouse about twenty miles into the hills, where Flossy is doing her back-to-the-land thing. I refused to join in meditation sessions or help weed the vegetable patch, but managed to get some serious sketching done, as there are some impressive views – hills and rivers, as well as all the different building shapes and plant shapes (I never realized vines were so expressively gnarled), and above all the light, which, at least these last few days, has been apocalyptically intense. The unreal, postcard feel is fading. It must have been just arrival.

While sketching I've been doing a lot of thinking about Julia. We grew up together, I pulled her hair, she used to tickle me till I was gasping. I got my first, apart from my mother, ideas of feminity from her I suppose; she was my big sister, she let me look in her pants a few times in return for little favours (taking the dog out when it was her turn, doing the washing up). I was usually the tearabout, she told on me, I spent my money, she didn't, etc. We were never particularly close and when she left home we hardly kept in touch at all until after father died and we had to discuss what to do about Mother – I think the funeral must have been the first time I'd seen her for a couple of years. Before that, after she left college, she went through a religious period right when I was at my most rebellious, so that for a while I thought of her as a pious old bitch who was always taking Dad's side over everything (now I realize this would have been the year or so after she had this famous abortion). We never really became good friends and I was never as close to her as I was to Brünhilde, or Trev or Lance, or even poor Mumsy in a funny way.

So why have I bothered to come out here and find her? I was never big on family values or duties. Perhaps I only came for a holiday really, that's the truth, to spend some of this money they keep pumping my way and to sort myself out finally post-B, face up to (decide?) who I am, etc. etc. (What a bore!) No, it was the holiday more than that. I remember feeling really very pleased about an hour after getting that letter from Alan, thinking here was a rare opportunity to take a trip, to meet some new people. I had no idea what I was supposed to say to this sister of mine who has discovered she can't have a baby and has apparently gone crazy or manic depressive or something. No idea at all. In fact I remember thinking it would be much more appropriate if you came rather than me, you know her much better, you could say the right things. But I never suggested it, because I thought, now I'm going to have a nice little holiday trip and show everybody what a nice bloke I am, going off to comfort my sister (also I was looking forward to telling her how successful I'm becoming). And, given that the trip was an emergency rather than a holiday, I could even in clear conscience ask you to pop in and see Mother from time to time (for all the difference it makes).

But while I've been here, after talking to people, and particularly after visiting the flat where she was, I've developed a quite urgent desire to see Julia again, to know she's okay and getting by, but most of all just to see and talk to her. I realize that, despite our never getting on that well, Julia is, has become, one of the most solid touchstones in my life. My opposite, perhaps. Or I always saw it that way. I'm not so sure now, not since she didn't come back to look after Mum. Anyhow, I simply can't imagine her not being around, it would be like removing part of the landscape, as if a couple of London suburbs (even though I'd never meant to live in them) were to disappear from

Nicholson's Guide. I know she is not what any of these people say she is: not a lesbian (or not <u>explained</u> by being that); not in search of a dominating male figure etc., and I know too that I couldn't say myself what or who she is; it's just that this morning, sitting with my notepad, smoking M.S. (not bad actually), sketching a cliffside here (where they say the Americans are hiding a missile base), I had such a clear image of her face that afternoon as she was coming out of school (why is it some images remain so vivid, is it because they are more true?) – the round cheeks, green eyes, long chestnut hair, solid jaw, very slightly upturned, pugnacious nose, with wry wrinkling about the bridge, sulky full mouth, heavy forehead that gave – but why have I used the past tense, for heaven's sake? – that gives her such a worried look – I had such a clear sense of her that I wanted very much to see her again, I suppose in part because one doesn't want to think of one's life as floating entirely free in time and space without any links at all, and then because it suddenly seems important to love (care for? cherish?!!) one or two people without knowing quite who they are or what they're up to, or what they think of you, but just because they have something to do with your life (the thought that she may be dead appals me). But most of all I want to see her because of this vision of her face which is completely hypnotizing me this morning (it really is most uncanny – as if we people were haunted, even when the buildings aren't), but which I can't seem to draw at all, which if I could draw would say more about her than any would-be analysis, more about her than I know myself.

S for Sentimentalism.

My conclusion.

I'll write again when I have further news or plans.

Love to yourselves and Joycie.

MIKE.

SKETCH OF FLOSSY

PS. Sorry, this is interminable. I just thought you might be amused to hear that Julia's old boyfriend Sandro came this afternoon with Beppe, the owner of the farm. He, Sandro, wanted to buy a dog off Beppe for this old dear he lodges with who's paranoid about rivals trying to steal her book proofs. Anyway, they're both quite beautiful men, these two (oh dear!) Beppe all he-man brawn, extraordinarily sensual rough-cut face, brilliant eyes in weatherbeaten skin, and Sandro your slim, classically well-bred, soft-spoken, smooth-as-a-groove North American. He, Sandro again, said Julia's problem was an inability to reconcile childhood fantasies fostered by a naive cultural background with the intransigence of real-life relationships, it made her impossible to live with ('Alan is an exceptionally nice man,' he tells me) and probably difficult for her to live with herself, and he said he wouldn't be at all surprised if she hadn't committed suicide. Flossy said, don't listen to him, he's taking a psychology course because they don't give him enough work to fill his time at the university. Sandro grinned and chose his dog. I thought I liked him. Beppe said he'd be perfectly happy for me to stay a while, I could do his portrait for rent (which will be fun).

So here we sits, as Mum used to say, and waits for news of Julia.

M.

———◦◦◦———

December 15th

Villa Verde
Via delle Pigne
Breccanecca
Genova

Dear Diana,

I am so sorry I didn't write and I am of course extremely sorry about poor Joyce. You do have all my sympathy and you can be sure I have been thinking about you a great deal.

Please don't think badly of me for not writing. I had one or two bad experiences that I don't want to go into. If you knew everything I am sure you would understand. Sometimes it just seems impossible to see or phone or write to those we feel closest to.

I am presently living in Breccanecca, a little village on the hills above Genoa where I shall soon be marrying a doctor whose previous wife was killed in a road accident and who has 3 young daughters, aged 10, 8 and 5. While they are at school I do medical translations for a friend of Franco's and when they come back we play in the garden or go for walks on the hills, or take the bus to the beach. Life is calm, joyous even, and I feel settled and very Italian, pickling aubergines and grinding olives from the twenty or so trees we have here. It's all turned out to be a very obvious and sensible solution.

Best love, Di, and to Stuart, and do tell Mike to forgive me – I do feel guilty about simply dumping Mother on him – and I will be in touch soon. I hope some time we will be able to come back and visit, but it will be very expensive of course with the three girls.

I was so sorry about Barry; do remember me to Kat-Kat.

Your old JULIA.

Julia was unhappy with this. She took two aspirins, lit a cigarette and, pouting with concentration, wrote:

December 15th   *219 Via Alserio*
Milano

Dear Diana,

I am sorry I didn't write and I am of course so terribly sad and sorry about poor Joyce. You do have all my sympathy and you can be sure I have been thinking about you a great deal.

Please don't judge me for not writing; I simply felt the need to cut off all contact with everybody. I felt all the old relationships were going nowhere, leading nowhere. And then I had one or two big disappointments that I don't want to go into. If you knew everything, I'm sure you would understand. One goes through these patches.

I am presently living in Milan where I'm sharing a flat with a French girl. I managed to get out of teaching and am working for Italian television in the department that selects foreign films and TV shows for the three public channels here. It's interesting work with plenty of nice people about (one particularly attractive American from Kentucky, tall, blond, my age, agonizingly polite) and most of all plenty of excellent career prospects, good pay and reasonable benefits.

The girl I'm living with, Agnès, is bright and breezy, reminds me of you sometimes, especially when she makes me answer the phone to check who it is before deciding if she will speak to them – you used to do that – and somehow the calls are always for her – as they were mostly for you. Anyway, we complement each other very well and what with the excellent job it's all turned out to be the obvious solution.

Best love, Di, and to Stuart, and do tell Mike to forgive me and I will be in touch soon. I hope I'll be able to come back and visit sooner or later, but just at the moment they're working me pretty hard and I never seem to get more than a few days off at a time.

I was so sorry about Barry; do remember me to Kat-Kat.

Your old JULIA.

But this was no better. She watched a fly buzz in her empty glass, ordered a Cynar with white wine.

December 15th

Dear Di,

I make no bones about not having written. Why should I? Sometimes it seems quite futile to contact even those we once felt closest to; one reserves every ounce of willpower for the simplest things: dressing, earning enough money to stay alive, feeding yourself, maintaining a minimum of self-respect. The truth is I rather envy you your handicapped child and busy missionary life. I envy the obviousness of it, the little rewards, the indisputable rightness.

I am presently living alone, for want of better company (actually one learns not to count on people nor on one's ability to judge them) in the city of Vicenza. I have a small furnished place, not unlike the first I had here, on a street with the tear-jerkingly apt name of Via dei Mutilati. Inevitably the furnishings include a madonna and a martyred saint (as if these were the only two possible outcomes in life), St Peter this time, crucified upside down. I rather enjoy the two of them: she smiles consolingly at him and he grimaces his agony at her, and there they both stay, imprisoned in their lugubrious frames, about ten dusty feet apart. I support myself with private lessons and the odd translation and spend a lot of time eating and drinking with one of my older students, a doctor widower in search of a new wife, though I shan't be obliging as he has the most appalling breath I've ever encountered, enough to send any woman to her grave. But he is good conversation, cultured as they say, and we frequently go to the cinema or theatre together. Otherwise I listen to the BBC (bought myself the wonderful new Sony shortwave portable, a revolution really) or read.

The truth is I have stopped trying to make things happen for me (though I do still apply for the occasional good job and have joined a volleyball team which trains Thursdays and plays Sundays – one of the members is a French girl who seems a possible friend). I have even stopped consciously waiting for things to happen to me, though I suppose one can never quite kill off the hope that they might. A war, for example, or earthquake, would presumably give me a chance to flower in an entirely new way.

Right now I'm sitting outside a café on Monte Berico, a steep hill that looks down over the city from the south and away to the Dolomites in the north. There's a big domed church at the top and it's a pilgrimage point, for some reason I haven't bothered to check up on. A porticade goes straight up at the steepest place from city to church, and every now and then you can see a pilgrim with some particularly urgent request labouring up on his, or more often her, knees, clutching a crucifix, muttering prayers. If the trick really worked, of course, everybody would be doing it.

My own experience is that events continually push your thoughts out and up towards religion, and your thoughts equally remorselessly return to base empty-handed.

Anyway, I'm under a beautiful pergola, I am overhearing a splendidly colourful conversation between two American blacks from the nearby airbase who obviously imagine I'm Italian and can't understand them; I have a breathtaking panorama spread out before me, the city, the mountains, sparkling sunshine, plus the intermittent amusement of a camp Neapolitan waiter trying to communicate with a party of decrepit Swiss pilgrims presumably raking in a few last indulgences before tackling the great divide. How it has happened I don't know, but I feel part of it all. I enjoy it. I live here. It's home.

Best love, Diana. I shall get across to see you sometime, if only I can manage to stir my stumps.

Your old JULIA.

PS. I was so sorry about Barry. Do remember me to Kat-Kat. You would be surprised how often I think of you all.

There, that was more her old self. Wait a couple of days though maybe, see if she really felt like sending it. Or perhaps everything would have changed by then.

Julia stood, paid and walked out of the empty bar. Forgotten her umbrella. She returned, retrieved it, unfurled it in the teeming rain. Visit Agnès? No, not this evening. She crossed the street, turned left and, stopping only to buy fresh batteries for her Sony, picked her way through puddled cobbles back home.